Nothing To Fear

by

Alicia Dean

Nothing To Fear

Contact Information: info@thewildrosepress.com

Cover Art by *Tamra Westberry*

The Wild Rose Press
PO Box 706
Adams Basin, NY 14410-0706
Visit us at www.thewildrosepress.com

Publishing History
First Crimson Rose Edition, February 2007
Print ISBN 1-60154-044-2

Published in the United States of America

Jade sensed a sudden movement.

She realized with surreal wonder that Bryce had sliced the knife across her neck.

Her hands flew to her throat. Blood gushed between her fingers. She sank to the floor, finally free of Bryce's grip.

Through a blur of pain, she was vaguely aware of El Lobo lifting his gun and yelling something unintelligible--shattering glass as Bryce hurled himself through the window into the rain drenched night--the booming echo of a gunshot--and El Lobo running to the window.

The man looked back and forth between Bryce's escape route and where she lay on the floor. Moving to her side, he tore off his shirt and pressed it against her throat, cursing under his breath.

The metallic taste of blood filled her mouth. Iciness twisted deep inside her--seized her skin. Her body convulsed. She clawed at the hands that held her. Dear God, she couldn't breathe.

In her delirium, she saw a blurred image of demonic red eyes and huge fangs.

This must be what death looks like.

The room faded in and out like the screen of a movie theatre as it switched frames. She tried to stay awake, afraid of what the blackness would bring, but her mind wouldn't focus.

"Hold on," a voice murmured. "Please don't die on me, please don't die."

She wanted to answer but couldn't. His words came from far away, then disappeared completely.

The world went silent as darkness swallowed her.

Dedication

This book is dedicated to my mentor, Mel Odom and to my fantastic critique partners, the Sooner Writers, especially to Jodi who has read over this manuscript more times than I have. To my sisters, Ruth and Sheri, my brother-in-law Tom, and my devoted friend, Paige, who are more excited about my being published than I am. To Rhonda...an amazing friend and editor. And, to my mother and three wonderful children, Lana, Lacey and Presley, whose love and support makes everything I do worthwhile.

Chapter One

The girl was a cutter.

Jade DiMarco had suspected it the first few times the teen had wandered into Safe Harbor Shelter. She'd noticed the girl scratching at the skin on the back of her hand, deeply, violently, as if wanting to inflict pain. Now, sitting in front of her was the disturbing, irrefutable truth.

The teen's sleeves rode up on her thin arms, revealing flesh so mangled it looked like the surface of the moon. Puckered scars, some more than four inches long, criss-crossed over deep pinkish-brown circles, obviously made by cigarette burns. A few wounds were new; others were just starting to heal. The coarse scabs were dotted with dried blood.

Jade winced as if she'd actually witnessed the mutilation. Her flesh tingled...tightened as if recoiling in apprehension of suffering the same fate.

Smeared black eyeliner circled the girl's clear blue eyes. Her pupils appeared normal. She wasn't high. She'd found another way to escape from reality. She'd traded emotional pain for physical.

The scent of French vanilla from the plug in air freshener mingled with the odor of sweat and cigarette smoke clinging to the girl. Laughter from a sitcom playing on the lobby television filtered into the office, contrasting starkly with the sad image of the lost young soul slouched in the black vinyl chair. She couldn't be more than fifteen or sixteen. What kind of thoughts went on in this child's head that she felt the need to mutilate herself?

A knot of pain coiled low in Jade's belly. She wanted

to reach out and hug the girl, tell her she didn't have to hurt herself, that nothing was worth that kind of torture. But she knew the girl wouldn't listen. For whatever reason, she'd created her own brand of hell and a hug from a stranger wasn't going to make it go away. If anything, it would drive her further inside herself.

The teen looked everywhere except at Jade, winding a strand of dark, unwashed hair around her index finger. "You won't call my parents?" Her tongue and lip piercings made the words almost indecipherable.

Jade shook her head. "No, Courtney. That's up to you. We want you to feel safe."

She was certain the girl had given a false name, but that was okay, at least she'd come back to the shelter. Jade had been trying off and on for weeks to get through to her. The girl would come by, hang out for an hour or so, then disappear. Each time she reappeared, there'd be new injuries, fresh sorrow in the girl's eyes.

Courtney pulled a near empty pack of cigarettes from the pocket of her denim shirt. The shirt was too large for her and was unbuttoned, revealing a frayed 'Daddy's Girl' tank top underneath. Jade had a feeling it had been a long time since she'd been Daddy's girl.

She put a cigarette between her lips. Jade decided against telling her there was no smoking allowed and passed an empty coke can over to her.

"Are you going to tell me about those?" Jade asked, pointing to the teen's wounds.

Courtney's gaze dropped to Jade's wrist, where a deep purple and yellow bruise stood out like paint on a white canvas. Hurriedly, Jade shoved her hands in her lap, hiding the evidence of her own injury.

"You first," the girl said, blowing a plume of smoke toward the ceiling.

Jade shook her head, fighting a wave of anger as she recalled the scene with her husband.

"I stumbled down the stairs and landed on my wrist. Stupid accident." Jade pretended an interest in the folder on her desk so she wouldn't have to meet Courtney's eyes.

When she looked up again, she saw the girl's face close, the light of trust in her eyes die. Courtney stared for a moment, then shrugged. "Yeah, I fell, too. Sucks,

2

huh?"

Jade clenched her jaw, looking down at her bruised wrists. She hated telling anyone what had happened. Didn't want to admit to the humiliating and frightening incident. But she knew if she wanted to gain Courtney's trust, she had to show her that she trusted her, too. Looking back up, she let out a breath and said, "My husband did this. He was angry because I said I might leave him."

The girl nodded slowly. "I know how that is. My boyfriend gets really pissed when I want to break up or when he sees me talking to another guy. Your husband must really love you."

Jade thought she'd heard wrong. She shook her head, a note of disbelief creeping into her voice. "You don't really believe that, do you? You really think that's what love is?" Her voice became more adamant. "People don't hurt the ones they love. Not on purpose. Not ever."

Courtney shrugged and dropped her cigarette into the coke can. A small sizzle sounded as the butt was extinguished. The girl stared at the can, not meeting Jade's gaze. "Sometimes I hurt so bad inside that I want to make it stop. I think that if I hurt myself on the outside, I'll forget about the inside pain."

Her lower lip trembled, but her eyes were flinty hard. She was a myriad of contradictions...a battered, ancient soul in the body of a child. Jade said nothing, afraid that if she spoke, the girl would stop talking.

Lifting a hand, Courtney swiped at her cheeks. "Do you know what its like to wonder what you did to make your family hate you? When I ran away, they didn't even look for me. I think my mom was glad."

Jade's heart squeezed and she tried to keep the tears from her voice. "Yes, I know what its like. It won't do me any good to say that I'm sure your mother loves you because I'm not. I don't know your mother. And not all mothers love their daughters. But, I can promise you that hurting yourself is not the answer. I can also promise you that the people here care about you. If you stay, you'll see that. You'll be safe with us here."

"You're the first person I ever told about this," she said quietly. "I don't even know why. There's something about you...like, you really do understand."

"I do. I was once a lot like you." The girls eyes widened in doubt and Jade continued. "Really. I ran away when I was sixteen. I lived on the streets for almost a year. It was awful." She didn't tell her that going back home was almost as bad. Or that she'd only gone back for a few months before she ran again. "When I moved out the next time, I stayed with my best friend, got a job and went to school to be an accountant. It was the best decision I ever made. I was finally, truly free and I never had to wonder where my next meal would come from, where I'd sleep for the night."

Courtney nodded. "Maybe I'll stay. For a while, anyway."

"Great. It's up to you. Just know that you're welcome here."

A tentative smile touched her lips. "Thanks. Are you here every day?"

"I'm a volunteer and I'm here just a few days a week."

"Oh." Courtney looked down where her fingers worried the buttons of her shirt. "I don't know the others. I'm not sure..."

"We have a staff counselor you'll really like. I promise. And the director, Mark, is awesome. All the kids love him." Jade shrugged. "I might come around a little more often, if you think you'll be here."

The girl nodded slowly. "Cool."

All these weeks of trying to get through to Courtney, trying to convince her to stay, worrying about what she might do to herself if she didn't. Now she was here. And Jade might be leaving. She couldn't stay with Bryce. Not now. But, could she leave the kids at the shelter?

She had money of her own, money she'd stashed away in case she ever needed her own funds. Bryce was wealthy, but his money was his. He'd insisted Jade quit her job before they married, and like a trained monkey, she'd acquiesced. After a year of marriage, she began to see that the secure, rosy picture she'd had in mind was a mirage. She knew that if she ever decided to leave him, she'd need cash. Unbeknownst to her husband, she'd begun keeping the books for Mark's father's construction

4

company. He paid her under the table, and Jade had saved almost every penny. She now had close to five thousand dollars. The five hundred cash in her purse would put it just over that mark.

Enough to leave Bryce and at least make a start in a new place. But, could she leave the runaways? Could she leave Melanie, her best friend since childhood? Plus, her father had been so thrilled when she and Bryce became engaged. Told her she was '*marrying well*'. That was the nicest thing he'd ever said to her. The only time in her life he'd been proud of her. What would he think when he found out she'd failed at her marriage? Never mind that he'd failed to protect her all those years while she'd grown up with her mother's abuse. After her mother's death, she and her father had forged a relationship she'd longed for all her life. Not your typical father/daughter bond but definitely more than she'd ever hoped for. Could she spoil that tenuous thread by leaving Bryce? The real question was, could she stay in her nightmare of a marriage now that she'd seen his true nature?

****

Jade pulled into the garage, noting that Bryce's white Mercedes was in its spot. So, he was working at home, not at the office. She didn't want to see him, not tonight, not this soon. Maybe not ever. Fortunately, his home office was separate from the main house. He could be there for hours, coming in anywhere from six o'clock on up to nine or later, expecting dinner to be waiting when he was ready. Expecting Berta, his faithful housekeeper but really more of a servant, to have the meal ready when he was ready for it. Which, she always did. After all, Bryce was king. The world and his home revolved around his wants. Berta had been with Bryce for years and adored him almost as much as he adored himself.

The air smelled of Italian food as Jade let herself into the house. Berta met her at the entrance to the dining room. She was backlit by the massive chandelier hanging over the oak dining set. The walls were papered with a French botanical pattern, elegantly offset by the muted terracotta mosaic tile.

"Mr. DiMarco is still working," Berta said unnecessarily. "Dinner will be later."

5

The woman was plump and ageless. Her unlined face and solid gray shock of hair could mean she was anywhere between forty and seventy. She wore a large apron over blue knit slacks and a shapeless blue and white striped blouse. Her lips continually pursed out, then back in. Jade was never certain whether it was her way of expressing disapproval, or a result of ill fitting dentures. Berta had never warmed up to Jade, but treated her with phony respect, underscored with contempt.

"Shall I make you a drink? I'm sure you've had a stressful day."

Jade didn't acknowledge the sarcasm underlying the woman's words. She knew the remark was 'Berta speak' for *You spend your days wallowing in the underbelly of filth while poor Mr. DiMarco toils to keep you in the lap of luxury.*

"No, thank you. I'll be going up to my room. You can call me when Bryce comes in."

The housekeeper's shrewd gaze behind large black framed glasses raked over Jade. She missed nothing, taking in Jade's blonde hair pulled back at the nape of her neck, dark circles beneath hazel eyes and the black silk blouse she wore over ivory slacks, no doubt making her fair skin look paler than usual. Did she notice the bruises? Would she attribute them to the man she worshipped? If she did, she'd probably dismiss it as Jade's having brought it on herself. In her eyes, Bryce DiMarco could do no wrong.

Berta nodded without comment and Jade escaped to her bedroom, eager to add the cash to her savings before Bryce came in the house. Silently, her feet moved across the plush white carpet to the mahogany four poster bed. She stood in front of the nightstand, the key to the drawer clenched tightly in her fist. She shivered as she remembered the way Bryce's face had contorted in rage. The way he'd stalked toward her and gripped her wrist so hard she thought he'd crush the bones. The fury in his eyes was beyond any she'd ever seen in another human being. Except maybe her mother.

During her two year marriage, Bryce had never shown even the slightest hint of physical violence. Especially not towards her. He'd been controlling, yes, overbearing, belittling, but never violent. Until she'd told him she thought they needed a trial separation.

She'd started out by saying that although she loved him, which she wasn't sure anymore that she did, their marriage had deteriorated over the past year. She didn't feel he regarded her as a partner, more as a possession. She'd finished by suggesting a trial separation and his look of annoyance had morphed into rage.

In that moment, staring into the eyes of her husband, the man who'd sworn to love and protect her, Jade had been terrified. It wasn't the same kind of fear she'd felt as a child, faced with the unrelenting rage of her mother. She'd learned to live with that kind of fear, learned to expect it. This was fear of the unknown, because she never expected Bryce to turn into a monster she didn't recognize. This fear was tinged with sorrow and despair. And the knowledge that once again, she'd put her trust into someone she shouldn't. Once again, she'd been betrayed and threatened by a person who was supposed to love her.

It was then that she knew she *would* leave him. Someday, very soon, but it wouldn't be just a trial separation and when she left, she'd have to disappear forever.

Tears of pain swimming in her eyes, she'd agreed to forget about the separation. She promised Bryce she'd never leave him. He'd released her, his voice colder than the icy wind howling outside, as he calmly said, "You're right. You won't. Because I'd find you. And I'd make you pay. You belong to me."

Now, twenty-four hours later, she could still feel the force of his anger...his cold determination to bend her to his will. Shivers of fear skittered along her spine and she realized she was gripping the key so hard it cut into her palm.

What had happened to the charming, loving man she'd married? What had happened to the fairytale life she envisioned, so different from the one she'd grown up in? As a child, she'd longed to escape, longed to be free of her hellish existence. What she hadn't known was, that like a rat in a maze, she'd land back in the same trap.

Bryce was flying out for a business trip to Los

Angeles in the morning. If she was going to leave, this weekend would be the time to do it. She would pack only the barest essentials. She wouldn't take the jewelry Bryce had given her, not even the custom made necklace with the jade and diamonds shaped in the letter 'J'. He gave it to her on their first anniversary. By then, she'd started to understand the nightmare she'd unwittingly walked into. She'd forced a smile to her lips, thanked him and claimed to love it. In truth, she despised it. It seemed another way for him to lay claim to her, branding her as his own.

That, and the other expensive pieces, would bring a hefty sum at a pawn shop. But, she couldn't take them. For one, she couldn't leave a trail for Bryce to follow. For another, she didn't want to take anything he had purchased. She wanted to be truly free of him. To be independent and know she could take care of herself.

She turned the key in the lock and pulled the drawer open. She froze in mid-motion as she looked into the drawer. Her mouth went dry and her knees nearly buckled. For a moment, she didn't quite comprehend what she was seeing. Or, what she *wasn't* seeing. She stared in numb disbelief, trembling as if an arctic wind had swept through the room. The drawer was empty. The money was gone.

Panic beat in her chest like the wings of a thousand insects. Bryce had found it. He'd taken it, which not only meant she was stuck here, her means of escape vanquished, it also meant he knew she had it. He'd have to wonder how she'd gotten that much money. When had he found it?

Dread settled in the pit of her stomach. She tried to remember the last time she'd been in the drawer. Mark's father paid her twice a month. She'd gotten her previous paycheck last month on the twentieth. This was the fourth. She hadn't been in the drawer for fourteen days. Bryce could have found it at any time during that period. Is that why he'd been so furious last night? He'd found the money, and she'd wanted a separation. Had he also discovered how she'd gotten the money? That she'd actually had the nerve to work without his knowledge? Had the nerve to disobey his orders?

He'd be livid if he found out his wife had lowered

herself to work for money. As if he couldn't provide for her, give her everything she could possibly need or want.

Oh God. He knew. She felt it, deep in her bones. He knew and he was playing some kind of game. What would he do?

Wait a minute. Why was she afraid? *Bryce* was the one who'd done wrong. He'd actually stolen money from her. How dare he take what she'd worked so hard to save? He hadn't done it because he needed the money, she knew that. He'd done it because she wasn't supposed to have anything of her own. She was his property, therefore, *her* property belonged to him.

All at once, her fear turned to anger.

Storming downstairs, past Berta and out the rear entrance of the house, she marched toward Bryce's office.

Almost without seeing the swimming pool as she passed by, without feeling the cold air through her ivory wool jacket, she arrived at Bryce's office, breathing heavily with her rage.

Not bothering to knock, she pushed the door open, stopping when she saw that Bryce was not alone.

Her husband sat behind the desk and a man she didn't recognize stood in the middle of the room. He was tall, with tightly coiled muscles beneath a black Harley Davidson tee shirt. His longish white-blonde hair was pulled back in a ponytail and a small gold hoop dangled from his ear. Whiskers a few shades darker than his hair covered his upper lip and chin.

"Hello, darling," Bryce said. "Is there something I can help you with?"

She nodded toward the stranger. "Hello." He responded with barely a nod and she turned back to Bryce. "I'm sorry. I didn't know you were in a meeting. But I need to speak with you. Now."

His brows lifted and a hint of the anger she'd witnessed last night surfaced. "Now? Are you certain about that? I believe you can see I'm busy."

"Yes, I can see that." Her gaze shifted to the man. He hadn't moved, hadn't said a word but his presence couldn't be ignored. Energy radiated from him like the current from an electrical charge. Normally, Jade would be intimidated by such a forceful presence, but right now, she was too angry to be effected.

"I had some money in my nightstand drawer. And it's gone. I wondered if you knew anything about it."

"Money?"

"Yes. Almost five thousand dollars."

A grin touched his lips, but his eyes were hard. "I didn't know you had that much money, darling. What an enterprising little soul I married. Did it occur to you that one of those derelicts from the shelter might have taken it?"

"That's impossible. They've never been here."

"They could easily find out where you live. They could have broken in while we were gone." The grin turned cruel. "When you feed strays, they often follow you home."

Strays? Jade's fists clenched in the pockets of her coat. "They're not animals. And I'm certain none of them broke in. You've got this place secured like an armored car. It was either Berta, or you."

The skin on Bryce's face visibly tightened. White lines appeared around his lips. Silence filled the room, sounding louder than the boom of a cannon. "You're accusing me of *theft*? Of pilfering your measly stash?"

She knew she'd pushed too hard when she saw a tic at the corner of his mouth. It wouldn't do any good to enrage him, especially in front of his guest. "I didn't mean that you'd stolen it. I thought maybe you'd moved it, for safe keeping."

"I'm sorry, dear." Bryce's voice was calm but a slight tremble in his clasped fists indicated a fragile hold on his temper. "I have no idea what happened, but I assure you, I'll launch a full investigation and get to the bottom of this *pressing* matter."

Warmth moved up her neck and into her cheeks. Bryce's attempt to humiliate her in front of his guest was working. But she wouldn't let it show. She swallowed back the anger before she spoke. "Thank you."

"Now, if you'll excuse me, Mr. Smith and I have business to discuss."

The stranger still hadn't spoken. His silence unnerved her. Jade felt an irresistible pull and flicked a glance at the man. She resisted the urge to take a step back when her gaze collided with the vivid green of his. The urge became stronger when his eyes moved up her body, then settled on her face. A chill skimmed her flesh.

The set of his firm mouth and the glint in his eyes was disconcerting and at the same time, riveting. She pulled her coat tightly around her, almost feeling the man's gaze penetrate the fabric of her blouse.

Dragging her attention from him, she turned back to Bryce and forced a smile through frozen lips. "Certainly. I didn't mean to interrupt you. I'll let you get back to your meeting.

"Thank you, darling. I'll be in shortly. Goodbye."

Jade recognized the tone. She'd heard it before. False affection tinged with anger. She'd been dismissed. She nodded and left the room.

As she made her way back to the house, her anger built once more. Was Bryce holding her money on his person or had he put it in his office? She wasn't sure, but she intended to tear the house and his office apart until she found it. Tomorrow morning he would leave for Los Angeles. She planned to use that opportunity to find the money. And be gone before he returned.

Chapter Two

Special Agent Delia Grimes could feel the eyes of her fellow agents burning a hole in her back as she returned to her desk. The room was silent. Too silent. The hum of computers and the tick of the clock were the only sounds to be heard. Somehow, the stillness accentuated the heavy scorched smell of coffee sitting too long on the burner.

What were they up to?

Then she saw it and she knew. Her body went still and her face flamed with embarrassment. Sucking in a breath, she took a seat, not acknowledging the 'gift' her co-workers had placed on the cluttered surface of her desk. She didn't look up, but when she heard the muted snickers, she knew they were aware she'd seen it.

A mug shot encased in a condom. Very funny. Very freakin funny.

The only reason she was here, at her desk, was because she'd fucked up. Yes, she admitted it, she'd fucked up. But, she didn't deserve this. Didn't deserve to be pulled out of the field and assigned to desk duty. Okay, so she'd been screwing a felon. And, okay, he was a suspect in a case they were currently working. Not good. She'd made a bad choice. She always made bad choices when it came to men, but this one had to be the worst.

She'd been a runway model before she became an FBI agent. Tall, with fiery red hair, ivory skin and green eyes, she'd had some success in the industry but she'd always wanted to be more. Wanted to prove she wasn't just a pretty face. She'd been so proud when she'd made it through the academy at Quantico, thinking now she'd automatically earn respect from men instead of them wanting to jump her bones. She'd been wrong. The respect had been a long time coming. But, she'd finally earned it. And now, she'd screwed it up. By the very thing she'd meant to avoid...hopping into bed with every man that desired her. She was certain a psychiatrist would relate her actions to not having a dad when she was growing up, trying to win the affection of men since she didn't have it as a child. Maybe that was true. Whatever the reason, she couldn't seem to say 'no'. And look where it had gotten her.

Her phone rang and she picked it up. "Special Agent Delia Grimes."

"Hey, you okay?" It was Luke Butler, her partner. *Asshole.* Even though he hadn't been the one to rat her out--she'd been caught in the act by another agent--he damned sure hadn't come to her defense. As a matter of fact, he'd told the Special Agent in Charge that he recommended desk duty until the case was over so she wouldn't further compromise the operation.

She stared at the mug shot, not wanting to touch it, but wanting to wish it away. "Fan-fucking-tastic," she responded, not even trying to keep the resentment out of her voice. She knew Luke had done the right thing but she wouldn't let him off the hook that easily. She had to take her anger out on someone. Besides, *he'd* been one of her bad decisions. It had turned out better than most, they were still friends, but nonetheless, still a mistake.

"I'm expecting a call." His tone became business-like. "I'm leaving my cell on silent but I had a message from an informant. He couldn't reach me so he said he'd call the office with the information. Didn't leave a number where I could call him back. Can you take a message and I'll call you when I get a chance?"

"Sure, no problem. Desk jockey Grimes at your service."

"Del, listen..."

"No. I'm tired of listening to you. Tired of getting stabbed in the back by my friends."

His heavy sigh spoke volumes. Regret...sadness...but righteous confidence that he'd done the right thing. *Whatever.*

"I gotta go," she said. "I'll take your message."

"Thanks."

She felt guilty when she hung up. Just a little. If he hadn't told her his phone was off, she might have called him back to apologize. He was involved in a dangerous undercover operation. The same operation she'd almost screwed up by sleeping with a suspect. Anything could happen to him. Agents often died in the field.

Luke was her best friend. He'd been nothing but kind to her, letting her cry on his shoulder after every failed relationship. And, he'd been the perfect gentleman when he'd ended their fling, somehow making her feel he was doing her a favor, while at the same time breaking her heart. When she spoke to him again, she'd be nicer. As bad as the situation was, it wasn't his fault.

An hour later, the call he was waiting on came through. The man's voice was hushed, disguised.

"This dude says the cargo's at a warehouse near the river."

Delia jotted down the information. "You have an address?"

"Yeah," sarcasm dripped from his tone, so thick it was unmistakable even through the phone line. "He gave me the address in case I wanted to mapquest it and pop in for a little look-see at the contraband." The man snorted, then continued. "Of course he didn't give me no address. He was just braggin' about how they got this high dollar cargo and they're all gonna be rich. This guy was switching off with a few other guys, guarding the goods. From what Butler was askin' about, it sounded like it might have something to do with the case he's got."

Delia was tempted to take her frustrations out on this smartass, to lambaste him with a few words that would make a sailor blush. But, she decided not to. What little help he gave was better than nothing, and if she pissed him off, he might withhold even that.

"Is there anything else you can tell me?" she asked with forced civility.

"Well, I don't exactly have the address, but I know pretty much where the warehouse is. When the guy headed out, I followed him, figuring if I got something real good, Butler might show his appreciation by way of cold hard cash. Tell him if he wants to know what I found out, meet me at Nick's pub on Manchester and I'll take him there after he shows me some green."

A thrill of excitement ran through her. They'd been looking for the girls for months. Girls who'd been snatched off the streets, runaways who wouldn't be missed because they were already missing. The bastards were selling the kids to Mexican whorehouses. Luke was undercover to bring down the big guns behind the operation. The guy Delia had fucked was small potatoes. The FBI wanted the evil master mind...the asshole in charge.

She didn't know how long it would be before she'd hear back from Luke. With only a moment's hesitation, she said, "Butler asked me to take your call and handle it. I'll meet you and you can take me to the warehouse."

"You got cash?"

"Yeah. I might share it if your info proves helpful."

"You don't share it, you'll never know."

She didn't know if what he had was legit, but it was worth a shot. Not only was Luke unreachable, if she discovered the girls herself, she'd get the credit. And this was big...maybe big enough to get her back in the field. And to wipe the smug grins off the other asshole agent's faces.

Delia pulled on her leather jacket and left without saying a word to anyone. She wasn't going to share this, not until she saw how it turned out. The last thing she needed was another stain on her record.

****

The informant traded his information for fifty bucks. She knew he expected more, but when faced with a choice of fifty dollars or a trip downtown for trying to squeeze a federal agent, he decided she had enough green to buy his information after all.

Now here she was, stealthily approaching the warehouse he'd directed her to. A sharp wind blew, biting through the leather jacket and into her flesh. She pulled her Glock and headed in a crouch toward the warehouse. So far, she'd seen no movement, no sign of life. If this was a dead end, it would cost her fifty dollars and a few hours, but she'd be spared the humiliation of the other agents

15

knowing she'd followed a bum lead.

Windows were set along the sides of the building, but they were blacked out. Even when she made her way to one of them, stretched up to where she was eye level with it, she still couldn't see inside.

She was debating whether to make a bold approach from the front, or give up and tell Luke his informant was full of shit, when she heard male voices coming from the west side of the building. She was on the north.

She crept alongside the wall, stopping when she reached the corner. Slowly, she peered around the building. Two men stood outside, one smoking a cigarette while the other stood next to him, hands shoved deeply in his coat pockets as he stomped the ground, trying to stay warm.

They moved away from the front door, in the opposite direction from her. Once they were far enough away, she turned the corner, keeping in the shadows, her back to the wall. She slowly made her way to the front door, eyes trained on the two men who moved further away. She didn't know where they were going. Maybe to smoke a joint? Or maybe they were into each other and were sneaking off for a little man on man action. Whatever the reason, she was glad they were making her reconnaissance mission easier. Things were falling into place. For once, the gods were smiling down at her. If she found what she thought she might, this could turn out to be the best night of her life.

The door was closed, but the knob twisted beneath her hand and she stepped inside. The room was a large open area, dimly lit with a couple of floor lamps, one on each side. Three sets of tables and chairs were scattered throughout. One table held a deck of cards, a six pack of Dr. Pepper and a Mr. Goodbar wrapper. The other tables were empty. A ratty blue recliner sat against the wall, facing a television. Two folding chairs were on either side of the recliner.

A door toward the back of the warehouse beckoned her. Sweeping her gaze around the room, she confirmed she was alone. Quickly, she made her way to the door. This one was locked. If she shot out the lock, the men would surely hear her. If she didn't, and the girls were inside, she couldn't very well get them out. She leaned her ear against the door but heard nothing.

"Hey," she said in a loud whisper, "Is anyone there?"

No response. Louder, she tried again, "Hey, I'm an FBI agent. I'm here to help you. Can you hear me?"

Still nothing. Making a decision, knowing that once she put it in motion, there was no going back, she fired two rounds into the lock. She heard a squeal from inside the room. Heart hammering with fear and excitement, she gave the door a kick and it swung open. Four young girls, looking dirty and frightened, crouched on individual cots, staring at her.

Relief whirled through her, closing her throat in a tight knot. She'd found the girls. They were okay. Not only had the tip paid off...she'd hit the freakin' motherload.

"Don't be afraid," she told them. "I'm an FBI agent, I'm here to help you. Do you know how many men there are?"

Slowly, almost in unison, the girls shook their heads but didn't speak. And didn't come toward Delia.

She would hope there were only the two men, but assume there could be more. She pulled her radio from her belt and motioned for the girls, "Come on, we've got to hurry. Follow me."

She led the girls toward the door she'd seen at the back of the warehouse. The men could possibly have gone around that way, but she was betting they'd enter the same way they left, through the front door. If they heard the shots, they'd enter sooner than later.

As she and the girls made their way to the back door, she keyed her radio. "This is Special Agent Delia Grimes, requesting backup at..."

The girls had slipped through the door and Delia was about to follow when she heard a shout from behind. "Hey...what the hell?"

She turned, aiming her weapon, dropping into a crouch. "FBI. Freeze!"

Just before the lights were extinguished, she assumed by the man still next to the front door, she saw that the man toward the front held a gun. Rather than following her orders, she saw a flash from the muzzle at almost the same time she felt a sharp, burning sensation in her shoulder. Then, numbness. She dropped the radio, throwing herself behind the door as she fired at the men. She didn't know if she'd hit both of them, but she was sure she'd hit one as she heard a grunt and a thump.

Damn. In the darkness, she couldn't find her radio. The red indicator light at the top should help to pinpoint its location, but she couldn't see even that. And she couldn't venture from behind the door, she wasn't sure if she'd hit either of the shooters. She was doubtful she'd hit both.

The girls. She had to get them to safety. Then, she'd figure out a way to call for backup. She could handle these two bozos on her own, or one if her aim had been true.

Slipping around the door and outside, she saw the four girls huddled together, shivering in the cold. They hadn't run because they didn't know where to run to. One girl seemed a little calmer than the others. She had shaggy purple hair and wore a thin red sweater over shiny gold pants. She stood with her arm around two of the girls while the other clung to her from behind.

Delia quickly approached the girl. "I need you to get away from here, get to a phone as fast as you can. My car's parked on the road a mile or so that way." She pointed the direction she'd come and handed the girl her keys. "Call the FBI and tell them to send backup." She searched in her pockets for a business card and pen. Jotting down the address of the warehouse, she shoved the card at the purple girl. "You can reach them at this number. If you can get in touch with an FBI agent named Luke Butler, I need you to give him a message for me. Can you do that?"

The girl took the card and slowly nodded.

Delia gave her the message and watched until the girls had disappeared completely from sight. She turned, raising her weapon, prepared to re-enter the building to make sure one or both of the goons were incapacitated.

Barely visible as a shadow in her peripheral vision, she saw that, apparently, one of the men was quite capacitated. She registered the thought just before something solid slammed against her head, dropping her to the ground.

A trickle of warmth traveled from her temple into her eye as dizziness assaulted her. The ground seemed to move like the surface of an ocean, but she planted her palms against it, preparing to rise.

The man planted a shoe in her head and speared her face into the ground. Pain seared, hot and sharp from her neck through her head, so severe she thought her eyeballs would explode.

"I don't know who the hell you are, lady. But the boss is on his way. He ain't gonna be too happy about what you did to my buddy, and he's gonna be downright pissed that you let those girls get away." His voice, although threatening, held a touch of fear. She figured he probably knew his ass was fried, too.

So, she was finally going to come face to face with the head honcho. A fatalistic voice inside her agony filled brain told her it might be the last face she saw.

****

Clouds shifted across the moon in a thin line as Jade made her way to the office behind the pool house. The swimming pool was covered with a black tarp and the moonlight glinting on the plastic gave the impression of a deep, black abyss. Rain had begun to fall, spattering onto the cement, shimmering like iridescent confetti in the glow of her flashlight.

She pulled her jacket over her head. She hadn't bothered with an umbrella, not wanting to encumber herself any more than necessary. Knowing Bryce's watchdog, Berta, might come out to investigate the lights in his office, she'd decided a flashlight would be a more useful tool than an umbrella. She was certain Bryce had instructed the woman to keep an eye on his errant wife.

Even from this great distance, she could see the glow of St. Louis' Gateway Arch as it rose above the city skyline, glistening in the drizzle falling from the clouds.

The sight always brought comfort to her. As if no matter how bad things were, how scary or how dark, the arch was there...familiar and solid like an old friend.

She let herself into Bryce's office with the spare key he kept in the study. His workplace consisted of a reception area and his private office. In daylight, the lobby's tile floors with swirls of silver and blue, landscape paintings and smoked glass walls exuded welcoming warmth. Tonight, with the reflection from the outer lights and the eerily moving shadows, the décor held a more sinister ambience.

She headed toward Bryce's office door, rain squelching beneath her feet as she dripped on the floor. She'd have to clean that up before she left, she didn't want to leave evidence of her visit.

A noise sounded behind her and she whirled, halfway across the floor. A quiver of anxiety traveled from her heart to deep in her stomach. She let out a pent up breath when she realized where the sound had come from. She hadn't closed the door fully and the wind had pulled it, clicking it shut. Quickly, anxious to get this done and get out, she made her way to Bryce's private office and turned the knob.

In the dimly lit room, the beam of her flashlight swept over the large oak desk, imported from Italy, the freestanding marble globe with fourteen karat gold inlay, and the photo of her and Bryce on their honeymoon in Cabo, San Lucas.

Shaking her head at what a naïve fool she'd been, she turned away from the photo and moved around the desk. Trying the top drawer, she found it locked. A bolt of anxiety shot through her as the magnitude of what she was doing dawned on her. She was taking a chance...a big one. But the money was hers. And if it was here, she'd find it.

Taking a deep breath, then expelling it slowly, she ignored the apprehension buzzing through her veins and tried the other drawers. All locked.

She searched through the key ring until she found a key small enough that it might open the desk drawers. She inserted the key in the lock, sighing in relief as it turned and the top drawer slid open. She was rifling through papers, absorbed in her task, when a sound penetrated the silence.

Her fingers stilled.

Had it been a door opening?

Raindrops pelted the office window as the storm outside intensified. She glanced toward the closed office door, wondering what was happening just beyond it. If someone were inside, the storm might mask their approach.

Another sound rose over the cacophony in her mind. She recognized this one immediately.

Footsteps.

Who could it be? The creepy guy from earlier? Had he returned to rob Bryce knowing he was out of town? Or, maybe it was Berta, coming to check up on Jade's illicit activities. Whoever it was, she didn't want to be caught pillaging her husband's office. If she were discovered, Bryce would be furious. At the very least she'd suffer the embarrassment of being caught. She was certain his fury from a few nights ago would seem like a ripple on the surface of the ocean compared to the hurricane of rage he'd express if he found her breaking into his office. Besides, if her presence were discovered, she certainly couldn't complete her search.

With trembling fingers, she slid the drawer shut, turned off the flashlight and slipped it into her jacket pocket. Glancing around the office for a place to hide, she spotted a slatted door a few feet from where she stood. She hadn't noticed it before, having only been in Bryce's office a few times. Was it a coat closet?

Only one way to find out.

Her fear of the dark, leftover from childhood, made her hesitate. The fear was so strong, she still slept with a nightlight burning, even at twenty-nine years old. She was being foolish, she knew. The light from the office window would filter through the slats enough that she wouldn't be in total darkness.

But a closet? How could she bring herself to purposely enter the scene of her childhood horrors? But did she have a choice? She didn't. The closet was her only hope.

On legs that were numb yet at the same time tingled painfully, she stepped to the door, then paused. Memories crowded her mind. Memories of being a small child locked in a dark closet, never knowing for how long, never knowing what was in the small space with her, never knowing when something would reach out and--

The sound of the doorknob turning broke her paralysis. In spite of every tendon in her body screaming in protest, she pulled the closet door open and slipped inside the darkened cavern. The walls seemed to shrink around her and a shudder ran the length of her body. She couldn't breathe. Willing air through her lungs, she closed her eyes and silently chanted the mantra she'd learned in therapy...*nothing to fear...nothing to fear...nothing to fear...*

She heard the office door close. Then silence. Unable to stand the tension a moment longer, she peeked through the panels. Aided by the light filtering through the office window, she recognized the intruder.

Bryce.

He was supposed to be out of town. He'd lied to her! Then, she almost laughed at the incongruous thought. Bryce's lying to her was the least of her problems.

From her hiding place, she watched him turn on the light. He walked over to the desk, his movements jerky and agitated. Now she saw him more clearly and she almost gasped out loud.

He looked rumpled and distraught. His suit was wrinkled and his tie hung loosely around his neck. His blond hair, darkened by rainwater, was mussed as if he'd been running his fingers through it. A heavy scowl marred his features.

His haggard appearance shocked her almost more than his outburst of violence had. She had never seen her husband looking anything other than elegantly composed.

He picked up the phone and punched some buttons. Not bothering with a greeting, he barked into the receiver, "Find them yet?" He listened for a moment, then shook his head. "Motherfucker." He dropped into his chair. "The cop bitch screwed us. El Lobo's people will go fucking ballistic. Not to mention the fortune we lost."

He was silent, then said, "Maybe I shouldn't have, but she wasn't going to tell us anything." He slammed his fist on the desk and cursed again. Jade jumped, covering her mouth to keep from crying out. "The bitch protected those girls to the very end. No matter what I did, she wouldn't break."

He rubbed a hand over his face, then drew back and stared at it with a puzzled expression. A dark smear appeared on his cheek. He pulled a handkerchief from his suit pocket and wiped his face, then his hands.

Dear God, was that blood? Jade's legs quivered and she planted her palms against the wall. The cold surface was solid and reassuring. A link to reality in a world that had suddenly become a surreal nightmare. She held on tightly...squeezing her eyes shut as hot tears threatened to spill.

The recent glimpses of Bryce's violent nature hadn't prepared her for this. She had no idea what was going on. No idea what Bryce was involved in, but she knew he'd done something bad. Something very bad. And she knew if he caught her here, listening in on his conversation, she'd find out exactly what he was capable of.

Her chest pulsed with the effort of holding back sobs.

Don't cry, don't cry, don't cry.

"El Lobo is meeting me with the cash. I won't take him to the warehouse until I hear from you. I'll stall him as long as I can."

Jade's lips parted as she tried to pull air into her lungs. Her breath hitched, a faint sound but one that seemed deafening in the dark silence of the closet.

Bryce lifted his head, peering around the office. "I need to go. Find those goddamned girls and I'll deal with El Lobo."

The blood in Jade's veins turned to ice. He knew she was here. If Bryce looked for her, he would find her. She pressed herself against the wall and waited, motionless, like a deer caught in the scope of a rifle.

His chair creaked so she knew he'd gotten up, but she couldn't tell if he headed in her direction. The thick carpeting would muffle his footsteps. He could be anywhere.

She heard him breathing and knew he had to be close--mere inches from where she hid. Her body tensed. Perspiration pooled in her armpits. She pressed further against the wall, her hysterical mind clinging to the foolish hope he wouldn't find her.

Seconds later, the closet door flew open.

A scream tore from her throat as her husband loomed in front of her, filling her vision. His face registered shock, then, what she thought was sorrow before he grabbed her shoulders and jerked her from the closet.

Underneath the scent of the expensive cologne he wore, she detected the odor of sweat and the river. She choked back the surge of nausea rising from her chest.

"Jade? For God's sake, what are you doing here?"

She couldn't speak. Fear raced through her body, numbing her vocal cords.

Bryce shook her roughly. "Answer me, damn you."

"Where did the blood come from?" she managed, her voice barely more than a whimper.

Something flickered in his eyes. "What blood?"

"I saw it. You wiped it off but I saw it. What have you done, Bryce?"

A gasp of air escaped from his clenched teeth. "You're my wife. You're supposed to trust me."

"Please let me go."

She tried to pull away but he held her tightly. He was so close, his hot breath seared the skin of her cheek. "I'm not letting you go until you tell me what the hell you're doing here." His voice held the warning hiss of a cobra.

She stared at him, not believing what was happening. "Who did you hurt tonight, Bryce? What's happened to those girls?" She dreaded the answer even as the question fell from her lips.

"What girls? What have you heard?" His fingers dug into her flesh. "You're working with the police, aren't you?"

Jade shook her head. "I wasn't working with the police. I don't know what you're talking about." The strength in her voice surprised her. Inside, she was a quaking volcano.

"Liar." Bryce snarled, shaking her once more. Fury emanated from him, exploding like fireworks in his ice blue eyes.

Seized by desperation, she pleaded with him. "You're hurting me. Please let me go."

He reached into his pocket. Grabbing her hair, he jerked her head back. Needles of pain shot from her scalp to her neck and tears sprang to her eyes. Something sharp and cold pressed against her exposed neck. Her horrified mind recognized the object.

A knife.

She was going to die. Her heart ached with betrayal at the same time fear kicked into high gear...into terror. The man who'd once swore he loved her, had promised to cherish and protect her, was about to end her life.

She'd always heard when people were about to die, their life flashed before them. But that didn't happen now. All she saw was her father...heard his voice telling her what a good catch Bryce was. Would he feel the same when he was looking down at the corpse of his daughter? She'd always wanted to please her father, and now it looked like she would die trying.

"How long have you known?" Bryce demanded. "Who have you told?"

Terror and disbelief squeezed her throat, rendered her mute. Her only response was a slight shake of her head. It was all she could manage with his grip fastened on her hair.

He released his hold and spun her around with her back to him. He clamped an arm around her shoulders and pulled her against his chest. He slid the dull side of the knife lightly along her cheek.

"I'd hate to mar your loveliness by cutting those beautiful green eyes out of your head, but if you push me, I will do exactly that." The blade moved to her neck. His harsh laugh vibrated against her ear. "You don't want to test me, darling. It would be in your best interest to tell me what I want to know. Understand?"

Jade's brain clicked frantically. She searched for something to say that would delay the inevitable. Terror overtook her. She couldn't think straight. Barely cognizant of the words tumbling from her lips, she began to speak. "I don't know anything. I just came here to look for..." She stopped. *I just came here to steal back the money you stole from me.* Wouldn't that infuriate him even more? "I mean...I just wanted to..."

His hold tightened. The tip of the knife pricked her skin. "Stop fucking with me, Jade. Spit it out or you die right now."

"DiMarco." A deep voice spoke from the doorway. Bryce wheeled toward the sound, still clasping Jade against him.

Mr. Smith stood inside the office with a gun pointed

at them.

Hysteria bubbled to the surface, coming out as choked laughter. If there had been any hope of survival, it was gone now. Between Bryce's knife and the stranger's gun, she didn't stand a chance. Hysteria changed to tears of despair that spilled down her cheeks. She slumped in Bryce's grip, facing the certainty of her impending death.

"El Lobo," Bryce breathed softly, his voice full of awe and...fear?

"Let her go, DiMarco."

"What? You must be crazy. She knows too much."

The man pointed the gun at Bryce's head. "I said let her go."

Jade detected a faint quiver in Bryce's body. "Why the fuck are you protecting her?"

El Lobo shook his head. "I don't give a damn either way but the last thing we need is the messy murder of a prominent citizen's wife to muddy the waters. Our goal is to make the exchange. Tonight. If I go back empty handed, I'm a dead man. We don't need a murder rap to draw attention to our transaction."

"Fuck you." Bryce stepped back and pulled her with him. El Lobo advanced too.

"This is between you and me." The stranger's voice was devoid of emotion. He seemed to be the only one in the room not on the brink of hysteria. "Take it easy. Think this through." He took another step.

"Stop right there or I'll cut her fucking head off," Bryce screamed. Jade could see him from the corner of her eye. His face was an insane mask of fury. "Drop the gun...now!"

"Bryce, please...for God's sake," Jade cried.

"Shut up, Jade. Goddamit, *shut up!*"

Bryce's hold tightened. If the knife didn't kill her, his grip on her windpipe would. She tugged on his arm, trying to loosen his grasp.

"I get it now," Bryce said to El Lobo, a note of realization in his tone. "You're fucking her. That's why you're protecting her. I saw the way you looked at each other last night."

El Lobo's eyes shifted to Jade, then dismissed her and went back to Bryce. "I never saw her before last night. You're out of your mind. Listen..."

"You're fucking lying!" Bryce cut him off. "You two are in on this together. You got the girls already, didn't you? That's why they disappeared. You found them and you're trying to screw me over."

El Lobo's face paled beneath his tanned skin. "The girls are gone?"

"Don't play dumb with me, motherfucker!" Bryce's trembling hand pressed the knife to Jade's throat. She tensed, letting out a whimper as she felt the tip of the knife pierce her flesh.

"Ok, let her go and I'll put the gun down." El Lobo squatted, the gun out in front of him but no longer pointed at Bryce.

"Drop the goddamned gun and move away from it!"

"Look, we can still go through with the deal." El Lobo stood, his hands held in front of him, palms up, showing Bryce he was no longer a threat. "She can't prove anything. Let her go. You stand to lose a lot if this goes bad."

Bryce maneuvered around with Jade still held in his grasp. He stopped when they were in front of the large window.

"You're right." His hold loosened. "I stand to lose a lot."

Jade sensed a sudden movement. She realized with surreal wonder that Bryce had sliced the knife across her neck.

Her hands flew to her throat. Blood gushed between her fingers. She sank to the floor, finally free of Bryce's grip.

Through a blur of pain, she was vaguely aware of El Lobo lifting his gun and yelling something unintelligible-- shattering glass as Bryce hurled himself through the window into the rain drenched night--the booming echo of a gunshot--and El Lobo running to the window.

The man looked back and forth between Bryce's escape route and where she lay on the floor. Moving to her side, he tore off his shirt and pressed it against her throat, cursing under his breath.

The metallic taste of blood filled her mouth. Iciness twisted deep inside her--seized her skin. Her body convulsed. She clawed at the hands that held her. Dear God, she couldn't breathe.

In her delirium, she saw a blurred image of demonic red eyes and huge fangs.

This must be what death looks like.

The room faded in and out like the screen of a movie theatre as it switched frames. She tried to stay awake, afraid of what the blackness would bring, but her mind wouldn't focus.

"Hold on," a voice murmured. "Please don't die on me, please don't die."

She wanted to answer but couldn't. His words came from far away, then disappeared completely.

The world went silent as darkness swallowed her.

Chapter Three

Luke Butler was a little out of practice when it came to praying, but he prayed now. He prayed that the woman bleeding to death before his eyes would survive. She might be his only hope of capturing her husband. She might also be his only hope of finding Delia. He'd called to see what she'd found out from the informant. That was when he learned that she'd taken off, called in briefly only to be cut short before she could give her location, and hadn't been heard from since.

He flipped his cell phone open with one hand, using his other to keep pressure on the shirt. As he punched 911 into the keypad, the storm outside intensified and the night sky sent a deluge of cold rain through the broken window.

"911 operator." A sudden crash of thunder nearly obliterated the voice on the other end of the line.

"This is FBI Special Agent Luke Butler. I need backup and an ambulance." He gave them the address and DiMarco's description and told them to dispatch units to search for him. After disconnecting, he called Special Agent Wayne Jackson's direct line, relieved when Wayne answered on the first ring.

"DiMarco got away but his wife is here with me. The sonofabitch tried to kill her." Sticky blood stained Luke's fingers, seeping from around the shirt and into the gray carpet.

"How'd he get away?"

Luke cursed as he was reminded of the choice he'd had to make a few moments earlier. Go after DiMarco and leave his wife to die, or stay with her and let the bastard escape, blowing his chance to find out what happened to Delia.

"I fired at him but I fuckin' missed. I had to stay with her," Luke replied shortly, knowing he'd made the right choice. Jade DiMarco was fighting for her life. There was no way he could have left her to die.

He hoped Delia was okay. He hoped this sick feeling in his gut had more to do with worry than with instinct.

"Is the woman going to be all right?" Wayne asked.

"Hell, I don't know. I'm not a doctor." She was pale and she'd lost a lot of blood. Her blonde hair was soaked with it.

"I hear sirens." Wayne told him at the exact moment Luke heard them too. "The ambulance must be there."

"Yeah. Its about time," Luke replied, although it had only been a few minutes since he'd made the call.

"I'll let you know if we catch DiMarco."

"I'm going after him as soon as I get her into the ambulance. I still haven't heard from Delia. I think DiMarco might have..." He couldn't finish the sentence.

"Don't worry, man. I'm sure she's fine."

"She'd better be." Luke almost choked on the words. DiMarco would pay dearly for what he'd done to the young girls he kidnapped, but Luke would personally kill the sonofabitch if he'd hurt his partner.

They ended the call as the paramedics arrived. Luke moved out of the way and let them take over, hoping with every fiber of his being that Jade DiMarco survived.

****

Luke arrived home as a sliver of daylight sliced through a purple haze of clouds. He stood in the silence without turning on a light and waited for the promise of a new day to seep through him and give him hope he would find Delia alive. The burst of optimism never came. His bones ached with weariness and frustration.

As soon as the ambulance left with Jade DiMarco, he'd gone in search of her husband but hadn't found a trace of him. Or a trace of what happened to Delia.

She wasn't supposed to be involved in the case any longer. Shouldn't have gone off on her own. But, knowing her, she'd probably felt she had something to prove. After

Luke helped in getting her assigned to desk duty, she'd been angry and aloof. He figured when the operation was over, he'd talk to her and convince her to forgive him. If something had happened to her and he didn't get a chance to gain her forgiveness, he wasn't sure how he'd handle it. But, if DiMarco had done something to her, he was certain how he'd handle him.

DiMarco had been kidnapping young runaways and selling them into prostitution. Luke had posed as a broker for a Mexican brothel and last night he was to finalize the deal. Once he received the money, DiMarco would lead him to the warehouse where the girls were held.

Now DiMarco had escaped, his wife had almost died and from what DiMarco had said, the kidnap victims had disappeared. And, to top it all off, Delia was missing. *Jesus. What next?*

Right now, he would kill for a shower and a long, dreamless nap. What he really wanted was to call his daughter, Samantha, but it was too early. She was in Atlanta, an hour ahead, but it was barely six-thirty a.m. His ex-wife would flip if he rang her phone at seven-thirty on a Saturday morning.

He and his ex-wife, Jessica, had divorced five years ago when Samantha was a little over a year old. Luke had arrived home from one of many extended undercover operations to find Jessica waiting for him, suitcases packed.

She calmly explained she'd found someone else. She and his daughter were tired of the lonely nights without him. The final twist of the knife was when she told him that she knew he wouldn't mind. He'd made it clear that the job meant more to him than they did.

Luke had been devastated but not surprised. He *had* spent too much time away from home but not because his job meant more to him than his family. It was just the opposite. He did what he did to make the world safer for them. He couldn't make Jessica understand that, so he hadn't even tried.

The man his ex-wife hooked up with had moved Luke's family to Georgia not long after the divorce. The guy was gone now, others had taken his place but his daughter still lived over five hundred miles away.

He walked into the bathroom and flipped on the light. The face that looked back at him was not his own but it somehow seemed more familiar. He'd worn the disguise for so long, he'd almost forgotten what he looked like. There was no need to wear it any longer. That phase of the operation was over.

He pulled off the blond wig, removed the green contacts and opened the medicine cabinet. Covering his face in shaving cream, he used a razor to remove the mustache and beard. Then he stripped off his clothes. Turning the shower on full blast, he stepped under the hot spray. He scrubbed his body and then shampooed his hair.

He toweled himself dry as he walked into the bedroom. His gaze moved to the bed. He was tempted to crawl beneath the covers. He wanted nothing more than to slip between the cool sheets and lose himself in the oblivion of sleep.

It had been a long night. It would be an even longer day. Sleep was the last thing he had time for. Besides, how could he sleep without knowing where Delia was? And without knowing if Jade DiMarco had survived the night.

****

When Luke walked through the doors of University Hospital, the sharp smell of antiseptic stung his nostrils, making him queasy. The hospital seemed almost deserted in the early morning hours. His footsteps sounded unnaturally loud in the still corridors as he approached room four-seventeen.

He badged the officer guarding Mrs. DiMarco and entered her room.

A network of tubes snaked from the machines beside her bed into her nose and to the IV in her arm. She looked so small, so helpless. Almost childlike. Her features were relaxed in sleep but once in a while, her brow would furrow and she would make little mewling sounds as if having a bad dream. He wondered if it was a sign she'd be regaining consciousness soon. She probably wasn't in a hurry to wake up. The reality she would face when she did wouldn't be pleasant.

Luke turned when the door opened. A heavyset nurse

with bright red hair and stern features entered the room. She was dressed in nursing whites as opposed to the colorful scrubs most of them seemed to favor these days.

"How is she?" Luke whispered.

The woman shrugged. "Too soon to tell. The doctor will be in this morning to check on her. We'll know more then. For now, her vitals are good and she's resting comfortably. That's about all we can hope for at this stage of the game."

He nodded and stepped aside to let the nurse perform her duties. She checked the IV and the monitors, then left.

Exhaustion burned his eyes as he stared down at the woman. His mind went over the events of the previous night. Was there something he could have done differently to keep her from winding up here?

His shock at finding DiMarco holding a knife to his wife's neck had propelled him into instinct mode. His first priority had been to prevent the woman from being hurt. He had failed miserably at that, but at least she was still alive.

He watched her for a few more minutes. Obviously, she wasn't going to wake up right away. She was in capable hands. He'd be notified as soon as she regained consciousness. No reason to hang around.

As he turned to leave, an anguished cry made him stop. Moving back to the bed, he saw tears trickling from the woman's closed lids. She lifted a pale hand and as if it were the most natural thing in the world, he took it, closing his fingers around hers. The lines on her brow smoothed and she seemed to relax. Her cold hand warmed to his touch. Suddenly, he didn't want to leave.

Without releasing her hand, he pulled a chair next to the bed and sat. The room was dark and quiet. A feeling of intimacy settled over him. What was it about this woman that made him want to take care of her? To ease her suffering? He was partially responsible for her being here in the first place, but he knew there was more to it than that.

Before he had time to analyze his feelings, his cell phone vibrated against his hip. Using his free hand, he took the phone off his belt clip.

"Butler." He spoke quietly into the phone.

"We got him." Wayne said abruptly.

"Where?"

"He sent one of his lackeys to his house, probably for some cash. The guy had ten thousand dollars on him. Snyder was on the stakeout and he tailed the dumbass right to DiMarco."

"Good work." Luke was sincere in his praise but he couldn't help wishing he'd been the one to nab DiMarco. "Where is he now?"

"They're booking him. Where are you?"

"The hospital."

"Doing your own stakeout, huh?"

Luke brushed his thumb along the soft skin of her knuckles. "Something like that."

"I figure by the time you meet me there, they'll have DiMarco in interrogation. You can get first crack at him."

"I'll be there in ten minutes."

Luke disengaged his hand from hers and left the room. He intended to get information about Delia from DiMarco, one way or another. Even if he had to beat it out of him.

****

Jade tried to open her eyes but the bright light hurt, so she closed them again. Ironically, she wanted to escape into the blackness that had always held such fear for her. Voices penetrated her consciousness and kept her from slipping away. Why wouldn't they just go away and let her sleep?

Reluctantly, she lifted her lids. Through a blur, she saw two men looking down at her. They were wearing almost identical suits. The only difference between them was that one was a lighter shade of gray than the other.

"She's awake," light gray said.

"Mrs. DiMarco." Dark gray spoke in a calm monotone. "Can you hear me?"

She nodded. Shards of pain screeched through her throat, causing her to regret the movement. She lay still for a moment until the pain eased, then carefully turned her head. A heart monitor beeped next to her bed. An IV stood beside it, hooked to the tubes in her arms and nose. She was in a hospital room.

"Mrs. DiMarco. Do you remember what happened? Do you know where you are?"

Jade tried to speak but her mouth was so dry her lips stuck together. Her tongue felt twice its normal size. "Thirsty," she croaked.

Light gray poured a glass of water from the pitcher on the tray next to her bed. He placed a straw in the cup and held it to her lips. She sipped gratefully. Nothing had ever tasted as delicious as the cool water sliding between her lips and down her throat. After letting her take no more than two or three sips, he pulled the glass away. She almost cried at being deprived of the soothing liquid.

"I'm sorry. You probably shouldn't have too much right now."

"Who are you?" Her voice was still hoarse but the words came out more clearly than before.

"We're with the FBI," dark gray said. "Do you remember what happened?"

Jade wrinkled her brow, trying to concentrate on a memory just at the edge of her consciousness. Then it came. She shut her eyes, feeling tears at the back of her lids. "My husband tried to kill me."

Dark gray looked at light gray and gave a slight nod. "I'm Special Agent Miller and this is Special Agent Connor. If you feel up to it, we need to ask you a few questions."

Before she could answer, the door opened and a nurse entered the room. "Give me a few minutes, gentlemen." The portly, red haired woman commanded. "I need to check on my patient."

The agents moved a few inches, barely allowing enough space for the nurse to squeeze through. "I guess I didn't make myself clear," she said. "I want you out of here. Shoo, go on, out!"

The men exchanged glances. "Miss, we need to..." light grey began.

"You need to get out, now!" She glared at them until they left the room.

"How you feeling, sweetie?" the woman asked, all traces of gruffness gone from her voice.

"I'm not sure yet."

"My name is Rosalyn and I'll be taking care of you. If

you need anything at all, just push this button." Rosalyn picked up the remote and showed Jade the nurse button. "Are you in much pain?"

"Not too much."

"Believe me, honey, you can thank the drugs for that." She placed a cylinder in Jade's hand. "Here's a morphine pump that you can use yourself. See this button on the end? If you start hurting, just give it a squeeze and you should be in la la land in no time."

"How bad is my injury?"

"It was a pretty nasty cut but, thank heavens, nothing vital was damaged. Missed your carotid artery. The doc put some stitches in you. Now it's just a matter of lettin' nature and the good Lord do their work. The doctor will be in later to check on you and you can ask him about it then. I know it doesn't feel that way to you right now, but you're a very lucky young woman. You're doing amazingly well considering what happened. You must be one tough cookie, although a body couldn't tell it by lookin' at ya."

Rosalyn fussed around her, readjusting her pillows and smoothing the hair off her brow. She checked the monitors and stuck a digital thermometer in Jade's ear. "Good girl, you're coming along fine. Do you feel like talking to R2 and D2 out there or do you want me to make them go away?"

Jade didn't think getting rid of the FBI would be an easy task but she had a feeling that if anyone could do it, Rosalyn could. "No, it's okay." She smiled at the older woman. "I'll talk to them."

"Ok, but if you get tired or start hurting, call me and I'll send 'em packin'."

As soon as Rosalyn was out the door, the agents re-entered. Standing next to her bed, they gazed down at her with matching looks of concern.

"Is Bryce in jail? Did you catch him?" she asked.

"Yes, he was apprehended this morning."

She nodded, feeling marginally better but not completely safe.

"Mrs. DiMarco, we need you to tell us, as accurately as possible, exactly what happened. Please start from the beginning."

Jade told them everything she could think of, starting with Thursday night when she interrupted the meeting between Bryce and Mr. Smith.

"I'm sorry. I don't really know much. I overheard my husband on the phone, but I'm not sure what it all meant."

"We're very sorry for what you've gone through and we appreciate your cooperation. I know that speaking is probably painful for you but if you could just tell us as much as you can about that night, it would be a big help."

Her throat had started to hurt even more but she didn't want to hit the morphine pump until she told the agents everything she could. She nodded and slowly, painfully, began speaking.

She told them what she'd overheard about the 'cop bitch'. When she said that, the two agents looked at one another and then back at her, waiting quietly as she continued.

"There was blood on Bryce's hands." She shuddered at the memory. "Or at least, I think it was blood." Pain and horror strangled her words. "I'm pretty certain he'd hurt someone that night."

Miller took a deep breath. He pursed his lips and expelled air. "Mrs. DiMarco, did your husband say anything about where the person was? Maybe something about where he left the victim?"

Jade shook her head. "No, not a thing. Can you answer a few questions for me?"

"We can try."

"What exactly was my husband involved in?"

"He kidnapped young runaways, girls who were living on the streets. His intention was to sell them into prostitution. Brothels in Mexico seem to favor young American girls."

Jade had braced herself for something horrible but never in her wildest dreams had she imagined something like this. Bile rose in her throat. She closed her eyes to hold the nausea at bay. She didn't want to humiliate herself in front of the agents. The heart monitor beat an unsteady rhythm as the reality of her situation filled her senses. She'd been married to a monster. "I should have known. Oh God, what have I done?"

"Your husband is the one we're after, ma'am. You didn't do anything wrong."

She opened her eyes but rather than look at the agents, she faced the wall. The images of the kids at the shelter were superimposed over the green surface. She thought of them in the clutches of a madman...taken from everything they know...forced into a life of pain and degradation with no means of escape. Her heart leaden with misery, she whispered, "I should have figured it out. I might have been able to help those poor girls."

"I'm sure there wasn't anything you could have done." Miller awkwardly attempted to comfort her.

"How many?" The guilt overwhelmed her. It seemed to overpower the physical pain she'd felt a few moments earlier.

"Pardon me?"

"How many girls? How many?" She turned back to look at them. Courtney's face and her battered arms rose to Jade's mind. Girls like that were already victims and the monster she was married to had made them even more so. Her voice rose and the pain sliced through her throat as she yelled hoarsely. "How many lives did he ruin while I stood by and did nothing?"

"Please calm down." Miller glanced at the door as if afraid the nurse would burst in and blame him for the state her patient was in.

Jade lowered her voice, attempting to regain her composure. Her neck felt as though a thousand needles tattooed it at once. "I need to know."

Miller sighed. "We don't know how many. That's part of our investigation. We're hoping this was his first attempt but we just don't know right now."

The door opened once again. Rosalyn bustled in. giving the agents a scathing look. "Time's up. This girl needs rest."

The men hesitated. Rosalyn planted her hands on her hips. "If I have to, I'll call the doctor. You can speak to her later when she's feeling more rested. She won't be any good to you if you wear her out."

The agents left and the nurse slipped an injection into Jade's IV. "This will help you sleep."

"I don't want to sleep," Jade sobbed. "I need to do

something. I have to..." Her words trailed off as her limbs began to relax. She no longer had the will to argue, she was so very tired. Her eyelids drooped.

As she drifted to sleep, she saw the face of a wolf; its red eyes gleaming, glistening fangs poised to rip out her throat.

Chapter Four

Luke stood next to Wayne and watched Bryce DiMarco through the one-way glass of the interrogation room.

The bastard looked perfectly relaxed, like he didn't have a care in the world. Other than the deep scratches on his face from the leap he'd taken through the office window, he seemed completely unscathed.

"Smug sonofabitch," Wayne muttered.

Luke nodded but didn't reply. A surge of fury moved through him. Shoving his hands into the pockets of his jacket, he fought the urge to kick the door in and smash his fist into DiMarco's face.

"You going in alone?" Wayne asked.

"Yeah."

"You should try to calm down first."

"I'm calm," Luke replied although his tone was everything but.

"Maybe I should go in with you."

Luke's eyes swept over his partner. Wayne was a massive black man with forearms the size of tree trunks. He was an imposing figure, but with his Brooks Brothers wardrobe and mild disposition, intimidation wasn't exactly his forte.

"I tell you what, if DiMarco needs any fashion tips, I'll be sure to give you a yell." He walked away, not giving Wayne a chance to reply.

DiMarco looked up when Luke entered the interrogation room, self-assurance radiating from his pores.

Luke flipped a chair around and straddled it, crossing his arms over the back. He wondered if DiMarco recognized him, if he could see any resemblance between him and El Lobo. There was no familiarity in DiMarco's eyes. That was good. The man was not as crafty as he would like to believe.

"Where is she, DiMarco?"

"I have no idea to whom you're referring."

"Bullshit. Tell me what you've done to her."

DiMarco clasped his hands together and rested them on the table. Giving a little shrug, he smiled. "I want to see my attorney."

"We all want a lot of things. Unfortunately, we don't always get them."

"You have to bring in my attorney."

"He's on his way." Luke leaned in closer to DiMarco as if sharing a secret. He almost gagged on the expensive cologne DiMarco wore. "I thought in the meantime, you and I could have a little chat."

"I won't say a word until he gets here."

"I'm sure you know you're in a lot of serious trouble. It might go a little easier on you if you cooperate with us before your attorney arrives."

DiMarco seemed to consider this for a moment. Then he shook his head. "I'm well aware of my rights. I don't have to talk to you without representation."

Quicker than lightning, Luke reached across the table and grabbed the man by his shirtfront. Leaning in, he spoke directly into DiMarco's face. "You'd better tell me where she is, slime ball. I could kill you right now and nobody would give a damn."

Luke detected fear in DiMarco's eyes, but his voice was steady when he replied. "You don't scare me, tough guy. You don't have a thing on me."

"What about attempted murder?" Luke spat, releasing DiMarco with more force than necessary.

The chair almost toppled over as DiMarco landed heavily back in his seat. "I don't know what you're talking about."

"You damn near killed your wife."

"Something happened to Jade?" DiMarco asked, his face plastered with a look of insincere concern. "Is she

41

okay?"

"You slit her throat, asshole. She barely survived."

DiMarco did a poor job of hiding his disappointment that his wife was still alive. "I did nothing of the sort. I don't know who did this to my wife, but I can assure you, he will pay."

"I don't need your assurance," Luke said. "*I'm* going to make sure he pays."

The man must have seen something in Luke's eyes that scared him because he looked away and swallowed loudly. "I have nothing to say to you."

"Where are those girls you kidnapped? Where is Delia Grimes? What have you done to her?"

"I don't know anything about kidnapped girls and I don't know any Delia Grimes. I will not say another word until my attorney arrives."

As if on cue, the door opened and Parker Williams entered, looking every bit the polished, successful criminal attorney he was reputed to be.

"What the hell's going on here, Butler?" Williams slapped his briefcase on the table and glared at Luke. "You can't question my client without my presence."

"Fuck you," Luke replied. He left the room, slamming the door behind him.

****

When Jade awoke, Rosalyn stood beside her bed, checking her vitals. "How you doing, sweetie?"

"Better, I think," Jade replied, although her neck was throbbing. She squeezed the morphine pump. "How long have I been asleep?"

"About four hours. You needed the rest. Best thing to start the body to heal, you know."

"Are the FBI agents still here?"

"Right outside. They're as antsy as a virgin on her wedding night. I told them they couldn't talk to you until tomorrow but they won't leave."

"It's okay. I'll talk to them now."

"Are you sure?" she asked, brows drawing together like a thundercloud.

Jade nodded. The nurse made grumbling noises but opened the door and told the agents they could come back in. They didn't speak until the door closed behind

Rosalyn.

"How are you feeling, Mrs. DiMarco?" Miller asked.

"Better, thank you."

"We need to talk to you again if you feel up to it."

She nodded. She knew they would talk to her whether she felt up to it or not.

"Were you able to remember anything more than what you've already told us?" Connor asked.

"No. Nothing. I'm sorry."

"That's okay. Something may come to you later. If it does, you will let us know?"

Jade nodded slowly, painfully. "Of course I will."

"We appreciate your cooperation. Now we need something else from you."

"What?"

"We need you to testify against your husband at his trial. Do you think you can handle that?"

Jade thought about seeing Bryce in a courtroom. Of looking into the face of the man who had done more than just betray her. The man who had destroyed her life and the lives of countless others. "I don't think my testimony will help your case that much. I don't really know anything about what Bryce has done."

"The details he revealed in the conversation you overheard are extremely important. And the fact that he tried to kill you, the things he said when he threatened you. All of that is evidence against him."

Her stomach clenched. She recognized the feeling. Fear. She was afraid of her husband. She felt like a coward and she hated herself for it. But there it was. "I'll do what I can," she replied without conviction. "Did you find the other man?"

"What other man?"

"The one I told you about. The man Bryce met with at our house on Thursday night. Mr. Smith, El Lobo, whatever his name is." She tried to remember everything she could about the mysterious stranger. "He came in when Bryce...the night he..." Her voice broke. The agents waited silently for her to continue. But she had already been through this. They knew what had happened to her. Now they needed to find El Lobo.

"We checked it out. There was no one matching the

description you gave in the area." Miller told her. "Maybe you were hallucinating."

"No, I was not hallucinating," she said firmly. "He was there. He helped me for some reason. I think he used his shirt to stop the bleeding. You've got to find him. He was involved in this thing with Bryce and he's still out there." Her voice shook as she thought about the innocent victims of her psychotic husband. "More girls could be hurt."

"Sometimes extreme trauma can cause us to imagine things. We assure you, we're looking for anyone who may have been involved in this operation with DiMarco but there was no one like you described with you last night."

"Then who helped me?" she demanded. "Who called the ambulance?"

"A neighbor was outside. He heard something and when he went to investigate, your husband escaped out the window. The neighbor called 911 and held a towel to your throat until the ambulance arrived."

She looked from one agent to the other. Why were they lying to her? She was certain about El Lobo. She remembered. Didn't she? Maybe she had imagined him helping her. But she hadn't imagined seeing him with Bryce the night before. "No, he's real. He was at my house. I'm telling you, he was involved in this and you need to find him."

"Don't worry, we'll check into it. Thank you for the information."

"When is the trial?"

"We don't know yet. Sometime next week, there will be a bail hearing and the judge will set the date for the trial. When you're released, we'll take you to a safe house and keep you there under federal protection until the trial is over."

"A safe house? Why?"

"Your husband is a very dangerous man with a lot of connections. We don't want to frighten you, but your life could be in danger. The FBI will make sure you're safe until all of this is over."

They may not have been trying to frighten her, but that is exactly what they did. She didn't want to stay at a safe house but neither did she want to go back to the

home she'd shared with Bryce.
****

Luke stood at the back of the crowded courtroom, directly behind the defense table. Almost as if equipped with built in radar, DiMarco swiveled and locked eyes with him. Tension gathered between Luke's shoulder blades. His hatred of the man was almost a physical thing. He must have conveyed some of what he was feeling in the look he gave because DiMarco was the first to turn away.

Judge White shuffled through a stack of papers. He looked at the defense table over his glasses. "These are serious charges. Would you like to state them?"

"We waive formal reading, Your Honor."

"How does your client plead?"

Parker Williams stood with DiMarco then smiled at the judge. "Not guilty, Your Honor. We'd like to request minimum bail."

"On what grounds?"

"Your Honor, my client is a respected businessman and an upstanding member of this community. He has no prior record and these charges are outrageous and unsubstantiated."

The district attorney spoke before Williams finished. "Your Honor, Mr. DiMarco is charged with attempted murder, racketeering, pandering, trafficking, and transporting a minor for prostitution. He is also the main suspect in the disappearance and possible murder of a federal agent. He has the financial resources to flee and we have no doubt that is exactly what he will do if granted bail. He's a danger to society and should be kept behind bars."

The judge removed his glasses as he addressed Parker Williams. "I will hold you personally responsible if Mr. DiMarco is not available to answer the charges, Mr. Williams. I am granting bail in the amount of one million dollars. No contact with the victims in this case."

Bryce DiMarco stood and shook hands with his attorney, grinning like he'd just won the lottery. Luke clenched and unclenched his fists, fighting an urge to leap across the benches. He wanted to wipe the smile from the bastard's face. He wanted to wrap his hands around his throat and squeeze until his eyeballs popped from his skull.

DiMarco looked back at Luke and winked. Black spots danced at the corner of Luke's vision...his rage almost blinding in its intensity. He could actually feel his body moving toward DiMarco, as if by a force that was beyond his control. Then he stopped. He couldn't do this, couldn't blow the chance of making DiMarco pay for what he'd done.

Luke glared at him, then turned away, The visions of beating the motherfucker to a bloody pulp were way too real and way too tempting. He quickly left the courtroom before he did something he and DiMarco would both regret.

****

The phone on Luke's desk was ringing as he walked into the station after the hearing. "Butler," Luke barked into the receiver.

"This is Anne at the front desk. There's a young lady here who says she needs to speak with you."

"Who is she?"

"She won't give her name but she said it's urgent. She said to tell you it's about Delia."

Luke's stomach clenched. A tingle that was part hope, part dread traveled through him. "Send her back."

A young girl with several facial piercings and spiky purple hair walked through the door. Luke rose to meet her. She looked no older than fifteen but the eyes that met his were those of a forty-year-old woman. Luke had seen that look before in the faces of young people on the streets. Most of them had seen enough to age them three lifetimes.

"I'm Agent Butler. Can I help you?"

"Can we talk somewhere private?" the girl glanced around warily. Luke guessed it had been difficult for her to come here. She probably didn't have a lot of trust in law enforcement.

"Come with me." He led her into an empty office and offered her a seat. She perched hesitantly on the edge of the chair. She looked up at him, tears brimming in her eyes.

"What can I do for you, Miss..."

"I can't tell you my name but I got some information for you."

"You mentioned Delia. What do you know about her?"

"Me and some other girls was kidnapped and held at a warehouse." Her lip trembled and her voice cracked as she continued. "Delia found us. She snuck us out and told me to call the FBI. I took her car and was going to a phone. Then I got scared. I figured, you know, I'm street people, I could be accused of stealing a car. Some shit like that. Plus, she had a gun so I figured she'd be okay." Her voice broke. "I didn't call. I just left her car in a Wal Mart parking lot and took off."

The air left his body in a rush. "Do you know where she is? Do you know what happened to her?"

The girl shook her head. "I heard about her on the news. That the cops was looking for her. Those assholes might've got her. She saved my life and now she's prob'ly dead. It'll be my fault cause I didn't call." The girl began to sob and Luke automatically offered her his handkerchief. She wiped her eyes and blew her nose. "I can tell you where the warehouse is. That's why I came."

Luke tamped down his anger and squelched the urge to berate the girl for her stupidity. After all, she'd come through now. And, he could understand her fear. Nonetheless, they had a lead. Hope sprang like a burst of sunlight. It wasn't everything they needed, but it was a start. It was damn sure more than they'd had. He took the address from the girl and told her to wait there, then headed for the door.

"Wait, there's more." The girl stopped him. Luke forced himself to turn and listen, even though he was anxious to follow up on the one slim lead they'd gotten on Delia. "She asked me to find you and give you a message. She said to tell you she was trying to fix her mistakes, but maybe she screwed up even more." The girl's forehead scrunched in concentration as if she were trying to make sure she got everything just right. "She said, 'Tell Luke no matter what happens, it wasn't his fault and he did the right thing.' She said to tell you if something happens to her, don't blame yourself."

Guilt settled in his heart like a stone. "Thanks...you did good," he told her, the words ending on a ragged breath.

"You gotta find her." The girl pleaded.

He nodded, then bolted from the room. He shouted at Marci, one of the female agents, "Take care of the girl. Find her some place to stay."

Wayne grabbed his jacket and followed Luke to the door. "What the hell's going on?"

"I know where the warehouse is," Luke spoke over his shoulder, not bothering to see if Wayne kept up.

"The girl was one of DiMarco's victims." Luke told him as they climbed into the car. Speeding from the parking lot, he deftly navigated through the downtown St. Louis traffic. "She gave me the address of the warehouse where the victims were held."

"I'll be damned."

"Delia got them out but the girl doesn't know what happened to her after that."

Luke knew from Wayne's silence that he feared the worst but Luke wasn't giving up hope. Not yet. He gave Wayne the rest of the details he'd gotten from the girl, leaving out the personal message from Delia. He wasn't sure he could say the words without tears.

A heavy downpour was in full swing by the time they reached the warehouse and pulled into the empty parking lot. Although every indication told them the darkened building was abandoned, they approached with caution.

Ducking into a crouch, guns drawn, they sidled along the wall of the warehouse until they reached a window facing the docks. Luke carefully rose and peered through the grimy glass, barely able to see through the smudges.

The lights from the marina illuminated the inside of the building just enough for Luke to confirm that it was indeed abandoned. He made his way to the door with Wayne following closely behind.

Luke reached out a hand and pushed against the door, relieved when it swung open. Cautiously, they entered the warehouse. Luke pulled the flashlight from his belt and shone it around the interior. The beam danced across the empty room, revealing nothing more than a few piles of trash and half a dozen folding chairs.

A door at the back of the warehouse stood open. With their backs to the wall, they crept toward the doorway. A quick look inside the darkened room told them that no one waited to ambush them but what they found confirmed their suspicions.

Lining the walls were cots covered in thin, dirty mattresses. On another wall were a toilet and rusty sink with a cracked mirror hanging above them. The stench of sweat and urine permeated the air. This was where the girls had been held.

Confident they had seen everything, they went outside and around to the back of the warehouse. As they rounded the corner, Luke's flashlight beam caught something that appeared to be a pile of clothing.

The rain had lessened but the ground was thick with mud that snatched at their shoes like a hungry crocodile as they stumbled through the muck.

Even before he reached the heap, Luke recognized Delia's copper hair and black leather jacket. Her crumpled form lay in the mud like a discarded rag doll.

A strangled cry escaped his throat. Chest heaving, in a voice he didn't recognize as his own, he moaned. "No, no, no..." as he dropped to his knees, pulling Delia onto his lap. He placed his fingers along the side of her neck and confirmed what he'd known the moment he saw her.

Holding her tightly against his chest, he rocked her gently, his tears mingling with the rain that fell onto her lifeless form.

Chapter Five

The drive to DiMarco's took an eternity. The scenery passed in a blur, but to Luke, it felt as if they were going in slow motion. He gripped the armrest, scowling at Wayne from the passenger seat. "Can't you drive any faster?"

"Not without killing us both." Wayne took his eyes off the road long enough to glance at Luke. "You're cool, right?"

Luke laughed harshly and clenched his hands into fists, imagining Bryce DiMarco's neck between them. "Cool as a cucumber, partner."

"Yeah, right. Promise me you won't do anything stupid."

"DiMarco's the one that did something stupid," Luke said. "And he's going to pay for it."

"We're taking him in by the book, right?" Wayne's tone held a warning. "You with me on that?"

Luke didn't reply. He wasn't sure what he had in mind. He just knew that he wanted DiMarco to suffer for what he'd done to Delia. The judicial system was too slow and not always effective. DiMarco deserved the ultimate punishment and Luke knew that if given the opportunity, he would make sure the punishment was carried out.

They drove through the gates of DiMarco's mansion. Two more FBI teams and two squad cars surrounded the perimeter of the property. The idea was not to converge on him and cause him to bolt, but in case he did, they'd be ready.

Before the Chevy came to a complete stop, Luke was

out and heading toward the front door. Wayne came up behind him, attempting to match his frenzied pace.

"Take it easy, man."

Luke ignored him, taking the steps two at a time. Still in motion, he pounded on the large oak door. There was no reply. The house was dark and Luke had a gut feeling DiMarco wasn't there. The bastard had skipped bail.

Luke pulled out his .9 mm and fired into the lock.

"Aw come on, man," Wayne said, coming up behind him. Luke didn't bother to acknowledge his partner's protests. He kicked the wood until the door swung open. Wayne followed him through the shattered door.

"FBI! Show me your hands you sonofabitch!" Luke shouted. No response.

They searched the entire estate, room by room. The place had an empty feel, like it hadn't been lived in for a while. DiMarco had been released on bail yesterday. He'd probably taken off as soon as they cut him loose.

"He's gone," Wayne said when they returned to the foyer.

"Yeah." Luke suddenly felt as empty as the house. His burning anger, the seething rage he'd felt since finding Delia's body, slowly left him like air escaping a balloon. All that remained was a sense of helplessness, and the overwhelming realization that once again, he'd failed someone he loved.

****

"Here you go, dear." Rosalyn smiled as she entered the hospital room with a wheelchair. Agents Connor and Miller followed behind. "I bet you're happy to be going home."

Jade looked up at the agents. They all knew she would not be going home, not ever again. She forced a smile for the nurse who had been so kind to her during her hospital stay, one that had proven much lengthier than her injury warranted. The truth was, they hadn't been sure what to do with her. She couldn't go home, and the FBI hadn't yet readied a safe house for her. They'd gone to the mansion and asked Berta to gather Jade's belongings, which almost certainly infuriated the housekeeper. She probably wasn't pleased at doing a favor for the woman who'd destroyed her beloved master. "Yes, I am. Thank you for everything."

"Sure, sweetie. It was my pleasure."

Jade stood. Her legs felt as if they had no more substance than a drinking straw. She held onto the bed for a moment, and made it to the wheelchair with a little help from Rosalyn.

Once she was settled in the chair, the nurse reached into the closet. She pulled out a hospital bag and placed it on Jade's lap.

Jade opened the bag and the first thing she noticed was her wedding ring. The two carat pear cut diamond glinted at her from inside a small, plastic zippered baggie. Suddenly, her insides were as cold as the jewel that seemed to hold an almost malevolent energy. She picked up the bag and turned to look up at Rosalyn.

"Here," she told the woman. "I want you to have this."

"What?" The look on Rosalyn's face was the same as if Jade had offered her a live grenade. "No, Dear. Heavens, no. I can't take that."

"Yes, please," Jade said. "I don't want it. I can't wear it anymore...can't look at it. You've been so kind to me. Please, it would mean a lot."

"I think I'd get into trouble."

Jade shoved it into the woman's hand. "Hold onto it. Check with your supervisor or whatever you need to do. But I don't want it back."

The woman didn't answer, simply took the ring and nodded, slipping it into her pocket.

Folded neatly beneath where the ring lay, like a scene from a nightmare, was the black clothing Jade had worn the night she broke into Bryce's office. An item she didn't recognize was visible beneath her clothes. Reaching in, she pulled it from the bag.

"Oh, my," Rosalyn exclaimed as she saw the bloodstained article clasped in Jade's hands. "That shouldn't have been in there. I know it must be upsetting. Let me get rid of that for you."

"What the hell?" Agent Conner murmured in disbelief. "That was supposed to be in evidence."

Jade looked at the agents. They exchanged glances,

obviously uncomfortable. The room seemed to close in on her. Her grip tightened on the item that had been used to stop the flow of blood coming from the wound on her neck.

Not a towel, but the blue shirt El Lobo had worn the night he saved her life.

****

Jade shifted restlessly against the seat, wishing she could see outside. The van was windowless in the back, which was probably intentional. The site of the safe house was top secret and the Feds didn't want her to know its exact location.

The trip had already taken over an hour. She had no idea how much longer it would be before they reached their destination. She was tired and with no one to talk to, she had entirely too much time to think. And thinking was something she didn't particularly enjoy these days.

Twisting as much as the seatbelt would allow, she reclined into the corner of the seat. She felt drained, her body aching with fatigue. The hum of the engine lulled her and her eyelids began to droop. Without realizing it, she slipped into sleep and didn't awaken until she felt the van come to a stop. She wasn't sure how long she'd been out, but she wasn't feeling particularly rested, so she assumed it had been for a short time.

Agent Miller opened the door and offered her his hand. She took it and let him help her from the van. She stumbled as she climbed out, then immediately righted herself, ashamed of her show of weakness.

"Are you okay?" the agent asked.

"I'm fine, thank you." She pulled her hand from his and took a deep breath. The aroma of pine trees and burning firewood hung in the night air. Jade stood a moment, letting the scents waft over her, not realizing until now just how claustrophobic she'd felt during the trip. They were in a wooded area. Large evergreen trees loomed above them, almost obscuring the moon that shone in the night sky. Several feet in front of them, a small log cabin sat in a clearing between the trees. A thin line of smoke drifted from the chimney. She was surprised to see lights burning inside.

She turned to Agent Miller. "Is someone here?"

"There are a couple of agents inside. They need to go

over some things with you."

Jade frowned, disconcerted at the thought of dealing with more strangers. Not that she'd exactly bonded with Connor and Miller. Agent Miller reached around her and retrieved her overnight bag from the van and led her into the cabin. They stepped into a living area where an overstuffed plaid sofa and matching recliner were arranged in front of a burning fireplace. A glass topped coffee table sat between the sofa and chair. Other than those items, the room was almost bare. No decorations on the walls, no knick-knacks. A functional, no frills room to conduct functional, no frills business.

Two men stood to greet her. One was a nice-looking light-skinned black man who wore a suit she recognized as Armani. He was large, but graceful in his movements as he stepped over and took her hand. "Mrs. DiMarco, Special Agent Wayne Jackson. I want you to know that we're very sorry for what you've gone through and we're grateful for your cooperation." His deep voice was melodious and hypnotizing. Rather than shake her hand, he grasped it between his large ones and smiled, a look of sympathy and respect in his coffee colored eyes.

"Thank you," she replied. He released her hand and turned to indicate the other man who'd stopped just behind him.

"This is Special Agent Luke Butler."

The man didn't take her hand. He simply stood with his arms crossed over his chest. He was tall with dark hair that showed a hint of gray at the temples. He wore a Cincinnati Reds baseball cap, blue jeans and a loose gray sweatshirt with the sleeves pushed up, revealing a black leather band on his left wrist. The eyes beneath the cap were a deep amber color and seemed to glow with an inner light. His nose jutted slightly to the left as if it had been broken at some time. His face wasn't classically handsome, but it had some quality she couldn't define...strength, toughness, with just a hint of vulnerability, as if he'd suffered sorrow in his life but held his pain deep inside.

"Mrs. DiMarco," his voice was low and smooth with a slightly raspy quality like grains of sand softened by an ocean wave. His eyes also held sympathy but the look was tinged with reservation. "Please, have a seat."

He motioned toward the sofa and Jade gratefully sank into the cushions. Her nap in the van had been way too short. She felt as if she'd just completed a marathon. Connor and Miller stood silently next to the front door like faithful soldiers awaiting their next orders.

Agent Jackson took a seat next to her while Agent Butler sat on the edge of the chair and rested his elbows on his knees. Butler was the first to speak.

"I know what you're doing can't be easy and, as I'm sure you've been told countless times, the agency is very grateful that you've agreed to assist us in putting your husband behind bars. You'll be here at the safe house for a while. There will be at least four agents with you at all times. You have my word we will do everything in our power to keep you safe."

"Is all of this really necessary?" Jade was dismayed to feel tears burning her eyes. She wanted to be strong but she was starting to feel overwhelmed.

"Your husband is a very dangerous man with ties to even more dangerous men. There's no telling what he is capable of and he won't be happy to find out you're testifying against him."

"Yes, but he's in jail."

Butler looked down at his hands where they hung loosely between his knees. Jackson was the one to respond. "Not any longer, I'm afraid. He's fled."

"Fled?" Her voice lowered, shock and the ache from her injury making it difficult to speak. "How did that happen? He was in custody."

"Yes. But he was granted bail," Jackson said.

She shook her head, looking from one agent to the other. "He tried to kill me. He's been selling young girls into slavery and may have committed murder. How could he be granted bail?"

"Bail is often granted in cases involving an *upstanding* citizen such as DiMarco," Butler replied bitterly.

"This is unbelievable."

"Yes, it is. After he was granted bail, we discovered the body of an FBI agent. We're sure she's the woman he referred to in the phone conversation you overheard." He stopped for a moment, a shimmer in his eyes that looked suspiciously like tears. When he continued, the raspy tone of his voice was more pronounced. "We attempted to serve a warrant on him for the murder of Delia Grimes but he was gone when we arrived. We've had agents out looking for him since, but so far, we haven't found him."

A bolt of anxiety shot through her, tightening in a hard band around her chest. Bryce was free. And very, very angry. "So what happens now? I mean, you obviously can't bring him to trial until you find him. I have to stay here indefinitely?"

"Actually, Mrs. DiMarco, we want to place you into WITSEC, the Witness Security Program," Jackson told her.

"Witness Protection? You're kidding?"

Jackson shook his head. "I'm afraid not. We can't keep you here forever. It could take a while to apprehend your husband, then to bring him to trial. We're filing an application with the US Marshals to place you into the program."

"What does that mean? Exactly what's involved?"

Butler spoke now. "You'll be moved to a new location. With a completely new identity, driver's license, social security card, the works."

Her scalp tingled as shock and apprehension whirled into a confused white noise in her brain. "A whole new life? In a strange place?"

"Yes. And in the meantime, you'll be safe here. There's no way he can find you."

"How the hell do you know that? You don't even know where he is." Jade immediately regretted her words. She knew it wasn't Agent Butler's fault that Bryce had escaped. "I'm sorry. It's just that I thought this might be over soon. That I could testify and send him to prison. Now I find out that Bryce has disappeared. He could be anywhere. And *I'm* the one who'll really be in prison."

"I know it seems that way. Unfortunately, right now we don't have a lot of options."

"What about El Lobo? Did you find him? Miller and Connor don't believe the man exists, but I *saw* him. He's in on this with Bryce."

The room grew silent, the crackling of logs in the

fireplace the only sound. Jackson cleared his throat and said softly. "We know he exists. We've been trying for years to discover his true identity...to capture him. He's an extremely dangerous man and his existence is something the bureau has tried to hide. We were hoping you wouldn't remember seeing him."

They didn't have to tell her he was dangerous...she sensed it in the man's demeanor...saw it in those eyes....

"Why do you think he saved my life? Why would he do that?"

Jackson flicked a glance at Butler. His partner didn't seem inclined to respond, so he continued. "We wondered about that, too. All we could figure is that he might have planned to take you as a hostage. Or maybe he wanted to get rid of DiMarco. Apparently, their plan had fallen apart. He may have planned to kill DiMarco and pin it on you. There are a hundred theories but nothing to back any of them up. So, as usual, we're left with a lot of questions and no answers when it comes to El Lobo."

"But you are looking for him?" she asked hopefully, relieved they finally acknowledged that she wasn't crazy.

"Absolutely. He's top priority, along with DiMarco."

She nodded and Butler spoke again.

"You'll be relocated as soon as the paperwork comes through and that shouldn't take long. I can assure you that your husband won't find you while you're here. Even if he did, he would have to go through at least four agents to get to you. We're not going to let that happen."

He said it with so much confidence that Jade felt reassured. "Where will I be going? I mean, when they relocate me. Where will I live?"

"I'm afraid we can't tell you that. Not until you're on your way. The US Marshals will take care of the details. The FBI won't even know your location."

"You can't tell me where I'll be living?" Jade threw her hands up in frustration. "What about the people I'm leaving behind? How will they know how to reach me?"

"You can't tell anyone where you are. You have to sever all ties with friends and family," Agent Butler said flatly.

Her voice thick with unshed tears, she said, "Will I at least be able to tell my friends goodbye?"

He shook his head. "There can be no contact from this point on. For their safety and your own, you will have to simply disappear."

Jade felt her chest squeeze as if crushed by a huge fist. Even though she'd planned to leave Bryce, start over somewhere new, she'd thought she could do so with her own identity. She thought she could choose where she went, and still keep in touch with her friends and family. Her father had moved to New York with his new wife. He and Jade spoke only a few times a year, but he would wonder what had happened to her.

And what would Melanie think? She couldn't even tell her best friend what was going on. She'd be worried sick. Jade thought things would settle down soon and she would be able to call and explain everything to Melanie. Now this man was telling her she couldn't contact anyone. Tears burned at the back of her lids, but she fought to keep them from falling.

"I can't believe that I'm supposed to uproot my whole life."

"Better to uproot your life than to lose it," he stated bluntly. He picked up an envelope from the coffee table and pulled a stack of photos from it. "Maybe these will help you to understand the gravity of the situation."

He passed her the photographs. Her hands shook as she thumbed through the graphic images. Each scene depicted victims of a range of violent acts. One showed a young woman bound by ropes and covered in so much blood it was difficult to tell exactly where her wounds were. Nausea clutched Jade's stomach. After viewing only a few of the photos she threw them onto the coffee table. "My husband did all of this?"

"We have reason to believe he and his associates were responsible for these crimes, yes. Do you see now why it would be best if you entered WITSEC?"

Jade nodded slowly. She couldn't escape the sensation of the earth crumbling beneath her feet. Even though she'd survived Bryce's attack, he'd still taken her life.

****

Jade paced the small bedroom, feeling claustrophobic and agitated. Like the rest of the cabin, the room was

58

sparsely furnished. On one side was a double bed covered in a starburst-patterned quilt. Next to it was a nightstand with a bronze lamp and near the window, a three drawer dresser. She walked over to the dresser and stared at her reflection in the mirror. The white gauze on her neck resembled a macabre necklace. The doctor had instructed her to change the bandage at bedtime and she reached up to grip the edge of the gauze. She hesitated, reluctant to reveal what lay beneath.

Just do it, dammit. It's only a scar. It's not the end of the world. Not like it was for those young girls.

Tears clouded her vision and she wondered if they were for herself or for the innocent victims of her husband. Dear God, how many lives had he destroyed? Were any of them girls Jade had actually met? Girls who'd come through the shelter seeking safety and love? The thought made her sick with grief and helplessness. And to think she'd shared a bed with him. She shuddered, a rush of bile rising to the back of her throat. Oh God, how could she not have sensed the kind of man he was? How could she have let him touch her?

Pushing those thoughts aside, she clenched the bandage and, gritting her teeth, gave one quick yank. A sharp sting, as if the flesh on her neck had also been ripped away, made her yelp with pain. Her eyes watered and she squeezed them shut, willing away the sensation while she searched for the courage to view Bryce's handiwork. Slowly, she lifted her lids. She gave an involuntary gasp as her gaze dropped to her injury.

The wound was about four inches long. The edges were puckered and red streaks ran through the center. It wasn't a straight cut; it angled from the middle of her throat and down the right side.

She wanted to turn away, but like a gawker at the scene of an accident, she couldn't. Waves of panic rose from her stomach to her throat. God, she was hideous. The doctors had said the wound would leave a scar but she hadn't been prepared for this. She trembled and her knees went weak. Gripping the edge of the vanity, she finally looked away from her reflection as hot tears burned down her cheeks.

She didn't know how long she stood there, head

bowed and weeping, but however long it had been was long enough. Looking back into the mirror, she saw that the eyes staring at her were red and swollen. She shook her head in disgust. She was tired of the pity trip, tired of feeling sorry for herself.

She had to be strong. She would get through this and start a new life. There was nothing for her here except hurtful reminders...and Melanie...and the kids at the shelter. The thought of never seeing Melanie or the kids again brought another lump to her throat, but this time, she fought back the tears.

She used a hand towel to dry her face and replaced the bandage with a fresh one. She put on her pajamas and climbed into bed, but she couldn't sleep, even after taking one of the sleeping pills the doctor had given her. She pulled the covers tightly around her shoulders and shifted to her side...but still, she lay wide awake.

Giving up in frustration, she climbed out of bed and dressed in sweat pants and a hooded pullover.

In the kitchen, she nuked a cup of water and dropped in a tea bag. She sat at the kitchen table and rested her elbows on the surface, covering her face with her hands. Tears formed in her eyes and seeped between her fingertips. She hated to admit it, even to herself, but she was terrified. Scared of starting a new life but just as afraid of the old one. She didn't want to run away but she knew that she had no choice, especially with Bryce on the loose. There was no telling what he would do to her if he ever found her. An icy chill swept through her, fear twitching like a living thing inside her.

"You should try to get some sleep."

She jolted, her hands flying from her face. Whirling, she found Agent Butler standing in the doorway. Quickly, she swiped at the tears on her cheeks. "I didn't hear you come in."

"I'm sorry if I startled you." He wore the same clothes he'd worn earlier in the evening. Apparently, just like her, he had no intention of sleeping tonight. He seemed taller in the dim light of the kitchen. There was something mysterious, even slightly dangerous about him.

She swallowed, her heart pounding. "You didn't." She told him but her quavering voice belied the words.

His eyes moved over her face and her hand subconsciously went to her throat.

A reassuring smile touched his mouth. "Mind if I join you?"

She minded. Very much. She was mentally exhausted and the last thing she wanted was to try to make conversation with this unsettling man. Most of all, she didn't want his pity. But she didn't tell him any of that. Instead she nodded toward the chair opposite hers. "Not at all."

He took the seat and watched as she dipped the tea bag into the steaming water. She took a drink and looked at him over the rim of the cup.

"We all have scars, you know," he told her enigmatically.

She wasn't sure if he referred to something personal, or if he was just making conversation to help her feel better. She nodded. "I guess some are just more visible than others."

"It's the internal scars that take the longest to heal." His amber eyes penetrated the darkness, gazing at her so intently, she had the sensation he was looking into her soul.

She dropped her gaze to her tea cup, feeling breathless all of a sudden as her cheeks flushed with warmth. Not knowing how to respond, she nodded and gave a nervous laugh. "I always thought the Witness Protection Program was just something out of a movie," she said, feeling dense as soon as the words were out of her mouth. She shrugged, hoping her discomfort didn't show. "I guess it never really dawned on me that it was real."

"Yes, it's real. It's not exactly something that gets a lot of press. There have been some problems with it in the past; some of the witnesses in the program are just as bad, or worse, than the people the government is trying to prosecute. Unfortunately, there have been several cases where a protected witness commits a crime while they're under the government's protection. One man murdered his entire family."

"Dear God, how awful. Why would they protect someone like that?"

Agent Butler shrugged. "He had the goods on some very bad men. Years ago, the mob literally ran the east coast. No one was willing to testify because anyone who tried, ended up dead before the trial started. Things changed once the program was put into place. It's very well run and once a witness is relocated, their safety is almost guaranteed. WITSEC has never lost a witness while in the program. As long as you follow the guidelines, they can protect you. If you violate any of the rules, the protection ends."

"Sounds like you've got it all figured out. Too bad I don't."

"You'll be fine. Just look at it as an adventure."

Jade grimaced. "I've had enough adventure in the past week to last me a lifetime."

"I know." He smiled gently. "Are you feeling okay? Does that give you much pain?" he asked, indicating her throat.

She reached up to touch the bandage. "Not too bad."

"I saw a light on in your bedroom so I figured you were having trouble sleeping."

"Not because of the pain. I always leave a light on, even when I sleep."

"Really? Why?"

"I'm afraid of the dark," she answered, then felt her face flush with warmth. Why had she revealed such a personal detail to a total stranger?

He nodded as if a grown woman being afraid of the dark was the most natural thing in the world. "There isn't a lot of nighttime left but you really should try to get some sleep."

"I can't sleep, even with the pills the doctor prescribed."

"You've got a lot on your mind and you've been through hell this past week, so that's understandable."

"Do you think you'll ever find El Lobo?"

Butler quickly flicked his gaze to hers. "We won't give up until we catch him."

Somehow, his words reassured her like Jackson's hadn't. "Thank you." She smiled gratefully. Knowing that Bryce was out there somewhere was bad enough, but the thought of both men on the loose, maybe looking for her...aware that she could identify them...

She shivered, the flesh on the back of her neck tingling with fear.

In spite of the terror that thought invoked, the realization dawned on her that for some reason, in the intimate coziness of this room, sitting next to Luke Butler, she felt oddly safe.

****

Jade's voice wrapped around Luke in the semi darkness, sending a shiver up his spine. He didn't recall that husky quality when he'd heard her speak before and wondered if it was due to her injury.

Her hair in the dim light of the kitchen reminded him of warm honey. Hazel in the light, her eyes now took on a deep green tint, like a jungle cat...a beautiful cat, trapped and forced into captivity. Her posture was like that of someone expecting a blow, but ready to withstand it.

He looked at her hands wrapped around the coffee cup and thought about how soft and fragile they'd felt when he'd held them in the hospital. He had an absurd urge to touch them once again, to wrap his arms around her and hold her body against his.

Damn, where had that come from? He couldn't afford to think about this woman like that. Couldn't afford the luxury of desiring her, of wondering what her skin would taste like, what it would feel like to kiss her.

Her voice startled him out of his treacherous reverie. "I still don't understand why he saved my life."

He cringed inwardly, knowing she was talking about Smith, about *him*. "Could be several reasons. Maybe he wanted to keep you alive. Use you for leverage in case they got in a tight spot."

She leaned her elbows on the table and pillowed her head in her hands. "God, it's all so crazy. So confusing."

He didn't like her asking questions about El Lobo. It was important he not expose his undercover role. He might have to use it again one day. It could also possibly jeopardize the undercover agents still out in the field.

He should have known she would ask. He had hoped that the trauma of her injury would keep her from remembering but obviously, that hadn't happened.

Jade rose from the table and moved to the window. She sipped her tea and peered outside. "It's so quiet out here. And so dark." She turned back to him. "How many agents did you say would be here at all times?"

"No less than four."

She nodded. "Will you be one of them?"

"Most of the time."

She nodded again, seeming satisfied with his answer. Moving back to the table she sat down, a haunted look in her eyes. "How am I going to live with all this guilt?"

"What do you feel guilty about?"

"Allowing Bryce to do what he did. To hurt those poor girls."

"It's not your fault. My partner, Delia, helped the girls escape. I don't think any of them were actually hurt."

"What about the other times? I'm sure he's done this before. How many other girls were there? Do you have any idea?"

Luke took his time replying, then reluctantly admitted, "I'm afraid we don't. But, our government has contacted the Mexican government and they're being very cooperative. They've agreed to let us send agents over there to investigate and have offered assistance in helping to locate any girls that may have been victims in the past. Or as many of them as possible."

"Good," Jade said quietly. Then she gave him a look of sympathy. "Delia? She was the woman Bryce murdered? She was your partner?"

Grief weighted his chest like a block of cement, but he kept his voice even. "Yes. We're fairly certain your husband is responsible for her death."

"You must hate me," she said, her eyes shimmering with tears and self-loathing.

"You had nothing to do with it."

"I should've stopped him."

An image of DiMarco holding the blade to Jade's neck flashed in his mind. He recalled the helplessness and the rage he'd felt as she slid to the floor, blood pouring from the wound. He gave himself a mental shake, wondering why the sight of her near death had affected him so profoundly when he'd seen more than his share of murder victims. Dragging in a breath, he said, "You did try and you almost died. Everyone did the best they could." He didn't acknowledge his role in Delia's death. The fact that she wouldn't have been out there, chasing the lead, if it hadn't been for him.

She nodded, but the hazel eyes were still haunted. "I'm just sorry it wasn't enough for your partner."

Pushing back from the table, Luke stood and looked down at her. He felt the need to escape. Not only from his grief over Delia but also from the inappropriate thoughts he'd been entertaining about a witness. "You should try to rest. You may only be here for a few more days. As soon as your application is processed, the US Marshal's service will take you to your new location. You should spend the time trying to heal."

"Ok," she replied.

Not looking back to see if she would heed his advice, Luke left the room and headed to the front door. Maybe he'd take a look outside, walk around a bit. He wasn't supposed to be on watch tonight but he knew he couldn't sleep. He was wound as tight as a spring, his body filled with a strange combination of sadness and desire.

Chapter Six

Solitaire, Colorado
One Month Later

Jade pounded the heavy bag with a series of quick thrusts, feeling the vibration travel through her gloves and into her shoulders. The pungent odor of sweat hung in the air and filled her nostrils. A few of her fellow jujitsu students had stayed after class to work out. Over the noise of her own heavy breathing, she heard the slap of flesh against leather, punctuated with an occasional grunt.

She stepped back and used the towel around her neck to wipe the perspiration from her scar. Her injury had healed but it still itched like a swarm of ants had invaded her skin. Ignoring the discomfort, she continued practicing and felt a keen satisfaction as she landed a solid roundhouse back kick on the helpless bag.

She'd been taking jujitsu lessons six days a week and had learned a great deal about self-defense. She'd also taken some private lessons from her instructor, Cal Steiner. She told him that she had fled from an abusive relationship and was afraid her ex-boyfriend might find her.

Aside from the regular lessons, Cal taught her a few groin attacks, knee stamping and gouging techniques, pointing out the parts of a man's body where she could do the most damage.

Although proud of the progress she'd made, she knew it wasn't enough. Sure, she may be able to defend herself against someone her own size who wasn't schooled in martial arts. But could she take down a grown man that meant her serious harm? Could she defend herself against Bryce? She didn't think so.

After a few more minutes, Jade's muscles screamed and fatigue gripped her limbs. She'd been working out for two hours and even though she was stronger than she'd ever been, she knew when it was time to call it quits.

Pulling off her gloves, she gathered her bag from the bench and headed to the front door. As she approached the basketball courts, she heard Cal's voice raised in anger.

"You kids aren't supposed to be in here after eight o'clock. I've told you that before."

Cal was an ex-military Special Forces expert and a stickler when it came to rules. Jade always felt sorry for the kids that encountered his wrath when one of the rules was violated.

Stopping in the doorway, Jade saw a young girl and two teenage boys walking away from Cal. The girl was dressed completely in black with blue-black hair that was obviously dyed. The taller boy wore baggie jeans low on his thin hips, boxer shorts visible above the waistband. The other teen was chubby with long hair and a bad case of acne.

Jade cringed when the tall boy tossed a basketball over his shoulder, barely missing Cal's head.

"Hey," Cal shouted but the teens ignored him. "Smart ass punks," he muttered.

"Cal?" Jade said from the doorway. He looked up, noticing her for the first time. "Is it really that big a deal for them to hang out here?"

The teens stopped, the girl eying her with suspicion and the boys with what looked like admiration.

"It's the rules, Jenna. No one under eighteen in here after eight p.m."

She still wasn't used to her new name. *Jenna Donovan*. The US Marshals had suggested that she use her own initials. They said it was easier to become accustomed to a new name when it started with the same letters as the old.

"Maybe so, but isn't it better for them to be in here

than out on the streets?"

Cal huffed a breath and shook his head. "It's not really any of your business."

She shrugged as if to say 'I tried' as the teens passed her.

"Sorry for intruding," she told Cal once the kids were gone. "I just feel like this is a safer place for them to be. Better than being out causing trouble."

"Maybe so. But rules are rules."

She didn't want to argue with Cal but she could have reminded him that those were *his* rules and they made no sense. The gym didn't close until eleven but kids had to be out by eight.

What the hell. He was right. It was none of her business. She'd done fine so far by not getting involved with anyone, why start now?

"I've been meaning to talk to you about something," Cal said. "I'm worried about this ex-boyfriend of yours. He hasn't been around, has he?"

She shook her head, guilt eating at her for lying to Cal. "He doesn't know where I am."

His gaze dropped to her neck and she wondered what he was thinking. He'd never questioned her about her injury, but she was sure he attributed it to the 'boyfriend'. "Well, I don't mean to scare you, but it's likely he could find you. Do you have any idea how many women are killed by abusive men?"

"I know. I'll be careful. The skills you're teaching me will come in handy if he ever does find me."

"There's something else I want to teach you. Something I've never talked to anyone about, but I worry about you. It's called 'Dim Mak'. The Death Touch."

"The what?"

"Death Touch. It's an ancient oriental method of striking certain vital points on an opponent, rendering them incapacitated, sometimes even causing their death."

She laughed but stopped abruptly when she saw the look on his face. He was serious.

"I appreciate your concern, but I think what you've taught me is enough. Besides, you surely don't believe in that, do you?"

"Do you believe in acupuncture?" he asked, a

defensive note in his tone.

"Yes, but..."

"It's the same concept. If there are points on your body that can help you to heal, why can't they cause the opposite effect?"

"I suppose they could," she replied slowly, still not convinced but wanting to appease him. "I'm sorry for doubting you. I'm sure you know what you're talking about but I really don't think I'm interested. Thanks, anyway. Listen, it's late, I really need to go. I'll see you in class tomorrow."

"Ok, see ya."

"Jenna," Cal called out to her when she'd almost reached the door. He looked around as if to assure himself they were alone. "I know it's real." His voice was a guttural whisper that carried to her across the expanse of the gym. "Because I've used it."

A chill raced across her skin. She nodded but not knowing how to respond, she left. She was eager to breathe in fresh air after being in the gym for most of the day; and, if she were honest, anxious to get away from Cal. She was a little freaked about the Dim Mak thing, even though she didn't really believe it worked.

When she stepped outside, she saw the girl from the basketball court sitting on the curb in the parking lot. The boys were gone and she was alone in the dark, apparently waiting for a ride.

Without speaking, Jade averted her eyes and headed toward her car. *She'll be okay. She seems pretty tough.*

Her hand stalled as she reached for her keys.

*What if she's stranded without a ride? It's late and she's just a ki*d.

Forget it. Like Cal said, it's none of your business.

Yeah, but you can't just leave her here alone.

Sighing, Jade retraced her steps. The girl raised her head when she approached. "You okay?" Jade asked.

"Fine," the girl replied but Jade heard tears in her voice.

"It's late. Do you have a ride?"

Her thin shoulders lifted in a shrug. "I was supposed to, but the asshole didn't show up."

"I could give you a lift. Where do you live?"

The girl gave her a narrow-eyed stare and after a moment said, "The same apartments you do."

"Really?"

"Yeah. I've seen you around the place."

Jade hadn't noticed the girl before. She usually kept to herself, choosing to ignore the neighbors. Up close, the girl was prettier than she'd realized. She had striking blue eyes, circled with heavy black eyeliner and her lips were smeared with black lipstick. But her pale beauty was there, underneath the 'goth' look she tried to hide behind.

Deep in her eyes was a wariness that shouldn't be in someone so young. She reminded Jade of some of the girls she'd met at the shelter. She didn't see any signs of cutting, but the wounded air about the girl made her think of Courtney.

"Well, since I'm going your way, you might as well come along."

The girl shrugged as if it didn't matter but got up and followed her to her car.

"I'm Jenna Donovan, by the way," Jade said as they drove out of the parking lot.

"Ashley," the girl said without looking up, as if reluctantly volunteering the information.

She didn't speak again during the drive. Jade tried to make conversation, but each question she asked was answered with a shrug.

They pulled into the parking lot of the complex and the car had barely come to a stop before the girl muttered, "Thanks," and practically leapt from the seat, slamming the door behind her.

Jade climbed out of the car just in time to see a young boy run toward them, throwing his arms around the girl's waist.

"Ashley, I was worried about you."

She hugged him back and for the first time, Jade saw a softening in her harsh features. It almost made her look human. "I'm fine, Jonathan."

"You're late."

"Dennis was supposed to pick me up but he didn't show."

"He's drunk with momma."

Ashley cut her eyes toward Jade and took the boy by the shoulders, steering him away. "Shhh, Jon. Don't say that."

The boy pulled away from Ashley and, as if noticing Jade for the first time, peered at her curiously. He wore a grass stained baseball uniform that was at least a size too small. The buttons strained against his round belly and the 'Panther' logo on the front was frayed and faded. "Who are you?" he asked.

"My name's Jenna." Jade stuck out her hand. The boy placed his pudgy fingers in it and squeezed.

"I'm Jon."

"Pleased to meet you, Jon."

"I'm not supposed to talk to strangers but thanks for bringing Ashley home."

Right. His mother teaches him not to talk to strangers yet lets him run around an apartment complex unattended in the dark. Not to mention, leaving her daughter stranded. *Great job, Mom.*

"Well, we're neighbors but that's a good idea not to talk to strangers. And, you're welcome."

Together, they walked toward the apartment building. As they reached the entryway, a man staggered out. When he saw the kids, he started toward them. He was thin but had a paunch that poked out of his too-tight Rob Zombie tee shirt. His filthy blond hair was matted with sweat, limp bangs hanging above mean eyes. His face was mottled with acne scars and what looked like meth sores; she'd seen them on some of the kids at the shelter.

"What the hell do you think you're doin'? I was gonna pick you up. If I'd gotten there and you was gone I'da been pissed."

"Yeah, well, *I* was pissed when I waited for half an hour and you didn't show. Besides, as drunk as you are, I wouldn't have gotten in the car with you, anyway."

"You little bitch." The man started toward Ashley but saw Jade standing behind her and stopped. His tone immediately became more pleasant. "Who's your friend?" he asked.

"Jenna," Ashley said shortly. "She's a neighbor and she gave me a ride."

"We'll have to have her over some time." His eyes moved slowly up and down Jade's body and a shiver of revulsion moved over her skin. "To thank her."

"That's quite all right," Jade said coldly. "Ashley thanked me already. It was nice meeting all of you. Goodnight."

Without waiting for a response, Jade headed to her apartment. She was a little concerned that the guy might hurt the children but Ashley didn't seem afraid of him, so it was probably okay. Besides, she'd already performed her share of Good Samaritan duties for the day and she wanted no more involvement with that family and their problems. She had enough of her own.

She stripped off her clothes in the bedroom on her way to the shower. As she passed the window, she noticed the blinds were open. A shiver of alarm skimmed her spine. She walked over to close them, but before she did, she looked outside. A figure stood in the courtyard. She couldn't make out his features but from his silhouette, she could tell it was a man and he seemed to be looking at her apartment. There was something vaguely familiar about him.

Bryce. Dear God, Bryce had found her. She quickly stepped back, trembling violently. Standing with her back against the wall, she once more looked outside. The man was still there. Her first thought was to grab her gun from the drawer of the nightstand but she was too frozen to move.

As she watched, the figure's hand went to his mouth and he flicked a lighter to the cigarette between his lips. In the glow of the flame, she saw his features clearly. Not Bryce. Dennis. The asshole boyfriend.

Her fear turned to rage and she jerked the blinds closed. She had a feeling the son-of-a-bitch was going to be trouble.

Walking to her bedside table, she opened the drawer. The moonlight coming in through the blinds glinted off the barrel of the Ruger P89, giving her an odd feeling of security.

She closed the drawer and smiled. "Bring it on, asshole," she whispered. "I'll be ready."

****

72

Luke squatted beside Delia's grave and brushed his fingers over her headstone. "I won't promise you that I'll get him," he whispered. "But I swear to you, I'll never stop trying."

Even as he said the words, he felt crushed by his own inadequacies. It had been over a month and not a sign. It was as if the bastard had ceased to exist.

The wind picked up and Luke stood, shoving his hands deep inside the pockets of his bomber jacket. Flowers on some of the other graves began to sway, reminding him he should have brought her some roses or something. She would have liked that.

Until Delia's death, the last time he'd been at a cemetery was to visit Angel, the younger sister he'd lost ten years ago. Like Delia, he should have protected her. He'd thought at the time he was doing the right thing. She had to make a choice. He could only rescue her so many times, right? After that, it was up to her. Again, like Delia, she'd made the wrong choice. And it had cost her life.

The cemetery was deserted. He came here once a week and it was almost always deserted. Some of the headstones were brand new, the graves fresh. Others were so old the inscription was no longer legible. Strange how the atmosphere was peaceful and at the same time tragic. How many of these deaths were natural causes and how many were the work of some depraved sonofabitch like Bryce DiMarco?

His hands clenched and he shoved them further into his pockets, taking a deep breath. Rage crackled like electricity through his veins. He wanted DiMarco, wanted to snuff the life from him as surely as he'd snuffed the life from countless others. Delia...the young girls whose lives he'd destroyed. How many others?

He shook his head, wondering what kind of person stood among the dead and wished death upon another human being. Maybe it was normal, maybe it was sick, either way, he didn't really give a damn. That was how he felt. And he didn't just wish death on the bastard; he wanted it to be slow and painful. And he wanted it to be at his hands.

He rubbed his palms over his eyes and turned away.

It was hard to look at a headstone and see Delia's name there. She should be alive. She had her whole future ahead of her. She didn't deserve this.

The sudden blast of his cell phone shattered the peace. He dug it out of his pocket and flipped it open.

"Butler."

"Hey," It was Jennings from headquarters. "Got a call from DiMarco's wife. I figured you'd want me to patch it through."

"Sure," he replied, ignoring the buzz that traveled through his system. It wasn't excitement at talking to Jade, he told himself, only the anticipation that she had some information about her husband.

As he listened for the clicks that would tell him the call had been patched through, a thought occurred to him. If Jade DiMarco was calling, something might have happened. Had DiMarco found her?

After several anxious moments, he heard the call transfer and quickly answered. "Luke Butler."

"Agent Butler?" A woman's high-pitched squeak came over the line and he knew immediately the caller was not Jade DiMarco. It had been a while since he'd spoken to her, but he could never mistake this voice for Jade's husky tones. That meant his worries were unfounded, nothing had happened to her. The relief he felt when he realized the caller was not Jade DiMarco was tinged with disappointment because...well...because the caller was not Jade DiMarco.

"This is Agent Butler. How can I help you?"

"I saw on TV where you're looking for Bryce DiMarco, right? Well, I was...I mean, I *am*, married to him."

"You're Bryce DiMarco's wife?"

"Uhm, not exactly."

He took a deep breath, struggling to control his temper. He seemed to do that a lot lately. "What do you mean 'not exactly'? Didn't you just say you were Bryce DiMarco's wife?"

"I am his wife." The caller paused. "But he's not Bryce DiMarco."

His grip on the phone tightened until his knuckles turned white but he spoke as calmly as he could. "Look, ma'am. I don't know what kind of game you're playing but

I'm not in the mood and I'm not very good at riddles. You have a nice day."

He started to disconnect but her voice stopped him. "Wait," she said with a hint of desperation. "I'm married to the man who calls himself Bryce DiMarco but that's not his real name. That's not who he is."

"Then who is he?" he asked, slightly interested but still wary.

"Not over the phone." There was another pause. "There's a reward, right?"

"Yes. If the information you provide leads to his capture."

"I can't believe I'm doing this." Her voice dropped to a shaky whisper. For the first time, he heard genuine fear and knew she wasn't a crank. This was the real thing. "The reward better be a damn good one cause I'm gambling with my life."

"Headquarters handles that, but I guarantee if you help us catch DiMarco, you'll be compensated. When can you come in and talk to us?" He headed back to the car, hopeful for the first time that they might have a real break in the case. This woman could very well lead them to Bryce DiMarco, or whatever the hell his name was.

"Oh, no. I can't come in. He'd find out and kill me for sure. Can you meet me?"

"Where?"

"I don't know. Somewhere safe."

"Has DiMarco been in contact with you lately?"

"No. He doesn't know where I am. Or at least, I don't think he does, but I'm not taking any chances. I'm calling from out of state. It's not far though, maybe we could meet halfway."

"That would be great, but since I don't know where you are, I sure as hell don't know what's halfway between us." His patience snapped. This woman was giving him the runaround and he'd had enough.

"I know." Her voice sounded like she was crying and he felt a little ashamed. Obviously, the woman was terrified. "I'm sorry. I'm just so confused."

"Don't worry," he said, "I'll do whatever you need me to do. Just tell me where you want to meet."

"Do you know where Bloomington, Illinois is?"

"Yeah." He didn't say it, but he knew she was probably in Chicago. Bloomington was about halfway between there and St. Louis. If she were trying to hide, a big city like Chicago would be a good choice.

"There's a zoo in Miller Park. Meet me by the rainforest exhibit in three hours."

Bloomington was a hundred and sixty miles from St. Louis. That gave him enough time to get there but not a lot of time to spare. "How will I know you?" he asked.

"I'll find you," she assured him.

"How will you know me?"

Her voice now held amusement. "You're an FBI agent, right? You all look alike."

Luke looked down at the jeans and bomber jacket he wore. "You might be surprised."

"Trust me, I'll find you."

They ended the call and Luke drove out of the cemetery. He wondered if this woman were telling the truth and if she had information that would help them find DiMarco. He also digested one other interesting fact that he found disturbingly satisfying.

If this woman were actually married to Bryce and they'd never divorced...Jade was not *actually* DiMarco's wife.

Chapter Seven

Luke arrived at Miller Park just before dusk. At the ticket counter, he paid admission and picked up a map of the zoo. Following the brightly colored arrows, he made his way to the rainforest exhibit. The smell of popcorn and the odor of animals combined in an odd mixture that was pleasant and at the same time repulsive. A group of cursing teenagers shoved past him, followed by a harried mother, one child on her hip and another in a stroller.

A woman paced at the entrance to the exhibit. She looked out of place in the family-oriented environment. She wore a red blouse stretched tightly over surgically enhanced breasts and a short black skirt. The roots of her bleached blonde hair were so dark that at first glance, she seemed to be wearing a headband. She looked like a hooker...and not the high priced kind. DiMarco had definitely traded up when he'd married Jade.

"Mrs. DiMarco?"

Her head flew up and eyes surrounded by too much make up met his. She looked nervously over her shoulder.

"His last name was actually Lyons but I haven't used it in years. You can call me Tracy."

Luke nodded. "Want to take a stroll?"

She fell into step beside him, not speaking for the first few moments. The path they took wound through the exhibit beneath a canopy of lush foliage dotted by exotic flora. Birds twittered and squeaked, accompanied by the deep croak of frogs. From up ahead, the distant laughter of children filtered back to them.

Just when Luke was growing impatient for her to

speak, she took a deep breath and began. "We met eight years ago. I knew right away he was trouble but that never stopped me before and it didn't stop me then." She paused, pulling a cigarette from her purse, and placed it between her lips. A soft mist from the rainforest showered them, but she still managed to light the cigarette, nervously blowing puffs from her lipstick-smeared mouth. "He was so handsome. I always wondered why he married me. I figured out later it was cause he had me pegged. I was used to being a victim and he liked having one around."

"Was he violent?"

She gave a humorless laugh. "Only when things didn't go his way. Fortunately, that wasn't very often. Especially once he went to work for Sal. He moved up quick after that, started making big bucks."

"Sal?"

She heaved a sigh, blowing out a stream of smoke along with it. "Sal Giamani, the man Bryce worked for. Hey, do I get that reward or what?"

"Only if the information you provide leads to his capture. Do you have any idea where he might be?"

She shook her head. "No clue. You mean I stuck my neck out to help you and I get nothin?"

"It's possible you'll get a reward." They stopped on a bridge and Luke leaned his hands on the rails. He watched a brightly colored blue and red bird fly from tree to tree. A *Crimson Rosella*, the tag on the glass identified.

"Possible?" Her lip trembled and he thought for a moment she was going to cry. "I need that money."

The ambience of the rainforest was strangely calming. It was probably the only thing that kept Luke from grabbing the woman and shaking some sense into her. "Look, we really need to find your husband. He's extremely dangerous."

"You think I don't know that?" Her voice lowered and she looked around as if DiMarco might be hiding behind a tree. "I damn sure want you to find him before he finds me."

"What about his friends? Anyone he was close to that he may be in contact with?"

"Maybe Sal. Last I heard, he was wasting away in a

nursing home. Hell, he might be dead for all I know."

"Do you know which nursing home he was in?"

"I got no idea but I'd bet my ass Bryce is the one paying for it. Once Sal got too sick to run the business, his son took over. He never gave a rat's ass about his old man but Bryce was different. Sal took Bryce off the streets and gave him a job. They got really close, like Bryce was his kid or somethin'." She took another pull from her cigarette and dropped it to the ground, crushing it with the toe of her stiletto shoe.

"What about his family?"

"Bryce's parents are dead. A murder suicide thing. His mom was screwin around and Bryce's old man went nuts." She shrugged. "Bryce never talked about it to me. But you hear things, ya know?"

"Is there anything at all you can tell me that might help me find him? Friends, hobbies, bars he liked to hang out in?"

"I'm trying. I want that money and I want the bastard caught." She shuddered, and then lowered her voice. "Especially now that I've talked to you."

Luke handed her his business card. "Call me if you think of anything that might help us find him. Then we can talk about the reward. I'll need a way to get in touch with you."

"Bryce won't find out I said anything, will he?"

"Of course not. If anything happens to spook you, if you think he might be around, call me. I'll take care of you."

Her laugh held a lifetime of bitterness. She shook her head. "Yeah, if I had a nickel for every time some asshole promised to take care of me, I wouldn't need your damn reward."

He chose to ignore the fact that she had just called him an asshole. "How can I get in touch with you?"

"You can't. I'll get in touch with you."

She left and he followed at a discreet distance, watching her slip behind the wheel of a beat up Toyota. He took down the license number and kept an eye on her as he went to his car. Fortunately, the parking lot was nearly empty and he was able to keep her in his sights. He followed her out to the main highway.

Traffic on I-55 was light, allowing Luke to hang back as he tailed Tracy, keeping the Toyota in sight. He called Wayne and told him what he'd been up to.

"You could have let me in on this, you know."

"Wasn't enough time." He dismissed Wayne's complaint. "I need you to run a check on a couple of names for me. Sal Giamani and Bryce Lyons."

"Got it. What are you doing now?"

"Following the woman. She wouldn't tell me where she lives, I figure it's something we might need to know."

"I'll save the lecture about going off on your own. It's not like you'd listen anyway."

"What the fuck?" Luke swerved as two men in a blue Mazda sped past, nearly sideswiping him.

"What is it?"

"Some dipshit nearly ran me off the road. Sorry."

"You okay?"

Luke let out a breath and turned his attention back to his quarry. "Yeah, fine."

"I'll call you as soon as I get something on the names."

"Thanks. You're a peach." Luke hung up the phone, eyes focused on the taillights of Tracy's car. The assholes in the Mazda were long gone.

****

Luke followed the woman's car to Chicago where she turned into a run-down neighborhood. She parked in the driveway of a dilapidated house that was about five years past needing a paint job. Shingles were missing from the roof and weeds had taken control of the flowerbed in front of the house.

Yeah, she could probably use the reward. Hell, he'd be willing to pay her out of his own pocket if she led him to DiMarco.

He watched her go inside and wrote down the address. He sat there for another ten minutes, wondering how long he should watch her and why Wayne hadn't called yet when a car squealed by.

He had just enough time to see that it was a blue car but not enough time to get the plates when glass shattered and the driver side window next to Luke's head exploded. The sonofabitch had taken a shot at him.

Then he saw that it was a Mazda. The same car that had almost taken him out on the highway. But now it looked like there was only one man in the car. Earlier there had been two.

Luke started his car and took off after the shooter, trying to keep him in sight without driving at a deadly speed. With one eye on the road, he punched 911 into his cell phone.

"This is Special Agent Luke Butler from St. Louis, badge number 2317616," he told the operator. "I'm traveling west on 11th street, just past the intersection of Juniper and 11th. I'm in pursuit of a blue Mazda. Shots were fired. I need back up."

"Dispatching back up now, Special Agent Butler," the operator replied. Luke thanked her then ended the call.

An elderly man walking his dog stumbled back onto a curb as the cars sped by. Luke gripped the steering wheel and swerved, tapping the brakes as he backed off his speed. The last thing he needed was to take out an innocent bystander.

The gap widened between Luke and the Mazda. He would have to either pick up a considerable amount of speed, or let the guy go.

He couldn't let him go. Not only had the asshole taken a shot at him, he might be a lead to Bryce. Hell, he might *be* Bryce.

The decision was taken out of Luke's hands in a matter of seconds. The Mazda tried to take a corner too fast and flipped, rolling twice before coming to a stop on its' roof.

Luke pulled up beside the wreck and jumped out of his car. He saw immediately that the driver was not Bryce. He was a large, dark skinned man and right now he was unconscious. Or dead. He bled profusely from a gash on his head. Something about the man seemed familiar but Luke couldn't place where he'd seen him.

The door was crushed but Luke wrenched it open and knelt on the cement. A green pine tree deodorizer swung from the upside down mirror, giving off a sickeningly sweet odor that meshed with the smell of burnt rubber and gasoline.

Luke placed his fingers on the guy's neck but didn't

get a pulse. It was then that he realized he knew who the man was. During his undercover operation to bust Bryce, he'd seen the guy a few times. The man had worked for DiMarco.

From the corner of his eye, Luke saw something flutter in the breeze. A blue piece of paper slid from the dash onto the ground. Luke rescued it before the wind carried it away. The ticket was stamped with the Miller Park Zoo logo. A parking pass. He and Tracy had been followed from Bloomington.

"Motherfucker." Jumping into his car, Luke headed back to Tracy's house.

Something struck him in the gut as soon as he pulled into the driveway. The house looked the same as it had a few moments ago, but it didn't *feel* the same.

He un-holstered his Beretta and crept to the front door. "Tracy." He shouted as he knocked on the door. No answer. Her car still sat in the driveway.

Luke tried the knob. Unlocked. He pushed the door open and stepped inside.

She was lying on her side in the living room floor, blood pooling beneath her head. Lifeless eyes, frozen in terror, stared at the ceiling. A wound on her neck gaped open in a grisly mockery of a smile. DiMarco had slit her throat and done a much better job than he had on Jade's.

"Sonofabitch," Luke whispered, slamming his fist against his thigh. The bastard had been here just minutes ago. Hell, he could be here now.

Luke once again called 911. In a low voice, he told the operator to send back up to Tracy's address. He also asked for an ambulance, although he knew it was too late for Tracy Lyons.

He crept down the hallway toward one of the three closed doors. With his back against the wall, he reached around and flung the door open. He entered the room, gun first, aiming it at one corner, then the next.

Stepping over a pile of clothes, past an unmade bed, he approached the open closet. Empty.

He searched the last few rooms, another bedroom and a bathroom, but DiMarco was gone. He'd done what he had to do in record time and escaped. But he had to be nearby. The bastard couldn't have gotten far.

Luke searched the immediate area as he waited for the police, but didn't find DiMarco. He felt like Tracy's death was partially his fault. Maybe on a subconscious level, he'd intended to draw DiMarco out by stirring up the people in his old life. He hoped that wasn't the case, but he had to accept that it was possible. It was a facet of himself he didn't like, so he didn't dwell on it. What was done was done.

An ambulance and squad car pulled up to the house at the exact moment Luke's cell phone rang. It was Wayne.

"Nothing on Bryce Lyons but we got a hit on Sal Giamanni," Wayne said, "He's in a nursing home in Cape Girardeau. Paid for by Bryce DiMarco. Apparently, DiMarco visits him once a week like clockwork."

"He's a helluva guy, that DiMarco."

"Yeah, a real winner. What's happening there? You find out where the woman lives?"

"Lived," Luke corrected, wondering how he was going to explain that two deaths had occurred right under his nose, in a span of less than ten minutes.

****

The air shimmered with the burning intensity of the hundred-degree temperature. Funny how much warmer Cancun was than Chicago this time of year. Bryce slid his sunglasses over his eyes and settled into the wicker pool chair. His only concession to the heat had been to wear ivory colored linen slacks and loosen half the buttons of his blue silk shirt.

Parker Williams sat across the table, looking miserably overheated in a black wool double-breasted suit, necktie and all. A power suit...never leave home without it. What Williams didn't understand, was that power wasn't in what you wore. Power was who you are. What you do. What you are *capable* of doing.

They could have talked inside but Susannah had begged and whined until Bryce agreed to join her by the pool. Considering she had provided him a place to hide out, giving in to her demands was the least he could do.

The sun's rays reflected off the smooth surface of the pool and shone directly into Parker's unprotected eyes. He squinted at the paper he held in his sweat-dampened fingers.

"As you know, the FBI froze your accounts. At least the ones they knew about. You can't touch the five mil in the Caymans as it's in your wife's name only." He took a handkerchief from his pocket and mopped the perspiration from his forehead. "Tell me again why you did that?"

"It was a cushion in case I ever found myself in unfortunate circumstances such as those I'm in at the moment." Bryce's lips twisted in a sneer. "What I hadn't anticipated was that Jade would be in opposition to me. I suppose I overestimated her loyalty."

Yes, and he'd underestimated her courage, or more accurately, her stupidity. Did she really think she could defy him and win? Apparently she did, but she was in for a most difficult and excruciating lesson.

He listened to Parker with half his attention, absentmindedly flipping a silver dollar between his knuckles while he watched Susannah's lithe body slice the skin of the water.

Fortunately for him, she owned this secluded beach house in sunny Mexico, and was desperately in love with him. Also in his favor was the fact that she didn't have an ounce of scruples in that delectable body of hers. His being wanted by the FBI hadn't even made her blink when he needed a place to stay.

"Then of course, there are the accounts in Sal's name of which you're executor. The feds can't touch those."

The mention of Sal brought Bryce's attention back to the conversation. The guilt he felt for abandoning the man who had been more of a father to him than his own was almost unbearable. But it couldn't be helped. No way in hell would he risk going to visit him. Bryce couldn't take the chance of being apprehended and sent to prison. Not even for Sal.

"You know, the wisest course would be to turn yourself in," Parker told him, sucking greedily on his lemonade spritzer. "The only charge I feel we can't beat is the bail jumping charge. I think I can get you minimum sentencing on that. There's absolutely nothing to link you to the agent's murder or the trafficking charges. At the most, you would probably serve a year."

The sun glinted off the silver dollar as it moved more rapidly between Bryce's knuckles. "I will not serve one *day* in prison, Parker."

"I know how you feel, but you're only making things worse. If you hadn't fled, you'd probably have gotten off completely. I still think there's a good chance of cutting some kind of deal where you only have to serve probation."

The man was so optimistic, so enthusiastic. Bryce didn't have the heart to tell him what he'd done to Tracy.

Try to get a reduced sentence for that one, counselor.

"We're not cutting a deal. I'm not turning myself in. You are going to continue to do what I pay you to do and save your advice for someone who needs it. Do we understand one another?"

Parker's eyes rounded. "Do you have any idea what they'll do to me if they find out I knew your location and didn't tell them?"

Bryce pulled his sunglasses down on his nose and leaned forward, looking directly into Parker's eyes. "Do you have any idea what I'll do to you if you do?"

The color seeped from Parker's face. He cleared his throat and gulped his lemonade. "Well. I guess we're through for now. I'll be in touch." He shoved papers into his briefcase and slipped a sweaty hand into Bryce's for a handshake. Then he was gone.

"Hey baby," Susannah called from a lounge chair next to the pool. "Come and rub suntan lotion on my back."

"I'm not your fucking cabana boy, Susannah."

She sat up and leaned forward, showing even more skin than the dental floss she wore was meant to do. "Pretty please." Her full lips molded into an enticing pout but Bryce was unaffected.

Her bronze bathing suit was almost the exact shade as her tanned flesh. It was hard to tell where one ended and the other began. Sun-streaked blonde hair hung to mid back. She was a strikingly beautiful woman but she left him cold. Put a five hundred dollar swimsuit on a whore and she was still just a whore. They'd had some hot sex in the past, but once he'd met Jade, he'd lost all interest in Susannah.

Besides, she was the type of woman who could never be satisfied with just one man. As much as she'd professed to love him, she'd screw anything with a penis...and some things without. Lucky for Susannah, he didn't give a damn about her. Otherwise, he probably would have killed her.

She uncoiled from the lounge chair and sauntered over to where he sat. Placing a hand on either arm of the chair, she leaned in close. She smelled of suntan oil and chlorine. Her bikini top gaped open, showing her nipples. She flicked out her tongue and moistened already glossed lips.

"Come on, baby. You've been here for weeks and you haven't touched me. Don't you remember how good it was between us?" One hand slid slowly over his exposed chest and slipped beneath his shirt to the waistband of his pants. "Don't you know how much I want you?"

He grabbed her wrist and pulled it away. "I'm married, Susannah."

"For God's sake, Bryce. The bitch is gone. She betrayed you and *I'm* the one here for you. What the fuck is this crazy loyalty thing of yours? You're a ruthless bastard in every way, yet you won't cheat on your missing wife?"

He stood so quickly she stumbled back but still, he held onto her wrist. He pulled her against him and twisted her arm behind her back.

"My wife is *temporarily* missing. I *will* find her. I *will* bring her back."

Her pupils widened, black nearly obliterating the blue. Her chin quivered and tears filled her eyes. "You're hurting me."

Blood surged to his groin and he felt the beginnings of an erection. Well, what do you know? She still turned him on after all. But she was the wrong woman.

He wanted to see that kind of fear in Jade's eyes.

His grip eased. "You understand? I *will* get my wife back."

"Ok, whatever. But surely you realize that she's fucking around on you? I mean, she *left* you. You don't think she's got the same fucked up views of fidelity as you, do you?"

86

Everything around him faded to nothing. A shadow passed over the sun. Words fired like missiles in his brain.

Jade with another man. Jade desecrating their marriage vows. Just like his mother had done to his father.

No! She goddamned sure better hope that wasn't the case. Because that would determine whether he took her back and simply punished her. Or whether he fucking killed her.

"Bryce! Bryce, goddammit, let go!"

Sunlight blazed once again and he looked down to where he still held onto Susannah. His fingers squeezed her arm so tightly, her flesh bulged between his knuckles. Tears streaked her cheeks. Pain had replaced the fear in her eyes.

He released her and stepped back. She stared at him and rubbed the angry red marks he'd left on her arms then turned and stormed inside.

Bryce shook his head. She was worse than Tracy. At least Tracy had been real. A low class bitch, but a loyal one. Until the end, that is. Tracy never should have talked to that fucking Butler. The sonofabitch thought he was so smart. He'd been so smug when he'd tried to intimidate Bryce after his arrest.

Agent Lucas Butler. A thorn in his side but obviously, the man was somewhat incompetent. After all, Bryce had murdered Tracy and escaped...with Butler less than half a mile away.

Unfortunately, Bryce had lost a good man in the process. Donahue had been loyal, an excellent employee. He'd been one of only a handful of men Bryce had trusted enough to take with him. Ah well, it couldn't be helped. Part of the cost of doing business.

The maid brought him a fresh Glenlivet on the rocks, then quietly disappeared. He took a sip of the scotch, capturing a cube of ice in his mouth and crunching it between his teeth. Something glinted in the sunlight at his feet. The silver dollar. He must have dropped it when he'd grabbed Susannah. He picked it up and once again began working it through his fingers.

It was the first dollar he'd ever made. The first time he'd had money that was all his own and he'd earned it when he went to work for Sal. He kept it to remind himself of where he'd come from.

And where he swore he'd never be again.

Chapter Eight

Jade stared at the computer screen and watched the numbers blur before her eyes. She had work to do, but she wasn't in the mood. Soon after she'd arrived in Solitaire, she'd begun keeping books for two different companies. They allowed her to work from home, which was perfect. The less contact she had with people, the better. In spite of the bizarre circumstances, it felt good to finally be free, finally independent, after all that time of living under Bryce's control.

She pulled up the spreadsheet for Magic Construction. No matter how hard she tried, she couldn't concentrate. Cutting herself off from human contact was a necessity but she grew lonelier with each day that passed.

The ache of no longer being able to see or speak with Melanie was almost a physical thing. Growing up, Melanie had been the only bright spot in Jade's horrible existence. Melanie's mother had welcomed Jade into her home as if she were another daughter. She was always in the kitchen, offering the girls a homemade snack. Jade especially liked the no-bake cookies. Melanie's mother would let them scrape the pan and eat the gooey treats while they were still warm.

Jade had thought that Melanie was the luckiest girl in the world. She was always amazed when her friend would complain about her mother. Didn't she realize how blessed she was?

Jade had secretly wished they could trade mothers. Funny how it never occurred to her that wishing her own mother on Melanie was selfish and cruel.

And now, she wanted to see her friend. Deeply and desperately needed to talk to her. Contacting family and friends was against the rules of the program, she knew that. And it could perhaps be dangerous. But God, she missed Melanie so much.

She stared at the computer screen now with a new purpose. Mel had an AOL account. Jade could add her screen name to the buddy list. Just to see if she was online. She didn't have to talk to her. Maybe seeing Melanie's name on the computer screen would help her feel connected to her friend.

She logged on and added Mel's name to her buddy list. Then waited breathlessly to see if the screen would show that she was online. Disappointment coursed through her when Mel's screen name didn't appear.

It was just as well. It had been foolish to even consider contacting her.

She minimized the AOL screen and once again stared at the spreadsheet. Concentrating on the numbers in front of her proved almost impossible. She kept clicking back on the Internet icon and her eyes kept straying to the buddy list box. Even when she had AOL minimized, her ears were pealed for the tone that indicated Mel had logged on.

But she didn't. Heaviness settled in Jade's chest. She had been lonely a few moments ago, now she ached with despair. Tears formed and in seconds, she was sobbing. She felt like an idiot but she couldn't stop weeping. She hadn't cried like this in a long, long time. The anguish came from deep within. From a hollow place inside her that had no end.

A noise filtered through her grief and the sobbing stopped when she recognized it. A barking dog. Mel's buddy sound. Excitement as intense as her grief coursed through her. Fingers moving frantically, she instant-messaged Mel.

Hello, how have you been?

A few seconds passed, then her reply. *Fine, thanks. Who are you?*

Of course, she had a new screen name. One Melanie didn't recognize.

It's Jade, she typed

Words appeared rapidly on the screen. *Oh my God! Jade! I've been so worried about you. I've missed you so much. What on earth happened? Are you okay?*

I'm fine. I had to leave and I'm sorry but I can't tell you where I am. It's too dangerous. I actually shouldn't have contacted you but I missed you. How have you been?

Terrible without you. When can I see you?

Fear that she was making a huge mistake warred with her elation at finally speaking with her friend. Oh well, the damage was done. If they found out, she would deal with the consequences.

I don't know. Not for a while. I'll call you soon and we'll have a real talk. I'll explain everything. How're your parents? Anything new with your love life?

Mom and Dad are fine. And the love life is the same. All quantity no quality. Have you talked to Bryce's uncle lately? I heard he's not doing well. He's been asking about Bryce.

Melanie had a cousin who worked at the nursing home where Bryce's Uncle Sal was a patient. Jade felt a pang of guilt. She really hadn't given much thought to Sal since all of this had happened.

Bryce had visited him once a week and occasionally, Jade went along, too. Sal never had warmed up to her, though. Sometimes he confused her with someone named Tracy. During those times, he treated her with more kindness. Whoever this Tracy person was, Sal must have liked her. Jade had asked Bryce about Tracy but he said he had no idea who Sal was talking about.

I haven't spoken with Sal, she typed back. *I hope he's okay. I'm sure he's wondering why Bryce hasn't been to see him.*

What's going on with that whole thing? They haven't caught Bryce yet?

Jade was beginning to wonder if they would ever catch the sonofabitch. *I really shouldn't talk about this online. I promise I'll call you soon. I'd better go now. Love you.*

Love you, too. I'm worried about you.

Don't worry about me. I'm fine. I promise.

They said goodbye and Jade logged off. After losing contact with Melanie, the loneliness came back full force.

As did her concern for Sal. At times he'd been crotchety with her, sometimes downright mean. But, he was a lonely, sick old man. Bryce had been his whole world. Now who would he have? She wanted to call him but couldn't take that chance, just in case Bryce had figured out a way to see him.

The thought of that psycho knowing she was in contact with his uncle sent fear spiraling through her. She would just have to get updates on Sal through Melanie.

Jade needed to do something to work off some of the tension that had gathered in her muscles. After changing into gray sweats and a t-shirt, she put on a Creedence CD and began her warm up routine.

Once she was loose, she went through the drills and exercises she'd learned in class. By the time she began her stance work, she was in the zone. So much so that it took a moment for her to realize someone was knocking on her door.

Who the hell could that be? She hadn't had a visitor since she'd moved to Solitaire.

She considered ignoring it, but with Creedence blasting from the stereo, they obviously knew she was home.

Yanking a towel off the couch, she dabbed at the perspiration on her face as she strode across the room.

"Who is it?" she called through the closed door.

"Ashley."

Dammit, what could she want? "Can I help you?"

"I just wanted to thank you for what you did the other night. Can I come in?"

A rush of breath left Jade's body and she hesitated for a moment, then swung the door open.

The goth look from a few nights ago had been toned down some. Ashley still wore black but the makeup was gone. Just as she'd suspected, the girl was pretty. But her eyes still held that haunted look.

"I'm kind of busy right now," Jade said, not inviting the girl to come inside.

Ashley's expression took on a pained look but she quickly masked it and shrugged her shoulders. "No prob. I just thought we could talk for a minute, you know, hang out, get to know each other, but that's okay."

I don't want to know you. I don't want to know anyone in this town. "Maybe some other time."

The girl nodded and turned away. Before she could close the door, Jade heard a man's voice roar from an apartment down the hall.

She thought the voice belonged to the jerk she'd met the other night. Dennis, yeah, that was his name.

Ashley had moved a few steps away but she stopped, crossing her arms tightly around her middle.

He's a sonofabitch and he's mean to the kids and their mother.

So, what can you do about it? It's none of your business, just ignore them.

Ah, take the easy way out? Don't get involved, just look out for yourself. Is that how things work now?

Yes, dammit. That's the way they have to work now.

Jade closed the door before she could see if Ashley turned back. She didn't think she could continue to ignore her if she saw her face again. The face of a girl who had experienced way too much anger, too much pain in her short life. She recognized the look because she'd seen it in the kids at the shelter...and she'd worn it herself. And ignoring Ashley's problems made her feel lower than dirt.

She tried to continue her workout but she was no longer in the zone. She kept seeing Ashley's hurt look. And she could still hear Dennis yelling. She couldn't understand what he was saying, but recognized the malevolence in his voice. And it made her want to hurt him. Damn thin walls in this place.

Just go check on them, make sure he's not hurting anyone.

Yeah, and what if he is? Put a little jujitsu on his ass? You think he'll take it easy on you like they do in class? Great idea, Jade. Great freakin idea.

But even as she tried to talk herself out of it, her feet were moving toward the door.

Locating the apartment was easy with the blast of Dennis' voice to guide her. She knocked loudly and in a few moments, an older, heavier version of Ashley opened the door. The woman's face was puffy and wrinkled. Her cheekbone was red with the obvious imprint of a hand. Slow anger wormed its way through Jade.

"Yes?" the woman barked, staring at her with a mixture of irritation and curiosity.

"Is everything okay in there?" Jade tried to peer around her without being obvious about it, but the door was only open wide enough for the woman's body, which was blocking her view into the room.

"Who the hell are you?"

"I'm your neighbor from down the hall, Jenna Donovan." A rush of warm air carried the stench of booze and sweat into the hallway from the open door. Jade resisted the urge to cover her nose. "I heard screaming. I thought someone might be hurt."

"Everyone's fine. It's none of your business."

From within the apartment, a man bellowed, "Deb, who the hell's at the door?"

"Just a neighbor, Dennis. I'll handle it," Ashley's mother called over her shoulder.

Jade lowered her voice. She didn't want Dennis to realize which 'neighbor' was at the door. "If the kids are in trouble, I'm making it my business."

"You a social worker or just nosy?"

"Look, I met Ashley and Jonathan. They seem like sweet kids. I wouldn't want anything to happen to them."

Deb crossed her arms and leaned in the doorway. "Yeah? You got kids?"

"No," Jade admitted.

"Then you don't know what the hell you're talking about. Leave us alone."

"Let me talk to Ashley and I'll leave."

"To hell with you."

She started to close the door but Jade stuck her foot inside, preventing her from shutting it all the way. "Look lady, I don't want to stand out here and argue with you all night. Let me talk to your daughter and I'll leave."

The woman's gaze was pure venom. Without taking her eyes off Jade, she yelled for her daughter.

Ashley came to the door. Her eyes and the tip of her nose were red from crying. Jade's gaze traveled quickly over the girl. She didn't see any marks.

"Ashley, are you okay?"

"Fine," Ashley muttered.

"Want to step out here for a minute?"

"What for?" she asked. Her look seemed to say *you had your chance.*

"I'd like to talk to you." When the girl didn't reply, Jade added, "Please?"

Shrugging, Ashley stepped past her mother and joined Jade in the hall. Jade looked expectantly at the woman and she finally slammed the door shut.

"I thought you were busy," Ashley said.

"Sorry about that. I was rude before."

"Whatever." Ashley shoved her hands in the pockets of her black jeans. She scuffed at the carpet with the toe of her boot. Apparently fascinated with the activity, she kept her eyes glued to the ground.

"Ashley, does Dennis hit you or your brother?"

She shook her head. "Not us."

"Your mother?"

The girl hesitated, then nodded.

"She doesn't have to put up with that. Why doesn't she get rid of him?"

Ashley gave another of her signature shrugs. "I guess cause she needs someone. I don't know. Ask her."

"What about your father?"

"He died three years ago." The scuffing stopped. The girl's entire body went still. "He was hiking and fell into an abandoned mine."

Jade sucked in a breath and her knees went weak. Dear God, what a horrific way to die. The image of falling into a black hole, meeting your death in such a terrifying manner made her physically ill. "I'm sorry."

"It's no big deal. We're doing fine." Ashley raised her head and gave a defiant look. She lifted a trembling hand to brush the hair back from her face. "I take care of Jon and watch my Mom get the shit beat out of her once in a while. Like I said, no big deal."

Something shifted inside Jade and tightened around her heart. The wall she'd built was starting to crumble, brick by brick. The girl needed her. She needed someone to care. Ashley's attempt at bravery made her seem even more vulnerable.

Jade knew from that point on, things would never be the same. Her carefully constructed plan to keep people at arm's length had just gone to hell.

****

Shady Acres Nursing Home was an upscale institution that catered to the wealthy but even money couldn't cover the odor of sickness and urine that lingered beneath the scent of pine cleaner. The smell followed Luke from the hallway into Sal Giamatti's room.

Artsy, expensive-looking paintings hung on the walls. The furnishings included a big screen television and a leather-covered sofa and recliner. The posh decor gave the illusion of a luxuriously appointed apartment. The heart monitor and IV stand with tubes snaking out of it quickly dispelled that image.

A mahogany nightstand next to the bed held a sterling silver picture frame with a photo of Bryce and Jade. Bryce was tanned and smiling, his arm slung casually over Jade's shoulder. She wore a bright yellow tank top and her blonde hair was pulled back in a ponytail. Rather than looking directly at the camera as her husband was, she stared adoringly at him, a half smile curving her full lips.

Luke's gaze moved from the photo to Sal Giammati. Looking at Sal's frail old body, Luke found it difficult to reconcile this image with the ruthless criminal Sal was alleged to be. His skin was the color of parchment paper and hung loosely on his frame. Age spots, some the size of nickels, freckled his forehead. His hands lay on top of the blankets and were dotted with the same discolorations. Long, yellowed fingernails gripped the bedspread. The man's sunken eyes glared at Luke.

"Who the hell are you?" Sal barked in a voice as dry as kindling.

"My name is Luke..." Luke began but the old man cut him off.

"You're a damned cop. I can smell 'em a mile away."

The old man's remark startled him. How had he known? "I'd like to ask you some questions about Bryce Lyons."

Sal struggled to a half-sitting position and scowled at Luke. "What the hell do you want to know?"

"When was the last time you saw him?"

"He was here yesterday."

Yesterday? Luke had stopped at the reception desk to

check Sal's visitor list and there hadn't been an entry since Bryce had been here over a month ago. He'd been surprised to see that Jade had also visited from time to time. He'd have thought Bryce would have kept his relationship with Sal a secret from his wife.

"Are you sure he was here yesterday?" Luke asked. The old man was suffering from Alzheimer's, but it was possible the information was accurate. He likely had lucid moments from time to time.

"Of course I am. He comes every week. Him and that pretty little thing he's married to."

Now Luke knew the old man was confused. He knew Jade definitely hadn't been there and he suspected neither had Bryce. "Are you close to Jade?"

"You betcha. She's like a daughter to me. Clever little thing, too. Why, she can run a scam like nobody you ever saw." Sal cackled and shook his head. "Bats those pretty eyes at a man and he doesn't know which way's up."

Luke didn't want to believe the old man, but his comments, combined with what they'd already learned about Jade DiMarco were starting to cast her in a bad light. The agency's investigation had revealed Jade had an account in the Cayman Island's with a balance of five million dollars. Jade had worked for Bryce's accounting firm before they'd married. How could she be that involved in his finances and not know, at least a little, about his activities?

Was it possible that Jade had been more aware of Bryce's crimes than she'd led them to believe? If that were true, then why had Bryce tried to kill her? Had she threatened to turn him in? Maybe Delia's murder was further than she was willing to go. Who knew? But one thing Luke did know. The more he learned about innocent little Jade, the less innocent she seemed to be.

His gut twisted with the realization that he'd been duped. Maybe if he'd thought like a cop instead of a hard dick, he would've seen beyond her attributes and figured out she was hiding something. The mistake knifed at him.

"Do you have any idea where Bryce is right now?" Luke asked, although he knew it was useless to question the old guy. He obviously wasn't in his right mind. But it was possible he had some valid information inside that feeble brain of his. And, he might be just crazy enough to tell Luke something he shouldn't.

"Do you think I'd tell you if I did?" Sal snarled as if reading Luke's mind. "You bastards'll never find him. Him and Tracy have a plan. They always do."

"Tracy?"

"His wife, dammit." Sal picked up the photo. He ran his hands lovingly over the image of Bryce and Jade. His fingernails made a clicking noise as they traveled across the glass. "Yep, they've got it all worked out. But I'll never tell you a thing. You can't make me talk no matter how much you sons a bitches beat me."

Luke shook his head. What the hell was he talking about now? Could it be that Tracy was the one he'd meant when he mentioned the scams? It seemed that he was confusing Bryce's two wives. Did Jade know about Tracy? If she'd been to visit Sal she almost had to. The way he rambled on about Bryce's first wife, he must have mentioned Tracy in front of Jade. DiMarco obviously wasn't worried that Sal would reveal the information to Jade or he wouldn't have brought her here to visit.

Maybe he hadn't been worried because Jade had known about Tracy all along.

****

Jade arrived home from her jujitsu lesson just before dark. Cal had asked her to stay after class so he could show her a few specialized skills to fend off an attacker. He was still concerned about her abusive boyfriend. He didn't bring up the 'dim mak' move again but she knew if she asked, he would be happy to show her the technique.

No thanks. What he'd shown her tonight had been enough to freak her out a little. She couldn't imagine actually *doing* any of those things to another human being.

Sure, she'd taken shooting lessons. She was learning how to kill with a weapon but this was different. To use Cal's methods, she would have to be very close to her target. She shuddered. Could she really do that? If the time came did she have what it took to put the lessons to use and actually *kill* another person? If that person were Bryce, then yes, she thought she could do it. After everything he'd done, if it came down to his life or hers, she was pretty certain she could kill him.

As she walked by Ashley's apartment on the way to hers, she heard a crash so loud it made her jump. Then she heard a man's voice raised in anger. The words were muffled but the message was clear. Once again, Dennis was on a rampage.

She started to pass by, then she heard a noise like flesh hitting flesh. Hard. Followed by a woman's cry. Then the shrill voice of a child and this time the words were clear.

"Leave her alone, shitball." It was Jon. "Leave my momma alone!"

"Get out of here, you fuckin' brat." Dennis' unmistakable bellow carried into the hallway. "Unless you want to be next."

Jade cringed and her steps faltered. She thought about calling the police but discarded the idea. It wouldn't be wise to bring attention to herself, not in a town this small, not while she was in hiding. No, this was something she should ignore or handle on her own. Hesitating for a moment, she sighed and rapped on the door. "Hey," she shouted. "Open up."

"Get the fuck away," Dennis growled through the closed door.

Jade tried the knob and the door swung open. The sight that greeted her was like a scene from a nightmare. Or from her own past.

Ashley sat in the corner, holding her little brother in her arms, tears streaming down her face. Jon's hair was matted to his head with sweat and his chubby cheeks were scarlet.

In the center of the room, Dennis held Deb by her hair, his fist raised, ready to strike. Blood streaked the woman's face and ran in a fresh pool from her nose.

"Let her go!" Jade shouted as she rocketed into the room.

The man whirled toward her. "You'd better get the fuck out, bitch, if you know what's good for you."

Jade's entire body shook and blood drummed through her ears. Enraged past the point of coherency, she advanced towards Dennis, her finger pointed at his chest.

"Let her go, you piece of shit."

He released the woman and she slumped to the floor. He hadn't done it because she told him to. He was simply shocked. Or maybe it was because she was next.

She soon found out it was the latter.

"Who the hell do you think you are?" He advanced toward her, swaying unsteadily, his fists balled at his sides.

Jade's first instinct was to step back, but she didn't want him to realize she was afraid of him. But she was. Petrified, in fact.

"Do you have any idea how despicable you are? Beating up on women and children." She shook her head, her voice quivering with rage and fear. "Does it make you feel like a tough guy or like the pathetic weakling you are?"

As she spoke, he'd gotten closer. A look of incredulity came over his features. His face turned so red, she thought he might explode.

He reached for her with both arms outstretched. In his drunken fury, he was slightly off balance. She quickly ducked to the floor and shot a leg out, taking his feet out from under him. He crashed to the floor but didn't stay down long. With a roar, he rose to his feet.

Behind him, Deb came to a sitting position. She watched as if she were a spectator, as if the tableau unfolding in front of her eyes had nothing to do with her. She didn't seem inclined to help.

Dennis came at her again. His hand shot out and with bone jarring force, he backhanded her across the face. Her teeth slammed against the inside of her cheek and she tasted blood, just before agonizing pain pounded through her head. She heard one of the children scream, she wasn't sure which. Maybe it was both of them. And then she went down.

She rose to her feet and Dennis was there, filling her vision. She wasn't sure why she no longer felt fear, but she didn't. Only a white-hot anger. And a desperate need to defeat this piece of shit.

He came toward her again, arms swinging wildly at his sides, a satisfied grin spread across his face. As soon as he came close enough, Jade reached up and grabbed his ears, twisting them as hard as she could. The grin disappeared quickly. He growled like a wounded bear and bent over, trying to break her hold. She brought her knee up into his solar plexus, hard and fast. She felt him grow heavy in her grip and when she released him, he once more went to the ground.

Somewhere in the back of her mind, she was amazed that the moves she'd learned from Cal had worked. But she knew it was temporary. Against a man Dennis' size, and as angry as he was, her domination of him wouldn't last long.

She glanced around quickly, looking for something to use as a weapon. Jon climbed from his sister's lap and ran to Jade, handing her a baseball bat.

She took it from him and turned back toward her opponent. Dennis was still on the ground, hunched over on all fours, breathing like a bull.

From behind her, she felt Jon reach for the cell phone hooked to her jeans. Although reluctant to get the police involved, after all that had taken place, Jade knew she no longer had a choice. Jon called 911 from her cell phone while she kept an eye on Dennis. After a few moments, he seemed to recover and rose slowly to his feet.

She lifted the bat over her shoulder, ready to knock a homerun in the sonofabitch's head. He hesitated, obviously having second thoughts about tangling with her *and* the baseball bat. He dropped his arms in defeat.

Flicking a glance back and forth between Dennis and the children, Jade saw Jon and Ashley run to their mother's side and help her to one of the kitchen chairs. Ashley wet a washcloth and began cleaning the blood from Deb's face.

The police and an ambulance arrived in less than five minutes. The EMT's treated Deb's injuries. She assured them she didn't need to go to the hospital and they left.

One of the officers, an attractive black man with a nice smile, took all their names. Looking around the room, he said, "I'm not sure exactly who the victims are here. Would someone mind telling me what happened?"

Jade explained everything that had taken place, realizing for the first time that *she* could be the one in trouble. She was the only person here who wasn't supposed to be.

The officer nodded. His partner, a tall, red-haired man, placed handcuffs on Dennis and read him his rights.

"What the hell?" Dennis sputtered. "She assaulted me in my own home."

"Is she the one that beat up Ms. Strickland?" he asked, nodding toward Deb.

Dennis lips clamped shut and he glared at Jade. Deb stood to her feet.

"Wait. I don't want to press charges, officer," she said.

"Sorry, Miss, it's out of your hands. Domestic violence is a crime punishable by law." He gave a brief, satisfied grin. "With or without the assistance of the victim."

"Ok, then," Dennis shouted. "I want to press charges against her." He nodded toward Jade.

The two officers looked at one another and chuckled. "I tell you what, partner," the red-haired one said. "You file a report when we get downtown. How about that?"

"You motherfuckers." Dennis jerked against his handcuffs as they led him out. When he passed Jade, he muttered under his breath. "I'll get you, bitch. Just wait and see."

Once they were gone, Jade went over to Deb. The woman's lip was busted and a large red mound was starting to swell under her eye. "Are you okay?" Jade asked.

Deb shook her head. Tears streamed down her puffy cheeks. "Why did you do it? Why?"

"What do you mean?"

"You should have minded your own business. You've made things worse."

"Worse? Worse than what he was doing to you?"

The woman smiled as if Jade were too simple to understand. "Yeah. Worse than that."

Jade shrugged. Not sure what to say. "Well, at least he's gone."

"He'll be back." Deb said quietly. Her face seemed to age ten years in an instant. "They always come back."

Chapter Nine

Luke walked into Supervisory Special Agent Madsen's office and dropped into the chair across from his desk.

"We need to set up an interview with Jade DiMarco," he told his superior.

"I'm glad you're here, Agent Butler. I need to speak with you and since you've been running around like some modern day Lone Ranger, doing your own thing, it's been kind of difficult to catch up with you."

Luke shrugged. "I followed some leads. There wasn't time to call in." This wasn't entirely true. There'd been time but Luke hadn't wanted to wait for Wayne before going to see Tracy Lyons. Yeah, sure, that had ended badly. But he'd done what he felt he had to do.

"Yeah. Well you doing that, not following protocol, makes what I'm about to tell you a little easier." Madsen leaned back in his chair and steepled his fingers beneath his chin. "You're off the case."

"What the hell do you mean? Things are starting to break. I've got new information that might lead to DiMarco." Luke had always gotten along with Madsen, although they'd had a few minor disagreements. Luke had a history of skating just on the edge of disciplinary action. Because of his success record, most of his faux pas had been overlooked. Apparently, this wasn't to be one of those times.

"Your partner was killed. You know that should automatically cause you to be removed from the case. But before we could make that happen, you go off like a crazy man, breaking every rule in the book."

Luke stood and began to pace. "Look, I understand where you're coming from and normally, I'd agree with you." Madsen snorted. Luke pretended not to notice. "I guarantee you, I'm fine over Agent Grimes' death. I'm thinking with a clear head and I'm starting to get some leads that need to be followed up on. I need to interview Jade DiMarco. I think she may know more about her husband's activities than we thought."

"Why would you think that?"

"First of all, she worked for his accounting firm until they were married. How could she not know anything about his business? And, that five million dollar account in her name in the Cayman Islands. You know that's got to be a cushion for him just in case he got into this kind of trouble. That way his loving wife could get her soft little hands on some quick cash."

SSA Madsen shook his head. "We've been over this before. As far as her job in the accounting firm, she only dealt with legitimate accounts. The account in Cayman Islands, she's never touched a penny of that money. We've kept an eye on it since we discovered it existed. Not one cent has been moved. Maybe she knows about it and maybe she doesn't. Either way, it's not a crime to have a lot of money."

"Ok, how about this? I went to see Sal Giammati. He went on and on about how DiMarco's wife wasn't as innocent as she seemed. She used to run scams for them. She was on the visitor's log. How could she be innocent if she associates with Sal Giammati?"

"Look, I'm not sure. The old man's got Alzheimer's. Doubt if he even knows his own name half the time, let alone remembers anything factual about Jade DiMarco."

"Why do you refuse to consider the possibility that she might be involved with her husband?"

"I'm not refusing to consider anything. For one thing, she's in the Witness Protection program and she's going to be a key wit once we bring in her husband. For another, are you forgetting he almost cut her head off? Doesn't sound to me like they're exactly tight."

"Maybe she was going to double cross him so he decided to take her out. I don't know. Maybe she *is* as innocent as she seems. But, bottom line, it wouldn't hurt to interview her one more time, right? With all the new info we have, could be she'd tell us something that might help us find DiMarco."

"You know, you have a point there."

Luke let out a long sigh and dropped back in his chair. "Great. You'll set it up then?"

"I'll have to review all the facts and decide if an interview is warranted. But no matter what, you're off the case. As a matter of fact, you really ought to take some time off. Use up some of those vacation days you've accumulated."

Luke stood again and slapped his palms on the desk. He leaned forward, trying to maintain his calm. "I don't want time off. I need to stay on this case. Keeping me in makes the most sense. I've got the momentum going now and I can find the sonofabitch. I know I can."

Madsen stood too. "I'm not interested in what you want. You're off the case, there's no debate. You can either take some vacation time or I can put you on administrative leave. Right now, you've got a choice. If you're still in my office sixty seconds from now, you won't."

Luke started to say more but vacation time was better than administrative leave. He held his anger, stared at Madsen for a few more seconds...fifty-five to be exact...then slammed out of the office.

He was almost to his car when his cell phone rang. For a moment, he had the ridiculous hope that it was Madsen and he'd changed his mind. He looked at the display. It was an unknown number.

"Butler," Luke answered the call.

"Hello, Agent Butler." A man's voice said. "How are you?"

"Who is this?" The voice sounded familiar but Luke couldn't quite place it.

"Now, now. You've gone and hurt my feelings. I thought since I'd occupied your every thought over the past several weeks, you'd surely recognize my voice."

Fucking DiMarco. Luke stopped in the middle of the parking lot, rage bubbling like a volcano inside him. "You motherfucker. Your ass is mine, you know that?"

"Take a deep breath, agent, calm down. You've seen what that impulsive nature of yours can get you, right? I was within six feet of you a few nights ago and you ran screeching off after my associate without thinking things through. I would think the outcome of that little incident would have taught you something."

The day was cool, yet Luke could feel a rush of sweat on his skin...hot beneath the jacket. There were a few people milling around in the parking lot but they seemed far away. He felt isolated from the world. He took deep breaths through his nose and slowly exhaled. *Don't screw this up. Maybe he'll slip and tell you something you can use.* "Why are you calling me, DiMarco? What do you want?"

"I just want to chat."

"Ok then, how about I tell you a story? Ever heard of what inmates do to guys like you in prison? They're fond of pretty boys, but its kind of a two edged sword. As attractive as I'm sure they'll find you, they have a tendency to do some violent things to perverts that prey on children. I don't think they'll be pleased with your penchant for forcing innocent young girls into prostitution."

There was a pause and Luke could hear the man breathing over the line. DiMarco's voice was a pitch higher when he finally spoke. "You know, Jade and Delia kind of remind me of each other. Have you ever noticed the resemblance?" When Luke didn't respond he went on. "Sure, Delia was a redhead and Jade's a blonde. But they sort of had the same innocence about them. Makes you wonder, doesn't it? Will Jade scream louder than the cop? She's probably not nearly as tough as your partner was. What do you think?"

"Fuck you, DiMarco."

DiMarco chuckled. The sound made Luke's skin crawl. "What's the matter, Butler? Don't tell me you have a thing for my wife like you did for the cop? I'll admit she's a hot little number but after the bitch betrayed me, she has to pay. I'd hate for you to get attached to another woman and then lose her."

"Look, you sonofabitch," Luke ground out, his jaws so tight his teeth ached. "No matter what, you're a dead man for what you did to Delia. You have my solemn promise on that. But if you so much as touch one hair on Jade's head, if you come within fifty feet of her, I'll kill you so slow you'll beg me to make it stop. You got that, DiMarco?"

Even as the words tumbled from his lips, Luke wondered where they'd come from. Five minutes ago, he'd been ready to crucify Jade DiMarco and now he was ready to kill for her? The only way he could justify his reaction was that he knew Jade wasn't evil like Bryce. Even if she had been a part of her husband's operation, Luke truly believed she wouldn't have been involved in trafficking those young girls. Her grief and shock over that had been genuine. And she probably wasn't a part of Delia's murder either. Whatever the truth was about Jade, Luke knew he didn't want DiMarco to get his hands on her.

"You don't scare me, Butler," DiMarco replied silkily. "I eat guys like you for breakfast."

"Trust me, princess." Luke growled into the receiver. "You've never met anyone like me."

****

Jade inhaled deeply, breathing in the scent of the Colorado morning and along with it, the smell of gunpowder. In the distance, the Rocky Mountains stood sentinel around the Blue Hills Gun Club. Large evergreens lined the fence that enclosed the pistol range.

She felt oddly at peace each time she came to shoot. Cal's gym and the range seemed more like home than her own apartment.

She planted her feet and aimed at the target. A lock of hair escaped her ponytail, a cool breeze blowing the errant strands into her eyes just as she squeezed off a shot. Missed badly on that one. She pushed the hair out of her face and took aim once more. This one came much closer to the bull's eye. In spite of the ear protectors she wore, the report of the weapon sounded loud in the stillness of the fall morning.

She and the Rangemaster were the only ones out this early. She liked having the range to herself. These days, being around other people made her uneasy. Even the tenuous friendship she'd formed with Ashley made her uncomfortable. It was amazing how moving to a strange place and living under an assumed identity had tarnished her social skills. Go figure.

She fired a few more rounds, then pushed the button to slide the target toward her. Not bad. Well, except for the few shots that had missed the shaded figure completely and imbedded in the white paper background. One round had come dangerously close to the heart. For a moment, her mind superimposed Bryce's face over the silhouette.

She replaced the target with a new one and slid it back out. She steadied and took aim, firing into the head of the silhouette.

"You're not following through."

"Jesus." Startled, she whirled and came face to face with Agent Luke Butler. "What the hell?" she gasped as the air left her body. She couldn't decide if she were more surprised or angry at his sudden appearance.

"You need to keep everything the same even after the shot breaks. Just pretend you're continuing to fire after the shot's gone."

"I'm not talking about the freaking lesson. What the hell are you doing here?" Her heart rate kicked up a notch and she blamed it on his scaring the hell out of her. "You know, it's not the smartest thing in the world, sneaking up on someone with a gun in their hand."

His eyebrows lifted in mock horror. "Were you going to shoot me?"

"I could have. How did you get back here?"

"FBI credentials can get you anywhere." He nodded toward the Ruger. "Wanna put that down?"

She placed the gun on the table and wiped her damp palms on her khaki cargo pants.

"What are you doing here? Did you find Bryce?"

"No, not yet." He shook his head but he said it with confidence. Like he knew it was only a matter of time. "Is there somewhere we can go to talk? Maybe get something to drink?"

"I don't drink," she blurted. "Well, not alcohol anyway." She felt her face flush, certain he hadn't meant alcohol. It was barely eight a.m.

He grinned. "Coffee then?"

"There's a coffee shop inside. Will that work?"

"Sure."

She slid the safety in place on her Ruger and slipped it back into the holster. Removing her protective glasses, she led him inside. They ordered coffee at the counter and settled into a booth.

She looked at him across the table, noticing for the first time that he'd lost weight. The skin on his face seemed tight and his eyes held a haunted look. But they were the same intense amber she remembered from their first meeting. His dark hair was longer and a hint of whiskers covered his cheeks and upper lip. She'd always found scruff sexy. Damn. She didn't want to find anything about him sexy.

"How did you find me?" she asked. "I thought the US Marshals were the only ones that knew my location. For that matter, how did you know I was here at the range?"

"I followed you from your apartment." He admitted without a hint of shame. "And as far as locating you, let's just say that I have friends that owed me favors."

"So you're not here officially?"

He didn't answer. He stared at her for a moment and she noticed something in his eyes she didn't like. Suspicion.

"How much do you know about your husband's past?" he asked.

She shrugged and took a sip of coffee. "Not a lot. Both his parents died. He was an only child. His father passed away about a year before I met him. He left the floundering family business to Bryce. Bryce moved the business to St. Louis and made it a mega million-dollar empire. I met him when I worked for his accounting firm."

"Did he ever mention someone named Tracy?"

Tracy. The name Sal called her from time to time. "What is this about?"

Luke studied her closely. "Did he ever tell you he was married?"

"Bryce was married before I met him?"

"He was still married *when* you met him."

"I don't understand."

He took a drink of his coffee. Once again, he didn't reply. He regarded her skeptically. Did he think she was lying to him? What reason would she have to lie?

"I don't understand," she repeated with an edge to

her voice.

"DiMarco was already married when he married you. He never divorced his first wife."

Stunned but not hurt, she shook her head. There was even more she hadn't known about her husband. Then the true implication sank in. That meant that Bryce *wasn't* her husband. She was never legally married to him.

"That's actually good news." She smiled in relief. "Wonderful news, in fact."

"I'm not sure the first Mrs. DiMarco would agree."

"Where is she now?"

"Dead," Luke replied bluntly. "She was found murdered a few days ago."

"Oh, my God." Jade's hands shook. She gripped the coffee mug tightly between her fingers. "Bryce?"

"We're pretty certain it was. Take comfort in the fact that she was far from innocent. Not that I'm saying she deserved what happened to her, but she had a criminal record a mile long." His eyes narrowed and his mouth turned down at the corners. "DiMarco seemed to have a way with women. A way to convince them to go along with his schemes."

Again, he gave her that eagle eyed look. As if he were trying to discover her secrets.

"Are you accusing me of something, Agent Butler?"

"Are you aware that there's an account in the Cayman Islands in your name with a balance of five million?"

She sat in stunned silence for a moment. Five million dollars? Why would Bryce do that? He hadn't told her about it, so obviously it was for his own benefit. She shook her head and looked at Luke.

She hadn't missed the sarcasm in his tone. His habit of ignoring her questions and asking his own was starting to wear on her nerves. "No, I wasn't. But I don't think it really matters what I tell you. You've already made up your mind about me."

"You seem pretty defensive for someone with nothing to hide."

She sat up and balled her fists on the tabletop. "That's enough," she exploded. "If you suspect me of something, just say it. Ask your damned questions, make your accusations and get it over with. I'm not going to sit here and play your sick little game of cat and mouse."

"Right now, I don't know what to believe. My main concern is finding your husband. No matter what it takes."

"Well, harassing me is probably not the best way to go about it." Tears clogged her throat. Damn the man. She wanted to be angry, not hurt. "You seem to forget that I was a victim too."

He leaned back in the booth and draped his arm along the rear of the seat. His eyes dropped to the scar on her neck, visible above the ribbed tank top she wore. His features seemed to soften a little. "You're right. I'm not accusing you of anything. I'm just trying to get to the truth."

Not exactly an apology, but at least a change of attitude. She'd settle for that at the moment. "I'd like the truth too. And I'd damn sure like for you to find Bryce."

"Why didn't you tell us about Sal Giamatti?"

Another accusation? To hell with him if he didn't trust her. Trust was overrated anyway. "I didn't think it was important. I never thought to say anything."

"It never occurred to you that we should watch him? See if DiMarco tried to visit him?"

She shook her head. "I guess I assumed you'd know about his family. Sal's his uncle. What kind of investigators wouldn't know that?"

"Sal's not his uncle. He's a crime figure who took DiMarco in and gave him a job. DiMarco did his dirty work until he proved himself and Giamatti made him his right hand man."

"Oh my God." Feeble old Sal a criminal? Was everything she'd known about Bryce a lie?

"Sal had some interesting things to say about you. He thought you were pretty...uhm...skilled. Pretty street savvy."

"Good Lord, the only time I was ever around him was in the nursing home. Half the time he didn't even know my name." Then it hit her and she breathed a sigh of relief. "He called me Tracy. He apparently confused me with Bryce's first wife. You remember...the dead one with a criminal record?" she finished sarcastically.

111

"Maybe." He nodded slowly, as if considering the remote chance that she *wasn't* a dangerous criminal.

Deciding to let him mull over the possibility of her innocence, she changed the subject. "What about Bryce's parents? Did he lie about them too?"

"Bryce's parents died in a suspicious fire when he was fourteen, although he told his first wife it was a murder/suicide. Neighbors that were interviewed claimed Bryce had changed after his younger brother died."

"Younger brother?"

Luke nodded. "The boy was in a wheelchair and apparently, their mother wasn't very sympathetic. Treated the kid like shit. After he died, Bryce became violent, prone to rages."

An unwelcome sliver of sympathy for Bryce wormed its way into Jade's heart. "You think Bryce killed his parents?"

"It appears that way but he was never arrested for it. He disappeared shortly after. Seems he hooked up with Sal at a very young age."

"So what now? What do you want from me?"

Luke expelled a breath and shook his head. "I'm not sure. Just grasping at straws."

"I have no idea where Bryce is and I knew nothing about his past. I'm afraid you've come all this way for nothing."

"You never know what might turn up." He leaned forward and drained his cup. "I saw a few motels in town this morning. Any particular one you'd recommend?"

"Motel? You're staying?"

"Does that make you nervous?"

"As a matter of fact, it does. For one, you think I was somehow involved with that bastard and the horrible things he did. For another, I'm going to have a hell of a time explaining why an FBI agent is here in town."

"We'll tell them I'm an old friend...an old boyfriend. How's that?"

For the first time in several moments, she smiled. "Since the story I've given everyone is that my ex-boyfriend is an abusive asshole, Agent Butler, I guess it will be just perfect."

****

Luke followed Jade down Main Street, staying several car lengths behind her red Grand Prix. He'd been following her since they left the range that morning, but so far, she'd done nothing that warranted suspicion.

He drove past a grocery store with a fruit and vegetable stand out front, past a barber shop with an old-fashioned red and white pole outside, and incongruously, a Starbuck's coffee shop sat next to it, mixing modern with the old. Across the street sat the small police station, one patrol car parked outside. Jesus. This sleepy little town was ill-prepared for the likes of DiMarco. It would be like a mouse facing off with a lion

When Jade's car slowed and turned, he increased his speed; afraid he'd lose her on a side street. Drawing closer, he saw her pull into the parking lot of a gym.

He cruised by at a crawl and watched as she walked to the entrance. A muscled up Schwarzenegger clone arrived at the same time and held the door open for her, earning a smile and a nod of thanks. Luke wondered if she would have given the guy that smile if she'd seen the way he checked out her ass. Not that Luke blamed him. She had a damned fine ass. The rest of her wasn't too bad either.

When he'd first met her, she'd been soft and curvy. The curves were still there, but she was more toned now. He wasn't surprised to discover she'd been working out; her body was tighter, more defined.

She'd changed in other ways, too. The way she'd met his gaze, tilted her chin and challenged him at the coffee shop showed a strength and confidence that hadn't been there before. She also seemed tougher, harder. Or maybe she'd always been that way. Maybe the meek damsel thing had all been an act.

Luke made a u-turn and parked in a strip mall directly across the street from the gym. The place was jammed with shoppers. Cars shifted in and out of the lot. He could hang out here without drawing a lot of attention.

He tuned the radio to classic rock, cracked the window to let in the cool air, and slouched down in his seat to wait. For a moment, he questioned his sanity. What was he doing here, really? Did he expect Jade to hook up with DiMarco right under his nose? Did he think he'd apprehend them both with one swoop and go home happy?

Not necessarily, but there was a chance. Even if she was innocent, he needed to keep an eye on her. It was possible DiMarco might find her. After all, Luke had.

He had called in more than a few favors to locate Jade and he was risking a lot by being here. The lady could cause him some serious trouble. One phone call and his ass was in a heap of hot water. *What the hell.* The payoff would be worth it if he got his hands on DiMarco.

It still infuriated him that the bastard had called. Luke had tried to trace the number with no luck. What was DiMarco's game? Had he simply called to taunt him? Rub it in his face that he'd murdered Tracy and Luke hadn't caught him?

You're home free now you sonofabitch, enjoy it while you can.

As it did each time he had too much time to think, his mind went to Delia. He should have been there for her. She'd needed him and he'd let her down. He blinked hard and wiped the corners of his eyes.

Stop thinking about it. Concentrate on one woman at a time.

Jade chose that moment to emerge from the gym.

Sweat had darkened the hair around her face and plastered the green tank top to her damp skin. She paused for a moment, lifting her face to the sun. Her breasts pushed outward as she took a deep breath. For a moment, he lost his.

His groin heated and tightened. He shifted in his seat. It had been too damned long since he'd had a woman. No way he should be this turned on by a sweaty chick in workout clothes. She finally ended the little exhibition and got into her car. Good...easier on the libido that way.

He followed her home and, idling a short distance away, watched her park the Grand Prix, retrieve her gym bag from inside and climb a flight of stairs. She let herself into the corner apartment and he parked where he could keep an eye her window.

He settled back in his seat and yawned. He'd been at it for how many hours? Driving straight through from St.

Louis, stopping long enough for bathroom breaks and to grab a quick bite. Over nine hundred miles. All he'd eaten in the past few days was fast food gobbled on the run.

Now he was hungry. And damned tired. Ready to find one of those motels and grab some shuteye. Maybe he'd wait until her light went off, then he'd know she was in for the night.

She was probably up there undressing for bed right now. How would it be to slide between the sheets with her? Of course, even as tired as he was, sleep would have to wait. If he were in bed with Jade, there were things he'd rather do than sleep.

This shit had to stop. He was fantasizing about a witness and possible suspect. Of all the women in the world he shouldn't get involved with, Jade was at the top of the list. Maybe just under Lorena Bobbitt.

He laid his head back on the headrest. Damn, he was tired.

The sudden chirp of his cell phone made him jump. Shit...he must have dozed off.

He flipped the phone open and Wayne's voice came over the line. "How's the vacation going?" His partner didn't sound like he really believed Luke was taking a vacation.

"Great. How's the investigation going?"

"Not worth a shit. Did a check on the guy in the Mazda. Came back with a list of priors but nothing big. Checked out his cell phone, bunch of one nine hundred numbers. Other calls are being traced now, but so far, nothing to link him to DiMarco. How's *your* investigation going?"

Luke hadn't lied to Wayne once in the almost thirty years they'd known each other. He wasn't going to start now. "So far, nothing."

"Have you talked to her yet?"

"Yeah."

"Find out anything?"

He rubbed his eyes and looked up at her window. The light was still on. "Just that she wasn't exactly thrilled to see me."

"I'm not surprised. You'd better watch your ass."

"I know what I'm doing."

"You always think you know what you're doing." There was a pause. "You need to realize something, buddy. She's not Delia...and she's not Angel."

"What the fuck is that supposed to mean?" Wayne was the only person in the world who could get by with a sucker punch like that. One of the few that even knew what had happened to Angel. Luke tried not to think about the little sister he'd let die. Tried not to second-guess the decision he'd made. Obviously, it had been the wrong one. Something large and painful settled in his chest.

"You're only human, man. It's not up to you to save the world," Wayne said quietly.

Luke cleared his throat but couldn't get rid of the lump blocking his windpipe. "Well, so far I'm not exactly batting a thousand."

"What happened to them wasn't your fault."

"I've tried to tell myself the same thing. I didn't believe me either."

"Cut the martyr crap. You're using your guilt over Delia and Angel as a crutch. An excuse to break all the rules and charge off like some kind of knight in shining armor."

Luke sat up straight, wide-awake now. The cheeseburger he'd eaten earlier churned in his gut. His grip on the cell phone tightened.

"Fuck you, man. I'm here because I'm *suspicious* of her, not because I think she's in trouble. Where'd you get your degree in psycho babble anyway?"

"I'm your friend, you know that. But I'm also an agent. You could fuck this thing up in a big way."

"I'm not going to fuck it up," Luke said, but he wasn't sure he was right.

There was silence, then Wayne said, "I loved her too, you know."

Luke wasn't sure if he was talking about Delia or Angel but it didn't matter. Wayne had loved them both. But he'd loved Angel in a different way than he'd loved Delia. In a different way than Luke had loved either woman. Remembering that caused him to ease off his anger. "I know you did."

"I just hope you know what you're doing."

"Yeah, you and me both. Listen, I gotta go."

They hung up and Luke stared out the windshield, watching Jade's window and thinking. About Delia, about Angel, about Wayne. And about Jade. Was she really guilty or was he trying to convince himself she was so he'd have an excuse to stay away from her? Hell, like he needed another one.

When her light went off, he started the car. Time to find a hotel, hopefully get a few hours sleep.

He wasn't sure how long he'd be in town. He'd hang around until he got a break in the case.

Or, until he was satisfied that he wasn't going to.

Chapter Ten

Jade fought off the blankets and flipped on her side. She shut her eyes...opened them. It was no use. She couldn't sleep. Again.

She peered through the shadows into the dark corners. Nothing there. The dim glow of the night-light mocked her. Almost thirty years old and afraid of the boogeyman. *Damn you, Mother.*

No, she couldn't keep blaming her mother. She was an adult now. Time to take control of the blame. Take control of the fear. She damned sure couldn't blame her mother for the insomnia. That hadn't started until this thing with Bryce.

She could count on one hand the number of times she'd slept a full night in the past six weeks. It wasn't only the fear. It wasn't only the fact that the monster of her nightmares finally had a face. Her mind just refused to shut down these days. Refused to let her rest.

She climbed out of bed and went into the kitchen for a Frappuchino, turning on all the lights as she went. She couldn't sleep anyway. Might as well OD on caffeine, sugar and calories.

The most difficult thing about these sleepless nights was the loneliness. The desire to call Melanie was so strong she almost couldn't resist. But she had to. She'd taken a big chance by talking to her friend the first time. Continuing to contact her could be a death sentence. For both of them.

Besides, it was time she stopped relying on Mel every time she was afraid. She would have to learn to face her fears on her own. Because, like it or not, she was now on her own.

Face her fears.

Was that what she needed to do? Confront the very thing that terrified her the most? Martial arts training and knowing how to use a gun were fine. But as long as she lived in fear, she would never truly be free.

She should confront her fear of the dark. Find a way to conquer it once and for all. She thought about what Ashley had told her. About how her father had died in an abandoned mine. Well, you couldn't get much darker than that. Or much scarier. She shuddered. Was it really wise to venture into one of those mines? Shouldn't she start out with something small, say, a nice deep pothole, and work her way up to the mine?

Unable to get the tragedy of Ashley's father's death out of her mind, she'd researched local mines on the computer. In the past fifty years, there had been seventeen deaths and twenty-one injuries in Colorado. The numbers were not that staggering. But good God, the terror those people must have suffered before they died.

She chugged the sickeningly sweet coffee drink, wishing it were something stronger. That's another thing she could thank her mother for. Because she'd been a drunk, Jade had sworn off alcohol, had never touched a drop. At times like these, she wished she drank.

She walked to the window and pulled back the curtain. Frost coated the glass and icy air seeped in from the edges. The sunshine earlier today had been a facade. Winter was here. Cold, dark winter. She let the curtain fall back into place.

Suddenly, the apartment was too small, the walls too close. She needed some air. She pulled a jacket on over her flannel pajamas and went out onto the balcony.

Leaning over the railing, she looked up at the sky. The stars seemed so near she could almost touch them. It was as if God had taken a handful of glittering diamonds and flung them onto black velvet.

She closed her eyes and breathed deeply. The scents of pine and honeysuckle floated in the frigid air. Her loneliness eased somewhat as a sense of calm settled over her.

Then her treacherous mind let thoughts of Luke Butler sneak in. How dare he accuse her of being involved with Bryce? The sonofabitch had almost *killed* her. Did Luke think they'd planned it together? Yeah, like she'd have gone along with *that*.

What really sucked was that, in spite of the accusations, in spite of his attitude, some small, secret part of her had been thrilled to see him. And that really pissed her off.

He hadn't answered her question but she was certain the Marshals' office had no idea he was here. For now, she wouldn't say anything, but if he continued to accuse her, if he caused her any trouble at all, she'd rat him out in a New York minute.

After a few moments, the cold penetrated deep inside her jacket. She shoved her hands into her pockets, her body shivering. She wasn't ready to go inside yet but she was freezing. She still wouldn't be able to sleep, but maybe now that her head was clear, she could get some work done.

She stepped back inside, startled when she heard a knock at the front door. For a moment, she foolishly hoped it was Luke, although she couldn't think of a reason in the world for him to be at her door at three o'clock in the morning. Of course, she couldn't think of a reason for *anyone* to be at her door at three o'clock in the morning.

"Jenna, let me in!"

Dennis. Apparently, he'd been released from jail but what the hell was he doing at her door? She didn't answer, hoping he would think she was asleep. No way in hell was she letting him in.

"Please. I know you're awake. It's an emergency. Something's wrong with Ashley. She's not breathing. Deb's not home and we don't have a phone. I don't know what to do."

All caution fled as Jade rushed to the door on legs that felt like rubber bands. "Hold on," she shouted. Numb fingers fumbled with the lock. It seemed to take an eternity but finally, she managed to open the door.

As soon as she did, Dennis shoved his way inside. She stumbled back and gaped at him. He didn't seem concerned at all. His eyes were blood-shot and he reeked of alcohol. Swaying, he narrowed his eyes and gave her an unsteady glare.

"Ashley..." she said, even though she knew it had been a trick.

"She's fine, you stupid cunt. The whole famdamily's sound asleep. I jus' got home an' saw you out there." His head jerked toward the balcony. "Thought it might be a good time for you and me to be alone."

"Get the fuck out," she screamed, backing away from him.

He kicked the door shut and came at her. Before she realized what was happening, he doubled up his fist and punched her in the jaw. Her head snapped back and pain exploded in her ears. She grabbed her face and glared at him, ashamed of the tears that instantly filled her eyes.

"You need to learn somethin', bitch. Put yourself in a man's place and you're gonna be treated like a man," he growled, staggering towards her. "Understand?"

"And I'm sure that ordinarily you're a perfect gentleman." Her words were distorted because her jaw was on fire, but apparently he understood her.

He snorted and shook his head. His eyes took on a feral gleam as he moved closer. "You're a mouthy bitch, aren't ya? I can think of a better way to put that mouth of yours to use."

On legs that trembled with fear, she continued to retreat. He came toward her unsteadily, his hands jerking at his belt buckle as he advanced. Her back met the dining room wall.

His mouth split in a parody of a smile, revealing a black gap where a tooth should have been. No great loss. The remaining ones were crooked and stained. The missing one probably hadn't looked any better.

"I've been wantin' to do this since the first time I saw you. At first, it was cause you're fucking hot." His eyes dropped to the scar on her throat and he shrugged. "Even with that bride of Frankenstein shit you got goin' on there."

He was so close now, she could smell him. The stench of cheap cologne, body odor and booze assaulted her nostrils. Her throat closed and she tried to make herself breathe through her mouth.

"Get out!"

He shook his head. "Don't think so. Ya see, now I wanna fuck you so I can show you how much of a man I really am. Last time we saw each other, you had doubts, right?"

He lunged at her, pressing his lower body into hers. He jerked her jacket off her shoulders, then pulled it down around her wrists and held her captive with one hand.

His fingers dug into her face and her injured jaw flamed. He planted a hard wet kiss on her lips. Her throat constricted with the urge to vomit. She almost wished she would. Maybe then he'd back off.

She tried to pull away, tried to fight him but her hands were trapped behind her. He was incredibly strong to be so skinny. He released her face and grabbed her pajama top. He ripped it open, scattering buttons, exposing her breasts.

God. He was going to rape her.

She screamed. His filthy hand clamped over her mouth.

"Shut the fuck up if you know what's good for you. Right now, I just want to have a little fun. You keep screaming and I'll knock your ass out. No telling what I might do to you then. Know what I mean, missy?"

Icy needles of fear danced on her skin. Panic surged through her and she struggled like a wild animal.

He released her face and used both hands to pull her arms together behind her back. The pain was so severe and so sudden she gasped.

He laughed. "No fighting this time, babe. Tonight, I'm the one in charge."

There was something about his lack of hesitation. Something about his attitude. Something about his out and out *glee*. And somehow, she knew. He'd done this before. And he would do it again.

The nameless, faceless victims flashed through her mind. Dennis' victims. Bryce's victims. All of them caught unaware. All of them at the mercy of these sick sonofabitches. Had this slime ball touched Ashley like this? Was she his victim too?

No more.

No fucking more.

She made her body relax. He froze for a second, caught off guard. Then he eased his grip on her arms, still pressing his body against hers. He grinned and grabbed her breast. Her skin tightened, recoiling from his touch. His fingers dug painfully into the soft flesh.

"You decided to play along, huh? Ready to find out what it's like to be with a real man?" Lust gleamed in his muddy brown eyes. But it was more than just lust. He was enjoying her fear.

With his other hand, he gripped the top of her pajama pants and tugged. Before he could get them past her hips, she made herself gag, loudly and deeply in her throat.

"What the fuck? You're not going to puke are you?" Then he shrugged. Maybe he was accustomed to that sort of reaction from women.

Her head fell back. He leaned in close, his hot fetid breath on the skin of her neck. She snapped her head forward and clamped her teeth down on his cheek. She didn't let go. Even when his guttural cry split her eardrums. He tried to pull back but she bit down harder.

Her teeth split flesh and she tasted blood, old sweat and booze. Now she gagged for real.

She released him and he stumbled back, still howling, his hands pressed to his mangled cheek. He stared at her, his eyes glazed with shock and pain. "Ya fuggin bith...galdan fuggin bith..."

She couldn't call the police. Once had been enough. Too much attention wasn't good. Especially an attempted rape accusation. The media in this one-horse town would be all over that. Besides, jail didn't seem to have much of an effect on this piece of shit.

She pulled her jacket back on and zipped it shut. She ran into the kitchen and spit into the sink, then rushed into the bedroom and came back with the Ruger.

Dennis was on the floor now, hunched over. He rocked back and forth, still cradling his wounded cheek. She hurried in front of him and kicked his shoulder hard enough to knock him over on his back.

She straddled his thighs, one knee on either side and shoved the barrel of the gun against his crotch.

"Here's how it's going to work, motherfucker. You're

going to disappear. Completely and totally disappear."

His wide-eyed stare fastened on the gun.

"That's right. Mine's bigger than yours, you sonofabitch, and I'll tell you a little secret. I'm not afraid of you. You got that? So you're gonna go. If I see your sorry ass around those kids, their mother or this town." She shoved the gun more deeply into his groin. He let out a yelp. "I'm going to blow your useless dick right off. You got that?"

He nodded hard, his greasy blond hair flipping back and forth in his eyes.

"I'm not afraid of you," she repeated. "Not fucking *afraid*."

"Ok, ok, ok. Juth let me outta here, you crazy bith. You won't see me again."

"Don't go back to Ashley's tonight. I'm going to check and if you're there..." She let the words hang in the air. He nodded more vigorously.

She climbed off, still aiming the gun at his crotch. He jumped to his feet but hesitated at the door. His eyes gave off more hate than she'd ever seen. But there was fear there too. He glared at her briefly and then was gone.

The gun slipped from her fingers. She barely made it to the toilet before she lost the contents of her stomach. She sat slumped on the floor, arms wrapped around the toilet, and continued to dry heave for what seemed like an eternity. Finally, the nausea passed. She got to her feet and filled her mouth with Scope.

She swished it around while she went into the front room to lock the door. She really wasn't afraid. She hadn't lied about that. But she desperately needed a shower and what kind of idiot would she be to get in there without locking the front door? Especially after what had just happened.

She knew she could have killed him. Would have killed him without a qualm. And that scared her a little.

Standing under the hot spray, she scrubbed her body over and over again. She could still feel his hot breath on her. Still smell him. She scrubbed again but couldn't get the oily feel of him off her skin.

She wasn't sure how long she'd been standing under the water when the trembling started. She couldn't stop shaking. Her mind was calm, but her body was a mass of quivering nerves.

Above the sound of the shower, above the noise of her teeth rattling together, she heard knocking. Someone was at the door.

Dennis. Sorry sonofabitch.

****

Keeping one hand inside the pocket of his jacket, fingers curved around the butt of the gun, Luke pounded on Jade's door.

His heartbeat dialed up a notch for each second that had gone by since he'd seen the blood trail. Not a lot of blood, but it was fresh...and it ended at Jade's door.

Earlier, he'd checked into a hotel, eaten some tacos, showered and gone to bed. But after an hour of tossing and turning, he knew there was no way he was going to fall asleep.

Feeling restless and claustrophobic, he dressed and went for a drive. And ended up back at Jade's. He'd seen the light on and decided to investigate. He hadn't planned to actually knock on her door, just wanted to see if he could overhear something. Maybe catch someone leaving her apartment.

Then he'd seen the blood. He thought about calling 911 but wasn't sure if there was reason for concern. The boulder-sized knot resting in his gut told him there was. Ten more seconds and he was calling.

He barely completed the thought when the door swung open. Luke wasn't sure who was more surprised, him or the wild-eyed half wet woman standing in the doorway with a gun in her hand.

"What are you doing here?" she demanded.

He stepped inside and gently took the gun from her. His eyes searched her body but she didn't appear to be bleeding. "Are you okay?"

She looked at him without moving, without speaking. Then he noticed she was shaking like someone in the grip of a seizure.

He shut the door and put the gun down on the coffee table, then put an arm around her shoulders and led her to the couch. He draped an afghan over her, not only for warmth, but also because he didn't think she wore anything beneath the blue silk robe. An added layer between him and a naked Jade was probably a good idea.

He wanted to put his arms around her, hold her until the shaking stopped but he knew she wouldn't let him. It wasn't wise anyway. She was too tempting and smelled too damned sweet. A light citrus fragrance mingled with the damp warmth from her shower and played on his senses like a drug.

"What happened? Where did the blood come from?" he asked, ignoring the sudden heat that drummed through his body.

She drew the afghan more tightly around her shoulders. "I asked what you're doing here."

He didn't want to answer her question so he asked one of his own. "Was Bryce here? Did he do something to you?"

She turned her face away from him. Moonlight filtered through the window and cast shadows on her profile. Slowly, she shook her head. "No. Bryce wasn't here."

"Then who was? What the hell happened?"

"I had a run-in with a neighbor, but everything's fine now."

She turned to look at him and he saw that an ugly red welt had bloomed on her cheek. He gripped her chin and turned her face to the light. He felt his jaw muscles clench. "Some asshole did this to you?" Spots danced before his eyes. Fury heated his veins but he managed to keep his voice calm. "Where is he?"

"It's nothing. I already took care of it. He won't be back."

"How do you know?"

Her mouth turned up in the ghost of a grin. "Because that was his blood out there, not mine."

He returned her grin, his chest muscles relaxing as anxiety left his body. Gently, he brushed his thumb along her cheek. She flinched and pulled away.

"Sorry," he said softly. "I didn't mean to hurt you."

"You didn't," she said, but he saw in her eyes that he had. And that a lot of others before him had too.

He felt like a jerk but the suspicion was still there. She wouldn't tell him what had actually happened and he

126

couldn't shake the feeling it might have something to do with Bryce. One thing he knew for sure. She was holding something back from him.

***

Jade stood and took the afghan with her. She needed to put some space between them. "Look, I'm fine. I still don't know what you're doing here, but you can go now."

He stood with her. "I hate to leave you like this. Are you sure you're okay?"

"I'm sure. Honestly. I just need to sleep. I haven't done a lot of that lately."

"Join the club." He moved closer to her and once more took her chin in his hand, looking at her injured jaw. "That thing's getting bigger by the second. Looks like you've been sparring with Holyfield."

The flesh on her cheeks warmed with humiliation and she wanted to move away from his scrutiny, but she stayed where she was. No way would she let him know how his words affected her. "Yeah," she gave an embarrassed laugh and her fingers instinctively went to the scar on her neck. "I guess I'll have to put off entering that beauty pageant I had my eye on."

Her lame joke brought a smile to his lips. A little lopsided grin where only the corner of his mouth turned up.

His fingers followed the line of her neck and touched hers where they covered the scar. The light touch sent a shiver snaking across her flesh. "You are beautiful," he murmured.

For a moment, she was held in the golden grip of his eyes. She wasn't able to breathe but suddenly, it didn't matter. There was only him and the sensation of his fingers on hers. Her skin tingled and burned in anticipation.

His touch slipped from her fingers to the pulse at the base of her throat. It began to beat a wild rhythm and she knew then that she was breathing after all.

The afghan dropped from her shoulders but she barely noticed. She didn't know which one of them moved, maybe both of them had. They were inches apart, so close she could feel the heat coming from him. The dark stubble on his jaw mesmerized her. His eyes fastened on her mouth and she knew he was going to kiss her. Her lips actually ached for his touch.

Everything in the room seemed to fade away, yet at the same time was more distinct. The ticking of the clock filled her ears. The lights blazed brighter and cool air wafted over her skin. Yet, she still burned.

His hands left her neck to caress her shoulders, then slide along her back, leaving a trail of flames in their path. His touch settled on her hips. The naked desire in his eyes held her captive and she knew her eyes mirrored that same desire.

As if in slow motion, his head dipped and her heart tumbled madly in her chest. This was insanity. While she had a smidgen of coherency left, she knew she had to stop whatever was happening.

She stepped back abruptly and the spell was broken. He blinked and almost imperceptibly shook his head. She saw relief in his eyes and knew she'd done the right thing. Both of them had come close to making a huge mistake.

He cleared his throat. "I'm sorry."

"For what?" she asked.

She bent on the pretext of retrieving the afghan, but she really just wanted to hide the color in her cheeks. Every move seemed awkward, the flutter in her stomach making her feel disoriented.

"I don't know." He shrugged. "I should have been here. Should have helped you."

"How could you have helped? You had no idea."

"No. But if I had stayed, I could have stopped it."

"Stayed? What do you mean?"

His eyes fell away from hers and he shoved his hands in his pockets. "I was outside earlier. Watching your apartment."

"You were what?" Her breath hitched in her throat as she realized what he was telling her. "You were spying on me?"

"I'm sorry."

He didn't trust her. He wanted to catch her at something...wanted to prove her guilty...of what, she wasn't sure. Slow tendrils of anger and hurt burned through her, replacing the desire. She shook her head and gave a short, bitter laugh. "It's too bad you left when you did. Bryce was here with me. You probably just missed him by seconds." As soon as the words were out, she realized how childish she sounded, but she couldn't help it. Seconds ago, he'd looked at her with passion and only moments before that, he'd been staking out her apartment.

"Look. I've got a job to do." He shook his head and brushed a hand through his hair. "I'm not sure what's going on, but I know you're not being completely honest with me."

"Yeah, and I'm sure you're just the epitome of truth and honesty." She sucked in a breath, holding back tears. "I don't know what the hell you're up to, but you need to make up your mind whether you trust me or not. Use that cop instinct I've heard so much about and make a decision. If you decide you don't trust me, then follow me all you want but keep your fucking distance. If you continue to harass me, I'll let the Marshals know you're here and you can explain your sick little theories to them."

He studied her silently. She could see a myriad of expressions come and go on his face. Then he shrugged. "Do what you have to do."

"Get out." She went to the door and swung it open. "Leave now."

He walked to the door but instead of leaving, he took out a pen and a business card, scribbling something on the back. "Here." He extended the card toward her, but she didn't take it. "This has my cell number and the number at the hotel. I want you to call if you hear anything...or if you need anything."

She gave a humorless laugh and said tightly, "Call...or just yell out my window?"

He seemed to wince at the blow, but didn't comment. "Please take it and I'll leave."

She snatched the card from his hand and averted her face, not looking at him as he walked out the door. She didn't want him to see...didn't want him to know he'd made her cry.

Chapter Eleven

Luke used his credit card to scrape the dried blood from the floor of the hallway, then slipped it into his hotel key envelope. Later today, he'd send the sample to Wayne to have tested against DiMarco's.

DNA testing sometimes took up to four weeks but Wayne could push it through in three to four days if he made it a priority. Luke would have to convince him of the likelihood the blood belonged to DiMarco. Something he wasn't even sure about himself.

He mentally replayed the scene in her apartment.

You almost kissed her. What the hell were you thinking?

He'd also told her she was beautiful. Sure, that was true, but did he have to say it out loud? Where was his head?

He knew where his head was. Lost in her. She'd smelled so good...looked so tempting in that damned robe. She'd acted so tough, yet seemed so vulnerable. No doubt about it, she'd gotten under his skin.

Face it, you're in trouble. Never had a woman affected him like Jade DiMarco. He knew he should stay away from her. But the more he told himself she could be involved with DiMarco, the more he wanted to prove she wasn't. The more he told himself she could be dangerous, the more he wanted to protect her. The more he told himself that making love to her would be a fatal error, the more his body ached for her.

The most difficult part of all was that she touched him on more than just a physical level. He was drawn to her deep in his soul. He almost hoped to discover she *was* involved with DiMarco. That might be the only thing that would keep him away from her.

He'd been with a few women since the divorce. But they were women who knew the score, women who wanted the same things he did. A good time, good sex, no strings attached. Even Delia's and his relationship had been purely sexual. They both knew nothing would come of it.

With Jade, it would be different. With Jade, it would be scary as hell.

****

Silver disco balls swung from the ceiling. Flashing strobes sent multi colored beams of light through the bar. Smoke blanketed the room like the aftermath of an atomic explosion. Nearly naked bodies packed the dance floor, moving to the beat of Madonna's "Like a Virgin."

Bryce grinned behind the phony mustache and beard. He'd bet no one in here had been anything *remotely* like a virgin in a very long time.

He sipped his club soda and grimaced. He'd prefer scotch but he needed to keep a clear head. Tonight was going to be a very special night.

He wasn't concerned about getting caught. He felt confident he could move freely around the city without fear of detection. He was certain the authorities didn't expect him to stick so close to home. Besides, the disguise he wore was virtually foolproof.

With lifts in his shoes, he'd added a few inches to his 6-foot height and dyed his hair black to match the fake whiskers. Gold tinted John Lennon glasses completed the ultra cool, urban look. His own mother wouldn't recognize him.

Of course, the bitch had been dead for twenty years.

A woman heading toward him caught his attention. She wore a low cut, red sequined blouse, ridiculously high heels and a short white skirt. He was pretty certain she was a hooker but that was okay. The 'who' didn't matter nearly as much as the 'where'. The strategic location of the sacrificial lamb was what would get Jade's attention. That was his sole purpose, after all. Wherever she happened to be, and he would know her exact location before long, he had to get her attention. He had to make sure she remembered his power. Because in spite of what she'd done to him, he still had power.

The prostitute slid onto the barstool next to him. Body odor and a sour smell he couldn't identify rolled off her like a malodorous fog. Good lord, how did she ever get any business? He didn't think he could get close enough to kill her, let alone fuck her. He damn sure couldn't imagine someone actually *paying* to have sex with her.

"Hey sugar, wanna buy me a drink?"

"Sorry." Bryce stood and quickly scanned the bar. His gaze fell on a woman he'd noticed earlier. "I'm with someone." He walked away before she could reply.

When he stopped at the young woman's table, she looked up at him uncertainly. She was around thirty and pretty in a wholesome way. Slightly plump, heart shaped face, pink fuzzy sweater, glossy brown hair with eyes the exact same shade. Not bad.

He'd watched her for a while and hadn't seen her speak to anyone. Odds were, she was alone. A half empty frozen margarita sat on the table in front of her.

"Hello." He smiled his most charming smile. "Can I buy you a drink?"

"Oh, no. No, thank you. One is pretty much my limit." She blushed and gave an apologetic smile.

He glanced over his shoulder and his voice took on a cajoling tone. "I was wondering if you could do me a big favor. There's a woman at the bar that won't take no for an answer. I hate to hurt her feelings but she's just not my type. I told her I was with someone. Then I looked around for the prettiest woman in the bar. That's when I spotted you. So here I am. How about it? Can I sit here just until she gives up? Please?"

A look of wariness came into her eyes. She probably wasn't often told she was the prettiest woman anywhere.

"You can sit, but you don't have to feed me a line of crap."

He slid into the chair next to her and shook his head. "It wasn't a line of crap. Most of the women in here are phony, vulgar. You're very pretty and you don't need all the artifice they use. You're naturally pretty." He leaned back in his chair and winked. "And that's the best kind of pretty."

Her smile beamed at him. He had her now. Let the games begin.

"So, tell me," he said. "What's a girl like you doing in a place like this all by yourself? Where's your husband? Boyfriend?"

She shook her head and the smile disappeared. "I don't have either. I was supposed to meet someone here but he didn't show up. I was just getting ready to leave."

"Well then, I'm glad I came over. I would hate to have missed out on meeting you. I'm Luke, by the way."

"Sarah."

A waitress came over and took their drink orders. Bryce asked for a club soda with a twist of lime. Sarah ordered another frozen margarita.

A slow song played and he reached his hand out to her. "Would you like to dance?"

She looked at him as if he'd asked if she wanted to lick the inside of a toilet "No." She shook her heard vigorously. "I can't dance. But thanks anyway."

"That's okay. To tell you the truth, I'm a terrible dancer. I just thought it would be nice...you know...with you. I figured it would give me a chance to be close to you." He ducked his head with what he hoped was just the right touch of shyness. It had the desired effect.

Sarah reached out and placed her hand over his. "How's this?" she asked softly. Her cheeks were now the same shade as her sweater. Perhaps he'd been hasty in his earlier 'virgin' assessment.

"Very nice." He squeezed her hand, ever so gently.

The waitress brought their drinks and Sarah took a sip of hers. "So, what do you do for a living?"

"I work for a company that procures rare gemstones for clients." He sipped his club soda and smiled. "We're mostly in the market for jade."

"Really? Fascinating. But I didn't know jade was rare."

"Oh, yes. Genuine jade is very rare. Too many people believe the color of a stone qualifies it as jade, but that's not true. The real thing is rare and very difficult to find."

Her eyes widened and she nodded solemnly. This was too much fun. She was his. No doubt about it.

"I'm a teacher. Boring, I know."

"No, not at all. A beautiful woman with a noble profession. Quite intriguing actually. What grade do you teach?"

A sparkle entered her eyes and for the first time, he thought she really *was* beautiful. "I teach special needs students."

An image burned behind Bryce's eyes. Dustin...his small body almost lost in the wheelchair where he spent every waking moment. Where he'd struggled, trapped and terrified, the night he lost his life. Bryce's grip on his glass tightened. "What did you say?"

"Special needs. I work with handicapped children. They're such a blessing. Just absolutely unbelievable. They're my life."

"That's great." His voice rang in his ears, sounding high pitched and uneven. He had to get away from her. "Listen, I shouldn't keep you any longer. I know you were trying to leave before. I don't want to hold you up."

"No. I'm actually finally having a..."

Bryce stood and swallowed his drink in one gulp. "Nice meeting you, Sarah."

Her eyes clouded over and she dropped her gaze. "Nice meeting you, too." He barely heard her over the pounding of the music.

She was hurt, disappointed. She would never know this was the luckiest night of her life.

He went back to the bar. The odorous hooker was gone. He ordered another drink and looked back at Sarah's table. She was gone, too.

The club would close in less than an hour. Didn't leave him much time. The crowd was starting to pair off, not many possibilities left.

He pulled the silver dollar from his pocket and began working it between his knuckles. Leaning his back against the bar, he sipped his drink and looked around. That was when he saw her.

Jade.

His heart crawled into his throat, obstructing his ability to breathe.

Then he got a better look at her. Not Jade, but she looked enough like her to make his knees weak.

134

Damn. He still loved her.

All the more reason why she had to pay.

The woman must have felt him staring because she met his gaze. He lifted his drink in a silent toast. She smiled and started toward him.

The closer she got, the less she looked like Jade. Where his wife's eyes were hazel and could go from green to blue depending on her mood, this woman's eyes were brown. And her hair was bleached, unlike Jade's natural honey blonde. She was also slightly thinner than Jade. A little younger perhaps, but more worldly looking.

She reached his side and her harshly painted red lips parted in a smile. "You look lonely. Want some company?"

"Sure. Can I buy you a drink?"

"Seven and Seven."

The bartender placed the drink in front of her and the woman slid onto the barstool. She leaned forward, allowing Bryce a good look at her ample cleavage and a whiff of her overpowering perfume. "How come I've never seen you in here before?"

He turned to face her, resting one elbow on the bar. "I don't get this way often. I'm here on business."

"Ooooh, a business man. I like that. What kind of business?"

"Tonight, you're my business, sweetheart." He looked into her eyes and ran a thumb down her cheek.

"You're a smooth talker, aren't you?" she giggled. Her eyes dropped to the coin he flipped between his fingers and she smiled. "I like shiny things. Can you show me a trick?"

"Most definitely, darlin'. You'd be amazed."

"I bet I would." She leaned closer and lowered her voice. "I bet you got something long and hard for me, too, don't ya, sugar?"

He thought of the knife tucked inside his boot, felt the weight of its presence. "Oh, baby," he whispered back. "You have no idea."

Her eyes widened and she gave a breathless laugh. "Let's get out of here."

She didn't act like Jade at all, but she looked just enough like her. It would be satisfying to punish her for Jade's misdeeds. A way to see fear and contrition in

Jade's eyes. A way to kill his wife without really killing her.

He smiled at the woman.

She smiled back.

Perfect.

Chapter Twelve

"You're still off. Try again." Cal turned from the martial arts dummy and came back to Jade's side.

Fingers covered in blue chalk, sweat dripping from her face, Jade nodded. They'd been at it for over an hour this morning. This was the third lesson she'd had this week.

The day after Dennis attacked her, she'd called Cal and asked him to show her Dim Mak. In spite of her previous doubts, she decided it damn sure couldn't hurt to know the technique, just in case.

Cal had marked the vital points on the dummy's body. The chalk was so they would know how close she came to the pressure points with each blow.

"There's more to it than hitting the right spot. You have to go in deep and fast, no hesitation. Got it?"

She brushed the hair back from her face. "Got it."

"If you don't hit the vital organs with the right depth, it does no good. Your opponent can overtake you. You must be quick and accurate."

She nodded. He'd told her the same thing each morning. He'd also shown her exercises to strengthen her fingers and hands.

When he'd first seen the bruises, his face had deepened to scarlet, a vein in the center of his forehead bulged and his voice had lowered to a menacing growl. He'd demanded to know if her boyfriend had found her. She told him she'd been mugged. He'd looked at her in disbelief but hadn't commented.

Jade took a deep breath and flexed her fingers. She

137

held her hands out. "More chalk." Cal quickly colored them blue.

"Concentrate...focus." His eyes bored into hers. "Accurate and deep. The neck is the most vulnerable of the points but the chest, wrist and elbow areas are sometime easier to access."

She stared at the dummy...at its neck, elbow, wrists, chest. She centered her mind; cleared it until the figure in front of her was the only think she saw, the only thing she felt.

She lunged toward the target. Her hands moved in a blur. She was aware of her flesh meeting the soft body of the dummy but her actions were controlled by something other than her conscious mind.

She stepped back and Cal moved around her to look at the chalk marks. He turned and smiled with the pride of a father who'd finally gotten through to a child.

"Perfect. You nailed it."

She wiped the sweat from her forehead, nodded, and held out her hands.

****

Jade walked out of the gym, zipping her jacket against the freezing air. She quickly headed to her car, stopping when she noticed a group of teenagers standing in the corner of the parking lot next to a tree. She recognized Ashley and walked over.

The girl wore a Breaking Benjamin t-shirt and blue jeans. The last few times Jade had seen her, the goth look was gone. Even though it might just be a harmless form of self-expression, the attire made her nervous. She hoped Ashley had given it up permanently.

The kids were smoking and one of the boys was drinking out of something inside a paper sack.

"Hi," Ashley said. She looked surprised, like she'd been caught at something.

"Hey. What's up?"

She shrugged. "Just hanging out."

Jade looked at the boys. They were the same ones Ashley had been with the first night Jade met her. They were a few years older than Ashley, but still not old enough to drink. They looked like trouble.

"Look," she told Ashley. "I've got some errands to run.

Thought I'd go by the coffee shop. Want to come?"

The girl glanced at her friends then back at Jade and shrugged again. "Sure."

At the coffee shop, they ordered cappuccinos and cinnamon rolls.

"How's everything going?" Jade asked as Ashley licked whipped cream from her cup.

"Okay. Dennis took off, so things have been better at home."

"Really? He's gone?"

"Yeah. He just left. Didn't even come by to get his stuff. He called Mom and asked her to take his things to work with her and he picked them up there. Way strange but awesome too."

"Hopefully, he'll stay gone."

"Yeah. He was a real prick."

"Watch your language."

"Sorry." She chewed a mouthful of cinnamon roll, eyes thoughtful. "You know, Mom wasn't always like this."

"No?"

She shook her head. "While Dad was alive, she was a great Mom. She took Jon to baseball practice; we went to all of his games. She cooked for us. It was cool."

"She took your Dad's death pretty hard?"

Ashley nodded and tears filled her eyes. "We all did. Jon hasn't played baseball since cause Mom won't bother with it. That's why he wears that damn uniform all the time. He misses it. Misses Dad."

"I'm sorry."

"After Dad died she started drinking. Then she went out with one jerk after another. Dennis hung around the longest. And he was the worst."

Jade knew exactly how bad Dennis was. Hopefully the bastard was gone for good. Hopefully there wouldn't be another to take his place. What a screwed up way to live. Ashley needed to get away from her mother as soon as possible.

"You know, you don't have to be like that, just because you live in that atmosphere." Jade was thinking about Ashley's friends. She wanted to tell her to stay away from them but knew that'd be as welcome as cops at a frat party. "What are your plans for the future? What are you going to do when you're out of school?"

Ashley shrugged. "Get a job, I guess. I mean, a different one from the freakin Tastee Burger. Working there sucks big time."

"What about school? College, or a trade school?"

"Yeah, right. How the freak would I get money for college?"

"There are grants, student loans, scholarships. There's always a way."

"I don't think so. I'll just get a job."

"Ashley, I came from a really bad home life too. Probably worse than yours." She knew it had been worse than Ashley's but she didn't want to give the girl details of her past. "I worked my way through school and acquired a degree in accounting. It was the best thing I've ever done. You can do something more with your life than just any old job. What do you really like? What would you like to do if you had all the money in the world?"

Ashley grinned. "If I had all the money in the world, I would do freakin *nothing*."

"You know what I mean." Jade smiled. "If you had the money for an education."

"I don't know. I never really thought about it."

"Well, you need to start thinking. You'll graduate next year and it's a big scary world out there. You can't depend on other people to take care of you. You've got to be able to take care of yourself."

"Ok. I'll think about it." She looked over Jade's shoulder and grimaced. "Shit."

"Watch your language. What's wrong?"

She nodded toward a television in the corner of the coffee shop. The weatherman was predicting snow and ice for the next few days.

"I freaking *hate* snow. Being cooped up in the house sucks."

After the weather, the anchorman came on with a report about a murder victim. Jade listened with half her attention until a line in his newscast made her turn back to the television.

The body of the young woman was found beside the swimming pool at the home of a senator from St. Louis,

Missouri. Cause of death hasn't been determined yet but there was obvious trauma to the body and police are treating it as a homicide. Senator Bomar is not a suspect in the case at this time, although police are questioning the senator, his family and staff.

The victim was completely nude except for a necklace. The police have released a photo of the necklace, hoping that someone will recognize it and can help identify the victim. So far, the police have no leads and are asking the public's help in solving this crime.

Jade's already shaking hands began to tremble more violently when a photo of the necklace appeared on the screen.

A jade necklace with the letter 'J' surrounded by diamonds.

Her necklace.

Jade's stomach heaved. For a moment, she thought the cinnamon roll and coffee were going to come back up.

"Jenna!" Ashley's voice penetrated her terror-numbed mind. "What's wrong? Are you okay? You look freaked."

"I'm not feeling well." She managed to croak. "I'll take you home."

"That's okay. I'm supposed to hook up with my friends again. Can you drive? Do you need a doctor?"

"I'll be fine."

Jade threw money on the table and left the café, tears blurring her vision on the drive home.

The necklace. Melanie's home. Bryce had killed that girl. *Dear God, he'd killed her because of me.*

Jade wasn't sure how she made it home. She stripped off her sweaty workout clothes and stepped into the shower, her mind screaming the words over and over again.

Bryce killed her because of me. Bryce can hurt the ones I love at any moment.

Melanie's family. Dear God, what if he does something to Melanie?

Suddenly, she couldn't breathe. She had to get out, had to get away. Only half aware of what she was doing, she dressed and grabbing her keys, escaped from the four walls that seemed closer than ever.

****

Fat snowflakes pounded the windshield, gathering in thick sheets as quickly as the wipers could clear them off. Definitely a night to be off the roads. Luke went through the McDonald's drive-thru and ate a Big Mac on his way back to the hotel.

He was at loose ends, bored out of his mind and unable to get Jade out of his head. Guilty or innocent? Victim or culprit? He wasn't sure and it was driving him crazy. *She* was driving him crazy.

Suddenly, he missed Samantha, needed to hear his daughter's voice. He thought about calling her but a phone call just wasn't enough. He needed to see her.

The snow reminded him of last winter when she'd stayed with him the week after Christmas. They'd made snow angels--his looked massive next to the imprint of her small body--then they'd had a snowball fight. She'd beaned him pretty good a couple of times. Not a bad arm for a four-year-old girl. Afterward, he'd made instant hot cocoa and had to hear all about how her mom made it with *real* milk. He grinned. She was kind of like her mother in that way, would settle for nothing less than the finest. His grin faded as loneliness seeped through his bones.

As thick as the snow was falling, as deep in concentration as he was, he almost passed the bar without noticing Jade's Grand Prix in the parking lot. What the hell was she doing in a bar? She'd said she didn't drink.

Drive on by, none of your concern.

But it was his concern. She was the reason he was here, after all. He needed to know what she was up to, especially if it was something out of the ordinary. Or at least that's what he told himself as he circled around and pulled into the parking lot.

He walked inside through a thick haze of smoke and the sounds of Dwight Yoakum blaring from the jukebox. His eyes slowly adjusted to the dimly lit bar. The only lighting came from neon beer signs hanging on the walls and suspended from the ceiling. The place was crowded with couples and a few lone patrons. A sea of cowboy hats floated like driftwood on fog-covered water.

He meandered through the room toward the bar,

looking for Jade as he zigzagged through the crowd. He spotted her sitting on a bar stool and made his way to her side.

She didn't notice him at first. She sat staring straight ahead, a Corona gripped between her hands like a lifeline. She wore blue jeans and a red lacy blouse. Her hair hung loose, the pink and blue neon lights giving it a purplish hue.

Their eyes met in the mirror behind the bar and her lips tightened into a thin line. She whirled toward him.

"What are you doing? Still following me?"

"Just passing by," he replied casually. "Thought a cold one sounded good."

"Right."

She turned away from him and lifted the Corona to her lips Her movements were slow and deliberate. Her eyes were glassy and her words slurred. He had a feeling that wasn't her first beer.

Luke ordered an O'Doul's. It looked like he might be her designated driver for the evening. He didn't want to be impaired along with her.

"I thought you didn't drink." He raised his voice to be heard above the music.

"I've done a lot of things lately I don't do."

She brushed her hair back, revealing the bruise on her cheek, stark and vivid against her pale skin. Who the hell had done that to her? His hands ached to get a hold of the bastard, whoever he was.

"Is something wrong?" he asked.

"What could be wrong? I mean, my homicidal husband wants me dead. I'm living in a strange town with a new identity and no friends or family. I've got an FBI agent breathing down my neck just waiting for me to make a wrong move. Could things be any better?"

"I don't know, but they could be worse. You could be dead."

She shrugged. "Would that really be worse?"

Damn, she was on a self-pity trip tonight. What had happened? He sipped his O'Doul's as she finished off her Corona and ordered another.

"How many of those have you had?" He nodded toward the fresh beer.

"Not that it's any of your business, but this is only my second."

"Really?"

"Yeah, really. My second Corona, that is. I started with strawberry daiquiris but they were too sweet. That cowboy down there bought me a Corona and I liked it so I ordered another." She pointed down the bar but there were so many cowboys in the general direction she indicated, he wasn't sure which one had bought her the beer.

"You like country music?" she asked suddenly.

The change in topic threw him off. "It's okay." He shrugged.

"I like it. Especially when I'm down. They really know how to hurt, you know? You can feel it in your soul...in your bones."

His gaze met hers and in her eyes he saw deep misery, a pain that was almost palpable. Quietly, he asked, "What's hurting you tonight, Jenna?"

Her eyes filled with tears. She brushed them away angrily, then took a deep breath, looked down, then back up at him. Her expression was like that of a puppy that'd been kicked a few too many times.

"Did you see the news?" she finally asked, her voice low.

"News? I guess not."

"The girl who was found murdered in St. Louis at Senator Bomar's house?"

He'd seen the report in his hotel room but hadn't paid much attention. "Yeah. I did see that. What about it?"

"It was Bryce."

"What? How do you know?"

"Senator Bomar's daughter, Melanie, is my best friend. Bryce left the girl's body there to send me a message. Show me how close he can get to the people I love."

"That's quite a leap, don't you think?"

Her mouth stretched into a grimace. She took a sip of her beer and shook her head. "Oh no, not at all. I didn't tell you the best part. You know how the girl was nude except for a necklace?"

"Yeah."

Her fingers made circles in the condensation on the bottle. She spoke so quietly he almost didn't hear her. "The necklace is mine."

"Jesus Christ. Are you sure?"

She nodded. "Bryce bought it for me for our first anniversary. I left it behind. He's sending me a message. It's my fault that girl died." Her voice choked and she took another long pull from the bottle.

Luke didn't know what to say. Of course it hadn't been her fault, but he could understand why she'd feel that way. "I need to make a quick phone call. I'll be back in a second. Will you be okay?"

"I don't need you to babysit me. I'm fine."

"Just sit tight. I'll be right back." He wasn't sure she'd listen to him but he needed to step outside to make the call. No way in hell could he hear well enough to call from inside.

Luke walked out front, at least that way he could see if she tried to leave. She had no business driving tonight.

He dialed Wayne's phone. When his friend answered, Luke said, "That body found at Senator Bomar's, I'm pretty sure DiMarco did her."

"What the hell? You sure?"

"Yeah, I think so. Jade said she and Bomar's daughter are best friends. Plus, the necklace on the body belonged to Jade. I'd say it's a pretty sure bet."

"Shit. Okay. I'll get right on it. You doing okay?"

"Yeah, I'm hanging in. You'll let me know if you come up with anything, right?"

"Sure. Yeah, I'll let you know."

"Thanks, man." Luke went back inside. Jade was still at the bar.

She glanced at him and turned back to her beer.

"You need to call the Marshal's office," he told her. "Let them know about your suspicions."

"I already did. They offered to place Mel and her family under protection but there's no way they'll agree."

She tilted the beer to her mouth. Her nipples strained against the lacy fabric of the red blouse. Breath stuttered in his throat...he almost groaned out loud as he shifted on the barstool, willing away the tightening in his groin. He looked away quickly, focusing on the lime bobbing up and down in the neck of the bottle with each pull of those moist, tempting lips.

"Hey," he said a bit too harshly. "Don't you think you've had enough? Maybe it's time to go home."

"I'm not ready yet."

"I think you are. You're not accustomed to drinking and it looks to me like you've reached your limit."

She wagged a finger in his face. "Listen here, mister, you're not my boss."

He expelled a breath. "The last thing you need right now is more booze."

"No. The last thing I need is you telling me what the fuck to do."

"It's not going to help anything."

"It already has. I never knew it before, but drinking makes the pain a little easier to bear." She held a hand in front of her face. "It makes the dark not so dark."

"It's going to be okay." His tone softened. "We'll find him."

"After he finds how many more victims?" She rested her elbows on the bar and cradled her head in her hands. Her eyes fluttered shut.

"It's time to get you out of here."

"I'm fine," she slurred, eyes still closed.

Luke took her by the elbow and helped her from the barstool. She didn't protest. They weaved through the crowd and outside into the fresh, cold air. He led her to his car and helped her inside, fastening her seatbelt for her.

As they pulled out of the parking lot, into the increasingly worsening blizzard, she laid her head back on the seat.

He thought she'd passed out but in a few moments, she spoke. "You got any kids, Butler?"

"I have a five-year old daughter, Samantha. She lives with my ex-wife in Atlanta."

"Yeah? You miss her?"

"All the time."

"Why aren't you with her?"

Where the hell had this line of questioning come from? He answered a little defensively. "She lives with her mother in another state. My job keeps me busy. I see her as often as I can."

She nodded. "Yeah. That's as good an excuse as any."

"What's that supposed to mean?"

"I just wondered who's protecting your little girl while you're out saving the world."

A rush of anger swept through his veins but was quickly replaced by guilt. She'd just verbalized the exact thing that had ended his marriage and caused him to lose his daughter. He didn't have a response. He kept his attention on the road, not wanting to discuss his personal life with her.

After a few moments of silence passed, he glanced over. Her eyes were closed. Maybe now she was finally out.

No such luck.

"My Dad was like you," she told him.

"Oh?"

"Yeah. He was a cop, too. All that mattered was the job. Not me, not his family. He didn't have anything to do with me until a few years after my mom died. Then, we sort of made up." She gave a harsh laugh. "He thought I was the greatest daughter in the world when I married Bryce. Who knew marrying a psycho is all it would take to make my Dad love me?"

Luke said nothing...wanting to comfort her yet at the same time wanting her to stop this soul wrenching confession. Hearing the words was like a physical blow. Knowing how much she'd suffered, how much she was still suffering, was hard to take.

She continued into the darkened silence as street lights shone through the window, casting shadows on her face that looked like tears.

"My Dad and I didn't speak for a few years before Mom died, or for several years after."

"Not even at the funeral?"

"I didn't go to the funeral."

"Why not?"

"Because," she said simply and without emotion, "I hated my mother."

He waited for her to say more but she didn't. They arrived at her apartment and he parked, then helped her out of the car. She was unsteady on her feet so he held her

147

upright, arm around her waist while he led her up the stairs and to the apartment. She fumbled for her key and after a few attempts, unlocked the door.

He led her into the bedroom. "You need to take some Ibuprofen. You'll feel better in the morning if you do. It also wouldn't hurt for you to eat something."

"I can't eat, no way. I'll be fine."

"If you've never drank then you can't imagine what's in store for you in the morning. You're going to wish you'd listened to me."

She shook her head and fell backwards on top of the bedspread. He wasn't sure what to do. He couldn't leave her here to pass out on top of the covers, fully clothed. He knelt down and slipped the shoes off her feet.

"Here, let me help you get under the blankets." He reached for her hand and pulled her up. She stumbled against him and his arms went around her.

Her head fell on his shoulder and his body tightened. She smelled like booze and cigarettes, yet he still wanted her.

He held onto her with one arm while he turned the covers back. The blouse she wore didn't look very comfortable. He noticed that underneath she wore a silky tank looking thing. Surely it would be safe to help her off with the blouse and leave the tank thing on.

"You might want to slip your blouse off." He tried to keep his tone neutral but the image those words invoked made it difficult.

She plopped down on the edge of the bed and began fumbling with the buttons. Her fingers weren't working so he helped, quickly undoing the pearl buttons while trying to ignore the way her warm body felt against his hands. His finger twitched, and he was overcome with the urge to flick it across her nipple. Taking a deep breath, he looked away as he slipped the blouse off her shoulders. Now for the jeans.

Hell, no. She could sleep in those. There was only so much a man could take.

Once her blouse was off, she lay back and he started to pull the covers over her.

"Hold on," she murmured. "I can't sleep with jeans on."

Damn. He was afraid of that. She was on her own there. He waited while she fumbled with the button and zipper. Unable to watch her slip the jeans over her hips, he went into the bathroom in search of Ibuprofen. He found it, filled a cup with water and when he thought it was safe, returned to the bedroom.

Big mistake.

She was lying on her side, one knee up, her hands under her chin. She wore nothing but the silky tank thing and panties.

Pink, cotton panties.

Nothing sexy about cotton panties, right?

Wrong. Somehow, the simplicity of them made her look vulnerable and so very hot. He reached for the covers and pulled them over her.

"Stay with me 'til I sleep?" she mumbled.

"Okay," Luke agreed, oddly reluctant yet at the same time eager. He sat on the edge of the bed. On the very edge, so he wouldn't accidentally touch her.

"Did you love her?"

"Who?" he asked, a little annoyed that she still wanted to chat. He figured she'd be passed out by now.

She turned over and looked at him, resting one arm behind her head. For the first time, he noticed a sprinkling of freckles across her shoulders. She also had a few on her nose. He'd never thought of freckles as sexy until now.

Jesus, you've got it bad when cotton panties and freckles are a turn-on.

"Your partner. The woman Bryce murdered."

His heart pounded. He didn't want to discuss Delia with her. He didn't want to talk to her at all. He needed to get the hell out of here. "I loved her, yes. But not romantically. We were very close. She was a good agent, a great person."

"I'm sorry. I'm sorry I had anything to do with the monster who took her life."

Luke nodded. She gazed up at him, emotion deepening her eyes to a dark green.

It was right then that he knew. His cop instinct finally kicked in. Jade DiMarco was innocent. There was no way she would have been involved with an evil piece of shit like DiMarco.

So, what did that mean as far as staying in Solitaire? What did he do now? Not a clue, not a lead. Not a damn thing to point to where the bastard was hiding. Obviously, he was still near St. Louis if he'd actually murdered that girl. Maybe he'd had someone else do the dirty work and he was miles away. Maybe the agents back home would find him. Maybe not.

"He's never going to stop is he?" her voice lowered to a whisper. "You're never going to find him."

Surprised that her words mirrored his thoughts, he answered, even though he wasn't sure he believed it anymore. "Yes. We'll find him."

Her eyes drifted shut and she murmured, "Thank you for saying that. Thanks for taking care of me."

He felt something loosening in his chest. Something that went way past desire and was more than just sympathy. A feeling for Jade that had no place in their current circumstances, a feeling he would have to control.

"You're welcome," he replied hoarsely.

"One more favor."

"Sure." Damn, was she never going to go to sleep?

Her voice was faint, but he heard the words clearly. "Would you please leave the light on when you go?"

Chapter Thirteen

Luke drove cautiously over the slick roads where snow had accumulated just in the short time he'd been inside Jade's apartment. Fortunately, there were few drivers out at two o'clock in the morning. He was almost relieved at the hazardous conditions. Gave him something to concentrate on other than Jade.

His cell phone rang and not taking his eyes off the road to check the number, he answered.

"I see I made the news." The familiar voice grated over the line.

He'd expected it to be Jade. Or Wayne calling with an update on the case. The last person he expected was DiMarco.

Spots danced in his vision and his body tensed like a boxer before a championship bout. In spite of the fury racing through his system, he managed to keep his voice steady. "What did you think would happen, asshole? Jade would suddenly go running into your arms because you're a twisted, murdering psycho?"

"I just wanted her attention. Wanted her to know I'm thinking of her."

"I'm thinking of you, too. Every minute of every day and I will find you."

"Not before I find another young girl." He laughed. "I wanted you to know it was me, Butler. Each girl I kill is one more you didn't save."

Luke pulled into a parking lot. He didn't trust himself to drive with the hot rush of blood pounding through his veins and his heart beating so loudly in his ears it overpowered everything else. He needed to concentrate, needed to beat DiMarco at his own sick game.

"What the fuck do you want, DiMarco?"

"You can stop this. You can stop the killings." DiMarco's silky voice grated on his already raw nerves. He silently waited for him to continue.

"All you have to do is tell me where Jade is. All I want is her. Just think, you'd be saving the lives of who knows how many young women. Sort of make up for the ones you didn't save." There was a pause, then another ripple of laughter. "That's right. I know about your past. About your sister and how it's your fault she died. Then there's Delia. Aren't you tired of people dying because of your fuck-ups?"

Anger flared, bright and hot inside Luke's chest. "You really think I'd sacrifice Jade to you? You sick motherfucker."

"I think you'll do whatever it takes to stop me. See, unlike the other girls, I won't hurt Jade. I want her with me, that's all. And, yes, there may be some type of punishment involved but you have my word I won't kill her." He sighed. "I know, I know. I did cut her throat, I'll admit that. But that was in a moment of panic, a fit of rage at her betrayal. I've calmed down since then. I'm not angry with her anymore. Everyone makes mistakes. In time, she'll come to realize just how serious her mistake was."

"Even a fucked up psycho like you can't possibly think I'll tell you where Jade is. I'll stop you all right, but it won't be by telling you where to find Jade."

"You've done a remarkably impressive job so far, Agent Butler. I'm sure it's just a matter of time, right? You know, if I were you, I'd worry that before you found me, I might find your little girl."

For a moment, Luke's rage was so immense, he couldn't find the words to express it. His breathing came in shallow gasps, fogging the windows. In spite of the icy wind buffeting the car, a cold sweat broke out on his flesh.

"You have no idea what I'll do to you if you even speak her name. You're a walking dead man, DiMarco."

"Save it, Butler. I've got power and connections you

can't even imagine. Your threats are as insignificant as a speck of fly shit."

Now it was Luke's turn to laugh. "I know all about your powerful connections. You're nothing more than a glorified street thug who moved up the ranks by sucking Sal's dick. Takes a big man to do that, right DiMarco?"

"Fuck you! Fuck you!" His voice was a scream of fury. All traces of composed mockery had fled. "You don't know what the fuck you're talking about! I'll kill you, you sonofabitch. Worthless stinking pig, how dare you talk to me like that!"

The tirade stopped abruptly as the call ended. Luke wasn't sure if DiMarco had hung up or if they'd simply lost the connection. Not that it mattered. DiMarco wasn't going to tell him anything helpful and Luke had some phone calls to make.

First, he called Wayne, waiting until his friend was fully awake before explaining what had happened and asking him to get Jessica and Samantha into protective custody.

Then he prepared for a fit similar to the one DiMarco had thrown as he dialed his ex-wife's number.

****

Jade slowly opened her eyes then wished she hadn't. Her head felt like it was being worked over with an ice pick. She was sick to her stomach. The inside of her mouth was coated with a dry, foul taste.

Bits and pieces of last night filtered in once she'd taken stock of how rotten she felt. Luke. She'd made a fool of herself. He'd had to take care of her, keep her from driving and killing herself or someone else. She owed him an apology.

She wished she'd taken his advice about eating. Her stomach felt queasy yet at the same time empty. She needed food but she couldn't think of anything she thought she could keep down. Dry toast. Maybe that would help.

She stumbled out of bed and her head really began to pound. She felt like total shit. So this is what it was like to have a hangover. No wonder her mom had been such a bitch all the time.

She started a pot of coffee and stuck a few slices of

bread in the toaster. She swallowed some aspirin and sat at the table to wait for the coffee. She wanted to call Melanie. Her friend must be freaking out about what had happened. But what would she say?

Hey, I think Bryce murdered an innocent woman and presented her to you as a gift just to fuck with me. Be prepared, because I'm pretty certain he's not finished with me yet.

Melanie not knowing Bryce had anything to do with it was best right now. She didn't need to be any more freaked than she probably was. And Jade didn't want to endanger her any more than she already had.

What she would really like to do is crawl back into bed and sleep until she felt human again, but she had work to do. The payroll for one of her clients was due today and she hadn't even started on it. She took her coffee to the computer and willed her mind to concentrate on the screen.

Three hours later, she'd completed the file. Unfortunately, this client was computer illiterate. Rather than send his files as an attachment, she always delivered them by hand.

A shower made her feel marginally better. She dressed and slipped on her coat, then called a cab to take her to the bar where she'd left her car. As she waited outside, a gust of icy air on her flesh revived her even more than the shower had done. Maybe she'd live after all. She knew one thing for damned sure. She'd never touch another drop of alcohol.

When the taxi dropped her off at her car, she trudged through the snow and climbed inside, sitting for a while to let the car warm up.

She drove slowly through the blizzard, peering nervously out her windshield as the snow pelted her car. The snowplows had been out to clear the roads, but patches of ice were still on the streets.

After she delivered the file, she ducked her head against the wind and ran back to her car. Once inside, she blasted the heat, shivering until the warmth finally penetrated the chill.

Anxious to get home, she accelerated too quickly when she turned out of the parking lot. She must have hit an icy patch because her wheels failed to grab and the car went into a slide. After a few harrowing seconds, she managed to straighten her wheels and come to a stop. Knees and teeth clattering, she rested her head on the wheel, muttering a prayer of thanks that she was still in one piece.

Snow fell in thick sheets. She could barely see two feet in front of her. To hell with this. She was near the café, so she slowly maneuvered her car into the parking lot. She'd hang out inside for a few hours. Maybe after the evening traffic had traveled the roads, conditions would be a little safer.

She ducked her head into her coat and ran to the door of the coffee shop. Locked. Dammit, they'd closed early. Probably because of the weather.

Luke's hotel was across the street. *You could see if he's there. It would give you a chance to apologize and get out of the storm.* She could also find out if he'd learned anything about the case.

She ran across the street and into the hotel. It was the same one she'd stayed at the first few days she'd arrived in Solitaire. Not exactly a five-star operation, but not bad either. The lobby held an overstuffed mauve couch and two hunter green wing chairs. Between them was a glossy oak coffee table. Seascape paintings hung on the putty colored walls.

She pulled the card Luke had given her out of her purse and walked into the elevator, punching the button for the fifth floor.

At the door of his room, she lifted her hand to knock but hesitated. Suddenly she was nervous. Being alone with Luke in a hotel room was almost as dangerous as driving home in this weather.

Memories of last night had slipped in periodically throughout the day. She remembered his touch as he'd removed her blouse. She shivered. It hadn't had that affect on her last night because she'd been too wasted to realize it. But thinking about it now...

She shook her head and knocked on the door. Best not to think about Luke that way. Or any man for that matter.

The door opened and Luke stared at her, his eyes

momentarily widening with surprise. He wore faded jeans and a khaki button up shirt with the sleeves rolled up to the elbows. His hair was rumpled as if he'd been running his hands through it. Her heart thudded unexpectedly at the sight of him. Coming here had probably been a bad idea.

"Hey. What's up?" he asked.

"I was nearby and my car went into a slide. I was kind of shaken up so I thought I'd stop by. I also wanted to apologize to you, about last night. And tell you thanks."

"Sure. No problem." He stepped back. "Sorry. Come in."

She walked past him into a semi-tidy mess. Housekeeping apparently hadn't come by yet because the bed was unmade and a damp towel lay across the back of a chair. A hint of some spicy masculine cologne hung in the air.

"Have a seat." Luke looked around and went over to clear a pile of clothes off the only chair in the room. "Would you like something to drink? There's a mini bar or I could make a pot of coffee."

"No, thank you." She sat on the edge of the chair, glancing up at him, then away. "Listen, I'm not sure exactly what went on last night but I remember bits and pieces." Her face flamed as she recalled him helping her into bed. "I wanted to thank you for not...well, you know. I was pretty bombed. You could have..." Her voice trailed off.

"How do you know I didn't?" He grinned. "Ah, I know. You didn't wake up with a smile on your face."

She laughed. "Yeah, that's it."

He settled on the foot of the bed, facing her. "How are you doing?"

"You mean as far as hung over or freaked over what Bryce did?"

"Both."

"The hangover finally went away. You were right, I should have eaten. As far as Bryce..." She looked down at her hands and shook her head. "I'm afraid of what he'll do next. I'm afraid of what I'll cause him to do."

"Hey. You didn't cause him to do anything. You're doing exactly what you should do. All of this is his fault, not yours. Understand?"

She looked up at him and nodded. "Does that mean you believe I'm innocent?"

There was only a slight pause before he said, "Yeah. I believe you."

No apology, she noticed. But her relief that he believed her was so great, she didn't mind. She also didn't ask what had made him change his mind. Best to let it go. "So what now? What do we do about Bryce?"

"I talked to my partner, told him you believe Bryce killed that girl. He's following up, checking on leads. If there's any evidence at all, he'll find it."

"He's got to be stopped. I know he doesn't know where I am right now, but he knows where the people I love are. And he obviously doesn't care how many innocent people have to die before he finds me. I also worry about the kids at the shelter. I volunteered at a halfway house for runaways before all of this happened. Bryce knows how much those kids mean to me. How vulnerable they are."

"I can see about putting some extra security at the shelter. Manpower is kind of limited but there may be something we can do."

"Yeah?" She smiled. "Thank you. But the way those kids come and go, it would be difficult to protect them. Anything you can do would be better than nothing, though." She shook her head. "When I was a kid, I had a pretty rough home life. I ran away a few times, lived on the streets. I think that's one reason I was so horrified when I found out what Bryce had done to those girls. I mean, any reasonably sane person would be horrified but for me, it was personal."

"I can understand that."

"You can't imagine how glad I was to hear I wasn't legally married to him." She shuddered. "But the truth is, I did marry him. What kind of person does that make me that I could ever love someone like him?"

"He fooled you. You're not the first person that's happened to and you won't be the last. You fell in love with the man you thought he was. And trust me, I've made my share of mistakes. I've seen and done a lot of things I wish I hadn't. Life's just that way. We learn from our mistakes and go on."

"Yeah. But I don't know where to go on to. I don't even know who I am anymore, what my future holds. When you're living a lie, you lose yourself. It wasn't as if I really knew who I was before. I mean, as Bryce's wife I was living the biggest lie of all, but this seems so surreal, so *temporary*. I read about a woman in the witness protection program whose little boy was killed in an accident while they were in the program." She looked at Luke and shook her head slowly. "They had to bury him with a different name on the tombstone. Can you imagine how that mother must have felt?"

"I know." His eyes held hers. She saw sympathy in them and turned away. She couldn't handle him looking at her that way. Couldn't afford to weaken toward him anymore than she already had. They fell silent and suddenly a rush of wind howled, rattling the windows.

She jumped, then gave an embarrassed laugh. "Sorry, spooked me a little." Beyond the window, night had fallen. The darkness was broken only by the glare of stark white snow coming down from the sky. She stood. "I'd better go before the weather gets really bad."

"I think it's already bad. Maybe you shouldn't try to drive in it."

Uncertainly, she glanced at the window, then back at Luke. How long would she have to stay before it was safe to go out? Was it safer out there than in here with this man?

Before, it had been easier to resist him. His attitude of mistrust toward her had been a buffer between them. But now, with that light of kindness in his eyes, the softening of his features and the way he knew exactly what to say...she found him more appealing than ever. And, this room was awfully small...

Indecision kept her immobile as she stood awkwardly in front of the chair. In the next moment, the room was plunged into total darkness.

Chapter Fourteen

Unable to prevent it, she let out a scream. "What happened?" The words trembled out of her throat. "Dear God, what's going on?"

"Don't worry, probably just a power outage." His voice came out of the blackness. "Are you okay?"

"How long will it be out? Can't they do something about it?"

"Hold on, I'll call the front desk."

She couldn't see him but she could hear him as he felt his way to the phone. Her entire body shook and her throat closed. She parted her lips, taking deep breaths through her nose and mouth.

After a short conversation, she heard him replace the receiver.

"It's a power outage and the backup generator failed. They're hoping to have it back on in a few hours."

"*A few hours?*" She noticed the panic in her voice but couldn't control it. She knew she was getting ready to totally freak out. She didn't want to do that in front of Luke but she couldn't stop. "I can't wait a few hours. I can't do this..."

"Hey, hey, don't worry." She sensed him move toward her in the darkness. Then his hands were on her arms, sliding down to take her cold fingers in his. "It's going to be okay. I'm right here. Nothing can happen to you."

She nodded but knew he couldn't see her. He lowered her beside him on the bed, briskly rubbing her hands between his.

"I'm sorry." Her voice was barely above a whisper. It

was all she could manage with the block of fear sitting at the base of her throat. "I've just never seen dark this dark before."

"Why are you afraid of the dark?"

She hesitated. "Just an experience from my childhood."

"It might help to talk about it."

Tell Luke about her mother? She'd never told anyone except Melanie. Not even Bryce knew, other than the few details that had slipped out when she'd been in the grip of a nightmare. "I can't."

"Okay. But if you want to, I'm here. And obviously we've got some free time on our hands. Not much else to do but talk, right? Unless..." He ended with an unmistakable leer in his voice.

She laughed. His teasing tone soothed her. She knew then that she could tell him. She *wanted* to tell him. She began slowly at first, then the words flooded out.

"When I was small, my mother had a nasty temper. My Dad was gone all the time. Like I told you, he was a cop. His job meant more to him than anything and he left me with her all the time, even knowing what would happen. Her favorite way to punish me was to lock me in a closet. It was so *dark*."

She trembled and felt his arms go around her. He pulled her against the strength of his body and silently waited for her to continue.

"I thought there were bugs crawling on me," she whispered. "That they were going to eat me. I thought a monster was going to suddenly materialize from the walls of the closet and take me away. She would leave me there for hours at a time. I kept waiting for my daddy to save me but he never did."

"God." His hands rubbed up and down her arms. Her body began to relax, the block in her throat slowly melted.

"I never knew what would set her off. I tried so hard to be good but there was no way I could be good enough. No matter what, I managed to make her mad."

"It's no wonder you're scared of the dark." His voice held sympathy but not the pity and aversion she'd expected. She was glad she told him.

The air in the room was chilly. The heat had stopped

working with the lights, but where her body touched his was warmth. Sweet, safe warmth. It felt so good, so right. Her heart slowed to a steady rhythm. For the first time in her life, she felt almost safe in the dark.

"I shouldn't have told you all that. I'm sorry I panicked. You must think I'm such a coward."

"No." His voice was husky. "That's not what I think of you."

Silence settled between them, unbroken only by the snow falling against the window and the sound of their breathing.

His touch slowed, burning over her back, her arms, becoming more a caress than comfort. Desire shimmered over her skin, settling low in her belly. She swallowed loudly, and closed her eyes.

"Feeling better?" He asked thickly.

"Mmmmhmmm." She nodded and felt her hair brush against his face.

"Ah, hell." He sighed a groan and his hand slipped to the nape of her neck, his fingers gently rubbing her scalp below her hairline. "You know what's going to happen if we don't stop this, right?"

She knew what was going to happen. Knew it shouldn't but her body disagreed. Her body screamed for him to touch even more of her. "You know what scares me almost as much as the dark?"

"What?"

"If I died right now, Bryce would be the last person I had sex with. The last man that touched me. I can't stand that thought."

Her heart slowed as she waited...for what? She'd just invited him to make love to her. But of the two of them, she was certain he was the one most in control...the one that wouldn't cross the line.

She was wrong.

She heard the surrender in his groan just before he tangled a hand in her hair and like a heat-seeking missile, his mouth found hers. He kissed her deeply, a melding of teeth, lips and tongue.

At the same time, his hands roamed down her sides to the edges of her shirt. They slipped beneath material and touched her bare skin. Breath hitched in her throat and she moaned, turning toward him.

He planted small kisses along her jaw line. His teeth caught her lower lip and gently tugged. She gripped his shoulders and pulled him to her, pressed her mouth against his, slipping her tongue inside, wanting more of him. Now.

Her fingers found the buttons of his shirt and she undid them, then skated her hands over his chest. The feel of his crisp hairs beneath her fingers sent a lightning bolt of hunger between her thighs.

He pulled his mouth from hers. She could feel him looking at her even though she couldn't see him.

"Damn. I didn't mean for this to...if you want me to stop..."

Somehow, the cloak of darkness made what they were doing okay. It didn't matter, anyway. She was beyond the point of reason. Her body cried out for his. "Please, no, I don't want you to...don't stop." She choked out the words.

He jerked her shirt over her head and the cool air slammed against her flesh. When he grazed his hand across her breast through her bra, she no longer felt the cold. In its place was a yearning, a hot aching need that consumed her.

He lowered her to the bed. His hands roved over her shoulders, arms, hips, creating electricity in her nerve-endings everywhere they touched. His callused fingers brushed over her belly, just below her navel and she gasped with pleasure.

"You're skin is so soft," he whispered. He kissed her shoulders, then his lips were on her throat.

She froze. Her hand flew to her neck, protecting the scar from his exploration. His hand covered hers and he linked their fingers together, dragging hers away. "You're beautiful. *All* of you."

She tensed as his lips moved over the scar, tenderly and without the slightest hesitation. She felt tears at the back of her throat.

Damn him for touching her in the only place that was forbidden. Her heart.

His mouth left her neck and found her nipple, sucking gently through the thin material of her bra.

"Yes," she whispered, arching against him. His fingers slipped behind her and unsnapped her bra, moving it out of his way. Then his tongue was on the skin of her breasts, sliding along the sides, quickly flicking across the nipple, then back to the sides, back to her nipples, over and over again.

"Please," she whimpered. His hands moved to the button of her jeans. He couldn't get them unfastened so she helped. In moments, they were off.

She heard him undressing, then felt his bare skin against hers as he pulled her close. He kissed her again, devouring her mouth while his hands continued to explore her flesh.

Unable to see him, not knowing where he would touch her next gave the moment an added edge, a disembodied thrill that spiraled her desire out of control. His hand cupped her over her panties, moving back and forth across her wet heat. Her hips came off the bed, pushing against his hand, craving so much more...

His mouth found her breast again and he took it in with his tongue, warm and hot, sucking, licking, driving her mad with need. His whiskers abraded the soft flesh of her breasts as his mouth traveled over her, creating a sizzling trail of fire.

She reached down and felt him, smooth and hard against her hand. "God..." His harsh groan reverberated over her flesh. He hooked a finger in her panties and tugged them off. His fingers slipped inside her, his thumb pressing against her center, stroking and kneading until she felt the first waves of release move through her.

"Oh, yes." Her entire body shook with the force of her orgasm. Her skin was like a living thing, aching, burning and pulsing from the tremors moving through her.

When the last of the quaking was over, she slid against him, smoothing her lips over his shoulders and chest, flicking her tongue along his skin.

His scent filled her nostrils, and she breathed deeply, reveling in the masculine feel and taste of him. She sensed him shift until he was over her. She held onto his biceps, feeling his muscles bunch and contract beneath her fingers.

Then he was inside her, moving slowly, filling her

with his warmth. She wrapped her legs around his back and arched to meet him. He moved more quickly, rocking his hips back and forth against her.

"I want you to come again," he groaned.

"Yes." Was all she could manage as the force built once more. Flames shot through her veins. A long shudder racked his body and his lips grabbed hers, kissing her deep and long while the explosion shook them both. The moment lasted forever, yet at the same time was over much too soon.

He relaxed against her, smoothed the hair from her face and kissed her forehead, tightening his arms around her. No longer distracted by passion, she became aware of the cold. The room was like a freezer, biting fiercely into her skin. Luke pulled the covers over them. She lay against him, listening to the thump of his heart against her ear. His chest rose and fell with long, steady breaths.

Now that she was sated, reality reared its ugly head. The dark couldn't totally erase what had happened. It was bad enough that she had given in to her desires, that she had made love to a man she wasn't sure she could trust. The horrible, dreadful truth was that he'd made her feel more than just passion. Something stronger than lust had invaded her body. She couldn't afford to feel that way about Luke. Couldn't afford to feel that way about anyone.

Loving someone made you their victim. And she'd sworn a solemn vow to herself that never again would she be a victim.

****

Luke hovered somewhere between awareness and oblivion. He'd never felt so completely satisfied. He'd never in his life experienced what he'd just experienced with Jade. Her every touch had been a shock to his system. A welcome and bone shattering shock. Sliding into her silky warmth had been like coming home. Like being where he was supposed to be. Where he never wanted to leave.

She felt so soft against him now. Her body conformed to his in all the right places. Just thinking about what had happened between them, feeling her soft breath on his skin...he felt a stirring once more and knew he could take her again, right now.

His tantalizing thoughts were shattered when she abruptly scooted away from him to the edge of the bed.

"What are you doing?" he asked.

"Getting dressed." Tension permeated her tone. "Dammit."

"What's wrong?"

"I can't find my clothes."

"You going somewhere?"

"It's cold so I want to get dressed and yes, I need to go home." Her voice was clipped, almost as cold as the air in the room.

He didn't point out that they'd both been plenty warm sharing body heat beneath the blankets. Apparently, the party was over. His growing erection began to fade. He swung his legs off the bed and felt for their clothing. He identified hers and tossed them to her.

"Thanks," she muttered.

"No problem."

They dressed in silence. He heard her move around in the darkness, then a thump.

"Shit."

She'd obviously bumped into something in her hurry to flee. To hell with her. They were mature adults and they'd had sex. No big deal yet she was acting like it was the end of the world.

"The weather hasn't improved and the power is still out. You might as well relax and wait until at least the lights come back on."

"I can manage. I need to go."

"Look, I'm not going to bite you or rape you or anything like that. I'm sorry about what happened since you're obviously pissed about it but I can guarantee you it won't happen again."

He wasn't sorry and he couldn't guarantee it wouldn't happen again. But he knew it had been a mistake. He'd been obsessing enough about Jade before he'd made love to her. Now that he'd had her...well, he didn't think it was going to be easy to let her go.

She heaved a sigh. "I know. I'm sorry. I guess if I'm pissed, it would be at myself. What happened between us was incredible, but we both know it was a huge mistake."

Well, he didn't think it was a *huge* mistake.

"What's done is done," he said matter of factly. "We got carried away and gave in to our urges. We can just forget about it and not let it change things between us." Forget about it, yeah, right. Like *that* was going to happen. "I'm probably leaving town soon anyway. I'll keep in touch and you can call me if something happens, but I need to follow up on a few leads."

He didn't have any leads to follow up on but there was no reason to stay. The results on the blood outside her apartment had come back and they didn't match DiMarco's. She obviously didn't know where DiMarco was. DiMarco didn't know where she was, and staying around her was starting to seem like a very bad idea.

"You're leaving?"

He thought he detected disappointment in her voice.

Women. For God's sake, who knew what they were thinking?

"Yeah. Probably in a few days. I'll say goodbye before I go."

The power flared back on in a blinding glare. Jade blinked against the burst of light. She looked tousled and gorgeous and utterly, devastatingly tempting. His body tensed against the desire worming its way back into his system and he wondered how much of this woman it would take to sate his appetite.

"Well, okay." She bent to retrieve her purse from the chair. "I'm going to head out. I guess I'll talk to you soon."

He nodded. "Call if you have any trouble getting home. You have a cell phone, right?"

"Yeah. I'll do that. Thanks."

"Sure." His heart thudded with dread as he watched the door shut behind her. Even in the light, darkness closed in on his soul and he wondered how he was going to forget what it felt like to hold her...to feel her satiny skin against his...inhaling her scent that still lingered in the room.

The truth was, he wouldn't, not in a million years.

Chapter Fifteen

Jade sat at the kitchen table, her coffee cup cradled between her hands. She hadn't heard from Luke since she'd walked out of his hotel room two days ago. Had he left Solitaire already? Left without telling her goodbye?

She should be relieved at the thought but instead, a hollow ache filled her soul. She would miss him. But his leaving was the best thing. For both of them.

A knock sounded at the door. She looked through the peephole. Luke. Her traitorous heart thumped a joyous rhythm.

She swung the door open. "Hi. Come in." Stepping back, she let him walk past her into the apartment, then shut the door and turned to him.

His eyes swept over her. She was acutely aware of how she must look in her tattered jeans, baggy sweatshirt and lack of makeup. Self-consciously, she brushed a hand over her hair, wishing she'd known he was coming so she could have fixed up a little.

They stood awkwardly in the middle of the room. "How are you?" Luke finally spoke.

"I'm okay. You?"

"Good."

She nodded. "So what's up?"

"Can we sit?"

"Yeah, sure. Sorry. Would you like something to drink?"

"No, thanks. I'm fine."

They sat on opposite ends of the couch but it was still too close for her peace of mind.

167

"They ID'd the body found at your friend's house. Do you know a Maureen Anderson?"

She shook her head. "No. Never heard of her."

"You never heard Bryce mention her name?"

"I'm telling you, it was just Bryce's way of sending me a message. He probably chose a complete stranger."

"It was a hell of a message. The girl's throat was cut. She was lying in a lounge chair next to the Senator's pool. Nude except for the necklace. Your necklace."

Goosebumps trickled along her flesh. She'd been *married* to the man. Good God, what was wrong with her instincts?

"They didn't find Bryce?"

"No. I'm sorry. Other than the necklace, there's no evidence linking him to the crime, but they're working on it."

"So what now?"

"Follow up on leads, although there aren't many."

"What about you?" The words rushed out of her. She'd meant to sound casual but knew she'd failed.

His voice was tight when he spoke. His eyes traveled over her face. "I'm leaving in a few days. Nothing left to do here. I need to see if I can help with the case."

She was surprised at how much his words upset her. She'd known he was leaving. Knew it was best for both of them. Then why did it feel like he'd reached in and snatched her heart from her chest?

Not trusting herself to speak, she nodded. Damn him, anyway. She wasn't supposed to feel like this about him. She wouldn't *allow* herself to feel like this. No way in hell. She'd learned what loving someone could do. She'd learned it as a very small child.

"Thanks for stopping by." She stood.

Luke hesitated, then stood with her. She didn't care that she sounded rude. Being around him was just too difficult. If he was leaving, he needed to just go. Now.

"I'll keep in touch. Let you know if we find DiMarco."

"Thanks."

"I probably won't see you before I leave but you have my number. Call if you need anything."

She nodded and led him to the door. He stopped at the open doorway and looked at her. "I'm sorry...about the other night..."

"It's okay." She interrupted. She didn't want to talk about what had happened between them. It was a mistake. It was over. Best to leave it alone.

"Well, then." He shoved his hands in his pockets. "I guess that's it. Goodbye."

"Bye." He left and she closed the door.

She went back to her coffee. It was cold. She dumped it in the sink. Through a blur of tears, she watched the dark liquid trickle down the drain.

She sat back at the kitchen table and dropped her head in her hands. Why the hell did it have to hurt so much?

Wallowing in her misery, it took her a moment to realize she heard the sound of angry voices outside her door, maybe coming from the hallway. She thought she recognized Ashley's but couldn't make out the words. Was she fighting with her mother again? It was never-ending.

Out of the muffled conversation, one word was distinguishable. *Dennis*. The sonofabitch was back?

She raced into the bedroom and tucked her Ruger in the waistband of her jeans, beneath the baggy sweatshirt.

She opened her front door and saw Ashley and her mother in the hallway. Ashley's back was to them as she stalked away.

"You come back here, young lady!" Deb yelled.

"Fuck you!" Ashley shouted, not turning back.

"Ashley!" Jade called after her.

Ashley turned at Jade's voice. She pointed at her mother. "She's going to marry him!"

"Dennis?" Jade asked, shooting Deb a look.

Ashley nodded and scrubbed at the tears on her cheeks. "I told her what he did to me and she's still going to marry him."

"Ashley," Deb admonished. "It's none of her concern."

"What did he do?" Jade spoke through gritted teeth.

"A few weeks ago, he grabbed my ass. Mom was right there but her back was turned." She shuddered. "I didn't tell her then cause I didn't want to start anything. And then he left, so I didn't worry about it. But now he's back and they're getting married!" Her voice ended on a sob.

An image surfaced in Jade's mind. She could almost

feel Dennis' hands on her skin...the smell of him...the sound of his hot breath in her ear...

Then she saw him doing the same thing to Ashley. "You can't marry him," she told Deb.

"It's none of your business. You've done nothing but cause trouble since we met you. We're moving away. You won't be able to butt in any longer."

"Me and Jon are *not* going with you." Ashley stalked over to her mother. "You go with that asshole if you want, but we're staying here."

"Watch how you talk to me, young lady. I won't have it. You *will* go with me. Dennis didn't mean anything by what he did. He loves you kids."

"You're out of your freakin mind!"

Deb raised her hand as if to strike Ashley and Jade rushed between them.

"Listen, you can't marry him. He's dangerous."

"What the hell do you know about it? You don't even know him."

"I know he tried to rape me!" The words were out before she could stop them. As much as she didn't want Ashley to know what Dennis had done, she knew it was best. They both needed to know what kind of low-life scum he was.

"Oh my God," Ashley breathed.

"Liar!" Deb whirled on Jade. "That's a filthy lie and you know it."

"That's why he left. I bit a chunk out of his cheek and threatened him with a gun if he ever came around again."

"That's how he got that scar?" Ashley asked.

Deb looked away uncertainly. She shook her head and turned back to Jade. "I don't believe you. You would have called the cops."

"I didn't call them because I knew he'd be out in no time. I just wanted him away from the kids."

"She's not lying." Ashley stared at her mother. "You know she's not."

Deb crossed her arms around her middle. Tears filled her eyes. "She's lying," she said softly.

****

Sorry motherfucker. Why couldn't you play along, Butler? You could save us all a lot of trouble if you'd lead me to my wife. She's *my* goddamned wife.

Bryce slammed his fist on the table and Susannah jumped, dropping her fork.

"What the hell is wrong with you?" she asked peevishly.

"Nothing. Just finish your breakfast and stay out of it."

For once, the woman listened to him. She fell silent.

Bryce pushed his plate away. He didn't have an appetite. He was sick and tired of them winning. He wanted Jade. He had no clue where she was. He wasn't any closer to finding her than he'd been the day she left.

He also hadn't found Butler's family. He'd gone to Atlanta, watched the house but never saw the woman or the little girl. Just some guy. Probably the ex-old lady's new hubby. Wouldn't do any good to fuck with him. Butler would probably appreciate Bryce taking him out.

Jade, where are you? Why are you doing this? You know you won't get by with it forever. You know I'll find you and the longer it takes me, the harder you'll pay.

Fuck her. She wants to play hardball, let's play. He stood and tossed his napkin on the table.

"Give me the keys to the Bimmer," he demanded.

"Where are you going?"

"None of your fucking business. Give me the keys." She pushed back from the table and fished the keys out of her purse. She handed them to him without another word. Maybe he'd get her trained yet.

Chesterfield on the west side of St. Louis boasted some of the most lavish homes the city. Senator Bomar's house was set back from the road and guarded by a wrought iron gate, but could still be glimpsed through the leafless trees at the front of the property. The home was a red brick Tudor with large bay windows, a massive chimney and sloping roof. Easily one of the most expensive in the neighborhood.

At one time, Bryce had lived in a home similar to this. Until that bitch had brought his world crashing down around him.

He parked across and down the street from the Senator's home. He waited for two hours. He'd just about decided he was wasting his time and would have to come back another day when the gate swung open.

A black Mercedes slid out of the drive and onto the street. He caught a glimpse of an attractive fiftyish woman behind the wheel. He'd met her a couple of times. Melanie Bomar's mother.

Staying a discreet distance behind, he followed her to an office building downtown.

He watched the woman--couldn't remember her name--go inside the building.

What to do now? It was just past noon so there would be other people around. He'd have to sit out here and wait for her to leave. Try to catch her in a less populated area. Maybe run her off the road on the way home.

He parked beside a meter and settled in to wait.

Five hours and a shitload of quarters later, she still hadn't emerged. Several others had. The building was dark.

What the hell. He hadn't gotten where he was without taking risks. He fed the meter once more and whistled as he headed toward the door.

****

Katherine Bomar sat back and massaged her right hand. In this day and age of computer-generated correspondence, she still preferred the old fashioned method. Gave it more of a personal touch. And, with everything that had been going on, she needed to do whatever she could to ensure her husband's donors remained confident in him.

This awful business with the poor girl found dead at their home. They had their work cut out for them to live that one down. Even though her main concern was the tragedy of the girl's murder, she had to think about the way it would affect her husband's campaign. She didn't mean to sound callous. But there was nothing she could do to help the poor girl now. She had to concentrate on damage control.

How had the body ended up at their pool? She couldn't imagine. The police didn't have a clue. They'd found no connection to anyone in her family or staff. Not a single lead.

The view beyond the fifth story window always soothed her. The silhouette of the Gateway Arch watched over the city like a benevolent keeper. Lights on the buildings seemed to float in the evening sky as the sun descended into the western horizon.

She sighed and picked up the pen once more.

The door behind her opened and she whirled around. Bryce DiMarco stood inside the office door, grinning like a maniac. At that moment, she knew precisely how the girl's body came to be at their residence. After what this animal had done to poor Jade, nothing would surprise her.

She stood and faced him, shoulders back, head high. "What are you doing here?" she asked, pulling herself up to her full 5'10 height.

He grinned and advanced toward her.

Without taking her eyes off him, she felt around on the desk until her fingers found the letter opener. She whipped it in front of her. "Do not come one step closer."

He stopped and his smile widened. "You don't mean to hurt me with that little piece of tin, do you?" His laugh sent a shiver of fear down her spine.

"I know what you've done. I know what kind of sick monster you are but I'm not afraid of you."

He crossed his arms and let his gaze travel over her. "Then you're not as smart as you look, are you?"

Even though he hadn't moved, she took a step back. "What do you want?" she demanded.

"Several things, actually. But you can't really help me with any of them." He took another step toward her and she reached for the phone. She punched the 'talk' button. Before she could dial 911, he was on her.

He wrenched the receiver from her grasp and threw it across the room. He grabbed her by the hair and pulled her toward him. She brought the letter opener up and into his chin. He howled with pain.

"Fucking bitch." He tightened his hold on her hair. Tears sprang to her eyes. Blood dripped from his chin onto her shoulder. Very little blood, unfortunately. She'd barely nicked him.

He grabbed the hand that clutched the letter opener and twisted until she released her hold. The useless weapon clattered to the desk. Shards of pain shot from her wrist up her arm. She was certain he'd broken it.

She'd heard the bone snap.

She felt his hot breath on her neck. Tears coursed down her cheeks...partly from pain, partly from fear.

He was so close, she could see her own reflection in his ice blue eyes.

What she saw in them frightened her more than anything had in all of her fifty-six years.

Chapter Sixteen

"Not so high and mighty now, are you, bitch?" Eyes wide with fright, the woman struggled in his grasp.

She grabbed his forearm with her uninjured hand, yanking to loosen his hold. "You filthy scum! Let me go!"

"Scum?" He released her hair and clamped his fingers around her neck. "I could buy and sell you *and* your husband, you stupid cunt. Who do you think you are?"

Her eyes bulged and her face reddened as he tightened his grip. She clawed at his hands, long red nails scratching his flesh.

"Please...just...let...me...go." She gasped for air and he eased his hold. "I won't tell anyone you were here," she promised desperately.

He threw his head back, a bark of laughter rumbling from his chest. "You must think I'm stupid. Do you really think I believe that? That I'll just turn around and go?" Melanie had always been such a bitch. Treated him like dirt. Like he wasn't good enough for her friend. What would she think when she realized the power he had over her world? No way Jade would stay away after she found out what he'd done to her best friend's mother.

He must have been distracted, loosened his hold more than he'd intended because the woman lunged away and the next thing he knew, she was free.

She raced to where he'd thrown the phone, amazingly agile considering the height of those heels she wore. He closed the short distance between them. Just as she reached her goal, he grabbed her hair and spun her around.

He punched her in the face. Blood spurted from her nose. Suddenly, she was like an enraged beast. She began to scream and flail her arms, catching him square in the jaw with a wild blow.

Carefully dodging her frenzied attack, he slipped the Italian switchblade from his coat pocket and flicked it open.

With one quick thrust, he felt the fourteen-inch blade penetrate her wool Valentino suit.

One more thrust and it sank into her flesh.

Blood sprayed onto his jacket. He'd have to leave it behind so as not to attract attention when he left.

One twist, then another.

She stopped struggling.

Funny, he still couldn't remember her name.

****

The snow had stopped falling but over a foot covered the ground. Icicles dangled from the roof, glinting like jewels in the slowly darkening evening. Jade sat in the window seat, using her finger to draw inverted smiley faces in the condensation on the glass.

Luke would be gone in a few days.

Deb was marrying Dennis. Would she really take the kids? Jade couldn't let her do that but she had no idea how to stop her.

Her cell phone rang. A woman's voice on the other end said, "US Marshal's service with a call for you. Melanie Bomar is on the line."

Melanie? Her spirits lifted. This was what she needed. To hear her friend's voice. The Marshal's service had allowed her to give her friends and family a number to dial in case of an emergency. They didn't know where they were calling, just that they could be connected to Jade. "Yes, thank you. Put her through."

"Jade?" Melanie's anguished cry filled her ear. "Oh my God, Jade."

"What is it, Mel?" Cold, numb fear swept through her body as she listened to her friend sob. "What's wrong?"

"Mother...she's dead. Oh my God, she's dead!"

Jade's body went weak and she sank to her knees, head bowed, the receiver gripped tightly against her ear.

"What? How?" She choked out the words, but they were so faint she wasn't sure Melanie heard them.

"Murdered. Someone killed her." Melanie moaned and her voice caught on a sob. "She was found in her office. Jade, what's happening? What does it mean? Did you hear about the body found at our house? What in God's name is happening?"

"I heard," Jade whispered. She didn't have to wonder if there were a connection to Maureen Anderson and Katherine Bomar's death.

With an icy, fatal dread, she knew.

She also knew what she had to do.

****

The red wig caused her head to itch, but Jade ignored the discomfort as she pushed the sunglasses higher on her nose and smiled at the balding salesman.

"This is the most amazingly gorgeous car I've ever seen." She leaned toward him and placed a hand on the sleeve of his jacket. His eyes shifted downward, drinking in the cleavage revealed by the unbuttoned leather jacket and tight blue blouse. She wore a silver choker around her neck to hide the scar.

"Glad you like it, ma'am." He told her breasts.

"Oh, my. Like it? I love it," she purred. Her fingers kneaded his flabby bicep. Her tongue flicked out to moisten her lips.

She'd taken a bus to Denver, then a cab to a mall where she'd purchased the outfit. She'd taken another cab to the car lot and approached the first male salesman she'd seen. One look at the lecherous gleam in his eyes and she knew she'd chosen well. The man was like a bar of chocolate left out in the sun. He practically melted in her hands.

She winked at him, then turned to lean inside the window of the mustang, giving him an eye full of her rear end in the tight white slacks. She made a show of checking out the interior, murmuring just the right amount of oohs and aaahs. She straightened and turned toward him, catching his gaze on her ass.

His eyes reluctantly moved to her face. He rubbed his hands together and cleared his throat. "How about a test drive, little lady?"

Her hips swayed as she sidled up to him. She took his tie in her fingers and leaned in until her lips were practically touching his. "How about I take it for a quick spin on my own, then swing by and let you...slide inside." The innuendo hung between them. She wanted to recoil at the odor of garlic coming from his panting breaths but she didn't flinch.

He smiled as if she'd offered him the key to the holy grail. "Yeah, sure. You do that. I'll see you in a few minutes?"

She batted her eyes and smiled. "You bet your ass, sugar."

She waved as she left the lot, feeling a moment of panic at what she'd done. The panic stayed with her as she pulled into the parking lot of a Wal Mart and switched tags with another Mustang.

It wasn't until she was gliding along I-70, lost in the sea of commuters that she relaxed. Guilt and fear flew out the sunroof of the red mustang. Melanie needed her. She was doing the right thing.

****

Fourteen hours later, Jade stood at a pay phone, fishing in the pocket of her over-sized jeans for coins. She had her cell but was afraid the US Marshals or FBI would have some kind of tap on her phone.

With her hair tucked beneath a Cardinals cap, wearing a baggy gray sweatshirt, from a distance, she could pass for a boy. Or, at least, a decidedly masculine female. Between the authorities and Bryce, she damned sure didn't want to be recognized.

Exhaustion caused her to slump against the wall as she listened to Melanie's cell phone ring in her ear. For a panicked moment, she thought her friend wasn't going to answer. She almost cried with relief when she heard her voice.

"I'm here, Mel. Can you come pick me up at the Denny's on Lindbergh Boulevard?" She was actually at a pay phone down the street but she'd only eaten once since she left Denver. She'd leave the Mustang here and walk to the restaurant so she could get breakfast while she waited for Melanie.

By the time Melanie pulled into the parking lot, Jade

was no longer starving but was now battling to keep her eyes open as weariness seized her body. How long had it been since she'd been to bed? She couldn't recall.

Melanie stepped out of the Corvette, her beautiful face crumpled with grief. Jade went into her embrace and the two women held each other and sobbed. After a few moments, they were starting to attract a crowd. They separated and slipped inside the car.

"How are you?" Jade asked once they were on the road. She knew it sounded hollow but she didn't know what to say.

Melanie shook her head, a fresh wave of tears pouring from her eyes. "She's gone, Jade. My mom is gone forever."

"I know, hon. I'm so sorry."

"Who would have killed her? Everyone loved her."

Jade hadn't wanted to tell Melanie about Bryce over the phone. She didn't want to tell her at all, but it wasn't something she could keep from her. Melanie had a right to know.

"There's something I need to tell you, Mel, and it's not going to be easy."

Melanie took her eyes off the road long enough to glance at her. "None of this has been easy lately. I'm sure I can handle it."

"I don't want you to hate me."

"Sweetie." She reached over the console and squeezed Jade's hand. "I could never hate you. Surely it's not that bad. Just tell me."

Jade stared out the window at the familiar sights of the city. Funny how she thought she'd missed St. Louis but now that she was here, she realized she didn't. Strangely, she missed Solitaire.

She took a deep breath, turned back to her friend, and said, "I'm pretty certain I know who murdered the girl found at your house. And I'm just as certain that same person killed your mother."

"What?" The look Melanie gave her was half uncertainty, half anger. Like she wasn't sure if Jade was joking and if so, didn't think it was funny.

"Melanie, I think Bryce killed them both. And, I believe he did it because of me."

"Oh, God." Melanie looked around and eased off the brake. She pulled to the shoulder of the highway, earning the blare of a driver's horn. Letting the car idle, she turned in her seat to face Jade. "Tell me everything."

Melanie was silent as Jade explained everything that had happened since she'd left St. Louis. The low hum of the engine was the only sound in the car for what seemed like an eternity. Melanie wouldn't even look at her, just kept staring out the window, still as stone.

"I'm so sorry. If you hate me, I'll understand."

Melanie shook her head but didn't turn around. "It's not your fault."

Relief swept through her. She knew it was her fault, but she couldn't have stood it if Melanie blamed her. She'd lost so much already. She wasn't sure if she could bear losing Melanie too.

****

A silver-haired man and a tall, graceful brunette walked arm in arm toward the green canopy. The woman's shoulders slumped in grief, taking a few inches off her height.

A smaller figure stood next to the tall woman and held onto her other arm. The figure was dressed in baggy clothing, a hat pulled low over dark hair. A large pair of sunglasses concealed most of the face but the man standing several yards away, watching through binoculars, knew what was behind those sunglasses. Those were the eyes he'd looked into when he promised to love and to cherish.

Til death do us part.

With his free hand, Bryce flipped the silver dollar as he watched the graveside service. He couldn't have planned it any better. Jade was here, just as he'd predicted. It was like a big beautiful orchestra and he was the maestro. He was the one in control. Just the way he liked it.

"What now, boss?"

"Shut the fuck up, Kenner," Bryce hissed. Even though they were several yards away, he wasn't taking any chances.

"Sorry." His voice lowered to a whisper. "You want me to follow her, right?"

"Yeah, right. I don't know how long she's staying but I want you to keep an eye on her. Follow her every move. She'll probably leave town soon. Follow her to the ends of the earth if necessary." He continued watching through the binoculars. He recognized Senator Bomar and Melanie as the people with Jade.

Loyal friend, aren't you, darling? Too bad you're not that loyal to your husband. Life would be a lot easier on both of us if you were.

Bryce wanted to follow her himself but he couldn't risk being seen by the Marshals. Or fucking Butler. Once Kenner nailed her location, he was to call Bryce. Then, Bryce had a very special surprise for his loving wife.

Kenner nodded. "You can count on me, boss."

"I know I can." Bryce slipped the dollar in his pocket. "After all, your life depends on it."

****

Luke stood at Jade's apartment door but hesitated before knocking. He was leaving town in the morning and had already told Jade goodbye. So why had he come back? He told himself it was so he could tell her he was sorry about her friend's mother, but he knew that was just an excuse. The truth was, he wanted to see her one last time before he left.

He *was* sorry about the Senator's wife. DiMarco had murdered the woman, he was sure of it. The next step was to prove it. To find the bastard before he hurt someone else. He knew how difficult it must be for Jade. To be here, hundreds of miles away from her best friend when she needed her the most.

He knocked on her door. No answer.

"If you're looking for Jenna, she's not here."

He turned. A young, dark haired girl stood outside an apartment a few doors down.

"Do you know where she is?" Luke asked her.

"Are you a friend of hers?" She eyed him suspiciously.

"Yeah. My name's Luke Butler. Maybe she mentioned me?"

"No. She really doesn't say much about her friends or her family." She walked up to him. "I'm Ashley. Nice to meet you."

"You, too. Do you know when she'll be back?"

The girl shook her head. "Not exactly. She went out of town. Some kind of family emergency."

Family emergency. "Sonofabitch."

He didn't realize he'd spoken aloud until he saw the expression on the girl's face. "What's wrong?"

"Nothing. Sorry. I've got to go." He stalked away, his mind going crazy with the possibility. Jade had gone to be with her friend. Back to St. Louis. He knew it in his gut.

He reached for his cell phone and punched in Jade's number. Then he stopped. No way in hell she'd tell him where she was. He called Wayne.

"I need a favor, buddy."

"Another one?"

Luke ignored his friend's irritation. "I need you to trace a number for me. Find out where the cell is."

"Look, this has gone far enough. You can't keep fucking playing cowboy. You need to get your ass out of there and let the agents on the case handle it."

"This is important. Stop giving me shit and trace the number."

"You're going to lose your job, fuck up the case and no telling what else. It's over, man. Let it be. You've used up all your favors."

"Listen, this is it, okay? Tell Madsen whatever you want. Tell him exactly what I've done. Tell him where I am. I don't give a shit. This is the last thing I'll ask but if you don't do it, Jade could die. If you've ever trusted me at all, trust me on this."

No response.

"Please," Luke added desperately.

"This is it? You swear?"

"I swear."

"Give me the number," Wayne sighed.

Luke gave him Jade's cell number as he climbed into his car. When he hung up with Wayne, he called Jade.

He listened to the phone ring, his chest tight with fear. What if DiMarco had already found her? Relief washed over him when she answered the phone.

"Where are you?" he asked, knowing she wouldn't tell him.

"I'm heading home. I had to take care of something."

"Like what?"

A heavy sigh traveled over the phone lines. "You know, it's really none of your business. I've had a rough few days and I just want to get home. I need to go."

"Wait." He didn't want to end the call. As if contact with her, even through the phone lines, could keep her safe. "I'm sorry about the Senator's wife."

"Thanks." Her voice was thick with tears. She swallowed, then continued. "Are you as sure as I am that it was Bryce?"

"I'm thinking it's a pretty safe bet."

"What are we going to do, Luke?"

"I'm not sure, babe." He clenched the phone, wishing he could tell her what she wanted to hear. He wondered when this had become more about Jade than Delia and he felt a twinge of guilt that it had. "All I can promise is that I won't give up. Not ever."

He hung up the phone, a desperate prayer buzzing through his brain. *God, please let me find her before DiMarco does.*

Chapter Seventeen

Jade closed her cell phone and lay back on the motel bed, staring at the water stains on the ceiling. Luke would be furious if he knew what she'd done. That she'd gone back to St. Louis for the funeral. She had a feeling he suspected but what could he do? Tattle on her to the US Marshals? Not likely.

And, she'd managed to get away without Bryce knowing she'd been there. Her heart filled with guilt that she'd escaped when Katherine hadn't. Jade was Bryce's target yet innocent people were dying. People who were nothing but pawns in Bryce's sick game.

Where the hell are you, Bryce? If she knew, she'd be tempted to go to him. Sacrifice herself just to get it over with. Stop the insanity once and for all. She shuddered. God, she wasn't sure she could actually do that. The man was a psycho...a freak...an abomination. The thought of being in his clutches...being at his mercy...

She forced the thoughts away. Alone in a motel in a strange town...not a good time to think about Bryce. About what he was capable of.

She was so very tired. She felt like she could sleep for days but she knew better. She'd be lucky if she slept at all.

She'd only made it halfway to Solitaire before she'd had to stop. She didn't see the point of making the return trip at the same breakneck speed she'd kept up on the trip to St. Louis.

Melanie had loaned her a car and arranged to have the Mustang anonymously returned to the lot, along with compensation for the time it had been gone.

As glad as she'd been to see Melanie, as much as she'd missed her, she was just as glad to be going home.

Home. When had she started thinking of Solitaire as home? Ashley, Jon, Cal. She missed them all.

Luke. Damn. She missed him, too. But it didn't matter; he'd be gone by the time she got back.

She didn't realize she'd fallen asleep until she jerked awake. She tried to figure out what had awakened her. She didn't remember hearing a noise, nothing other than the sounds of semi's roaring by on the highway. And an overly exuberant lovemaking session somewhere above her head.

The lamp was burning. The door was locked. Nothing to fear. She looked at the clock. Four a.m. She'd been asleep for almost seven hours. A deep sleep up to now.

So what had awoken her?

Then she remembered. It was the dream. The one that was so real, it had her heart clamoring to escape her chest. The dream she'd had several times since the night Bryce had slit her throat. A wolf's head coming at her from the dark. As it flew toward her face, fangs bared, the image switched from Bryce's face, then back to the wolf's. But this time...

Her breath caught in her throat. A torrent of chills raced over her skin. She pushed herself to a sitting position and dropped her head in her hands, rubbing the image from her eyes.

This time, her dream was different. This time, the wolf's face became Luke's.

****

Luke sipped the tepid coffee, then put it back in the cup holder. He squinted at the headlights of the oncoming traffic and turned up the volume on the radio.

Only a few more miles to go and he'd be with Jade. *Almost there, Jade. You're not going to like it but I'm almost there.* The trace had shown her to be at a Travel Inn in Salina, Kansas. He couldn't pinpoint the exact motel room but once he got that close, he'd find her.

What the hell had she been thinking? She'd wanted to be with her friend. She'd been close to Katherine Bomar, but good God, risk her life? If DiMarco found her...

No. She was okay. She had to be.

He cruised through the parking lot of the motel, looking for anything that might indicate which room Jade was in.

In a parking space at the rear, a man sat in a dark red Cadillac, smoking a cigarette. The car had Missouri license plates. It was four-thirty in the morning. Through the curtain in a room directly across from the Cadillac, the muted glow of a lamp burned. Jade was afraid of the dark.

He was pretty certain he'd found her.

He thought about going to the room, confronting Jade, telling her enough is enough. She'd screwed up by going to the funeral; DiMarco's goon had found her. Now it was time for Luke to call the shots. She was going to listen to him...do exactly what he told her...

At that moment, Jade emerged from the motel room. She climbed inside a blue Camaro and headed out of the parking lot. Sure enough, the guy pulled out behind her. Luke followed them.

Jade drove a few miles down the service road and pulled into a convenience store, parking next to a gas pump.

Gassing up at this time of the morning? Alone? In a strange town? The woman was out of her mind. Terrified of a dark room but rushes boldly where angels fear to tread. If he could get his hands on her right now, he'd shake some sense into her.

The stalker pulled into the parking lot of a closed bank across the street. Jade's back was to him while she pumped gas. The window of opportunity was small at best. Luke pulled in behind the guy, climbed out of his car and approached the driver's window.

"Hey buddy, got a light?"

"What the hell..." Before he could complete the thought, Luke had him by the throat. Just enough pressure to knock him out. He quietly went to sleep. Luke dragged the guy from the Cadillac over to his car and popped the trunk. The guy was large and squarely built. His dead weight was difficult to handle but with a little effort and a lot of grunting, Luke managed to get him inside.

He drove across the street and parked at a pump next to Jade. She looked up and instant fury came over her face. Over her entire body.

"What the hell are you doing here?" Cold wind whipped her hair across her cheeks and she shoved it away. "How did you find me?"

"The question is, what the hell are *you* doing?" Now that he knew she was okay, his concern turned to anger. "Are you fucking out of your mind? Do you even understand the *concept* of the Witness Protection Program? It was set up to *protect* you. It's pretty goddammed hard to do when you pull a stupid ass stunt like this."

She thrust the pump into the holder and whirled on him. "Stupid ass stunt? Going to be with my friend who needs me was a stupid ass stunt? Apparently, I'm not as stupid as you think. I covered my tracks pretty well and Bryce didn't find me so you can go straight to hell."

She stormed around to the driver's door and Luke followed. He grabbed her by the arm and turned her to face him. "Didn't find you, huh? The unconscious asshole in the trunk of my car might disagree."

"What are you talking about?" Her gaze flicked to the rear end of the car.

"Come on." Luke tugged her arm. She jerked away.

"Leave me the hell alone. I don't need you and I don't need the Witness Protection Program. They might have protected me so far, but Bryce has been on a rampage, killing everyone in his path. What the fuck good does it do to stay alive when that sonofabitch takes away the people I love?"

"Getting yourself killed isn't going to help anyone. We need to end this once and for all, but we need to do it together. Come on. Just trust me."

Her laugh was bitter, on the verge of hysteria. She wiped at the tears in her eyes and shook her head. "I don't know what to do."

She looked so lost, so beautiful. Luke wanted to take her away from all of this. He wanted to be her hero.

"Come on, hon. Come with me. Please."

She shrugged, then looked down at her feet. Gas fumes drifted to him as he waited for her answer. He didn't know how much force he'd be willing to use but he was determined to convince her to come with him. Finally, she looked up at him and nodded. "I'll follow you. This is Melanie's car. I can't leave it."

"Call her and she can have someone pick it up. Tell her you had an emergency. Just park it over there away from the pumps."

"Where are we going?"

"You still have your room, right?"

"I was heading back to Solitaire."

"Did you check out?"

"No. But I left the key in the room."

"We'll go back. You can tell the manager you locked yourself out."

They didn't speak on the way to the motel. Luke knew she had plenty to say but for now, she was silent.

He backed up to the door to Jade's room and waited in the car until she came back with the key. The parking lot was deserted at the moment, he had to move quickly. He took a roll of duct tape from the trunk and shoved it in his pocket before heaving the man onto the sidewalk. Jade unlocked the door and held it open while Luke dragged him into the room.

When the door closed behind them, Jade shook her head, eyes wide as they went from the man to Luke.

"Jesus," she whispered, as if she hadn't really believed Luke until she actually saw for herself.

Luke propped the guy in a chair and handcuffed him to it. He filled the ice bucket with water and threw it into the man's face, then slapped him until he moaned and his eyes flew open.

"What the fuck?"

The guy looked at Luke, then over at Jade. His broad face paled. He knew he was screwed when he saw that his quarry now had him captive.

"Where's DiMarco?" Luke asked.

The man grinned beneath his fu man chu mustache. His bald head looked oily in the lamplight. "She's right over there." He shrugged toward Jade.

"*Bryce* DiMarco, asshole."

He shrugged, then went mute.

Luke gripped him by the throat. "This can get ugly

very quickly. Tell me where the fuck he is."

"Go to hell."

Luke relaxed his grip. "What's your name?"

No answer.

Luke dug in the man's pockets and found his wallet. He flipped it open and smiled. "Reginald Kenner. Okay, Reggie. You see, at the academy, they taught us that it creates an air of trust when you use a subject's name. You trust me, Reggie?"

Still no response. "No? Well, maybe it's because I haven't introduced myself. My name is Luke Butler. I haven't slept in almost twenty-four hours. I'm a bit cranky and I'm about to cause you a great deal of pain. You can avoid that by answering my question."

"Go to hell," Kenner repeated.

Luke slammed his fist into Kenner's nose. His eyes watered and blood squirted from his nostrils.

"Luke!" Jade gasped. "For God's sake."

"Let me handle this, Jade."

He went into the bathroom and got a washcloth. He shoved it in the guy's mouth. Using the duct tape, he secured the gag. He dug in his pockets and pulled out a small pair of nail clippers. Flipping open the pointed nail file, he walked behind the guy and pulled his bound hands upward until he growled a scream through the gag.

He gripped one hand tightly. Then he looked at Jade. She had her fingers clamped over her mouth. Her eyes were wide with horror. And disgust.

"You may want to leave for this," Luke told her.

She shook her head but didn't speak.

"Seriously, Jade. Go wait in the car."

She stared at Luke for a moment, then at Kenner. She grabbed the keys from the nightstand and fled.

"You have one shot. One shot only. Tell me right now where DiMarco is and I'll let you go. All you have to do is nod your head. I'll remove the gag and you can tell me. You don't tell me...well, let's just say you'll wish you had."

The guy mumbled around the gag but Luke understood him. "Fuck you."

"Fuck me?" Luke laughed. "You're the one that's fucked." Luke jabbed the file underneath his index fingernail. His body convulsed. He nearly came out of the chair. A muted scream of agony filled the room. "It's your lucky day. I'm in a generous mood. One more chance."

Head lolling on his chest, snot, blood and tears streaming down his face, he shook his head. Luke shoved the file underneath another fingernail, then another. Kenner's body convulsed a few more times and then he was still. Passed out.

Loyal sonofabitch. Stupid, but loyal.

Or maybe he was just more scared of DiMarco than he was of Luke.

Luke took the man's cell phone and looked at the recent received and dialed numbers. One of them had to be DiMarco's, but which one?

"Shit," he muttered. This couldn't go on any longer. Luke couldn't watch Jade every minute and she obviously didn't always make the wisest choices. Samantha and his ex-wife couldn't hide forever. How many more innocent people had to die?

More than likely after this latest stunt, WITSEC was over for Jade. Even though they still needed her to testify, they may decide not to protect her.

Once again, Luke tossed water in the guy's face. He came to quicker this time. "Lucky for you, I've decided I don't want to know where DiMarco is."

Eyes filled with pain, hate, and confusion, the man glared at Luke.

"Instead, I want you to tell DiMarco where to find me. Where to find his wife. That should make both of you happy, right?"

His eyes narrowed. Suspicion emanated from him. Luke held the cell phone out. "Call DiMarco and tell him that Butler caught you. Tell him you're afraid I'm going to kill you, that I tortured you to get his location but you didn't give him up. Tell him I stepped out of the room but you overheard us talk about where Jade is. Tell him she's in Solitaire, Colorado." Luke knew he and Jade could get back to Solitaire before Bryce arrived. Luke was going to be ready for him.

The guy still looked confused. Luke removed the gag and switched his hands to where they were in front of him so he could dial.

"Tell him exactly what I told you. If you tell him I

told you to call, I'll kill you." Luke pulled the Beretta from his pocket and pointed it at Kenner's heart, just so the guy would know he wasn't lying.

Eyes glued to the gun, the man dialed a number. "Boss," His voice was low, desperate. "Butler caught me." He listened for a moment, then went on. "I know. I fucked up. Listen, I don't have long. I think he's going to kill me. He tried to make me give you up, tortured me. But I didn't tell him anything, I swear. He stepped out for second but he'll be right back. Your wife is here."

Apparently, there was a reaction to that because once again he stopped speaking. He closed his eyes and nodded. "I know, boss. I'm sorry. Listen, I don't have long. I overheard them talking. She's in Solitaire, Colorado." Luke grabbed the phone from his hand and punched the end button.

"That's enough sweet talk. You did fine. I might even let you live." Luke looked at the number Kenner dialed and stored it in his own phone. He shoved the gag back in his mouth and went outside.

As soon as Jade saw him, she threw the car door open and jumped out. "Did you kill him?"

"No. Come on, we need to get out of here."

"I don't believe you." She brushed past him and headed toward the door.

"Jade, wait. We need to go. I didn't kill him. He's fine. I'm leaving him here until we get away then I'm calling the police. We don't have much time."

"Don't have much time for what? I want to see for myself." She crossed her arms and stared mutinously at him. *Stubborn damned female.*

Luke heaved a sigh. "Ok, you win. Come on." He fished the motel key from his pocket and opened the door. Jade stepped inside and Luke followed.

"See? You happy now?" Luke asked.

The man stomped his feet, mumbling and jerking against his restraints. He cut his eyes toward Luke and gave Jade a pleading look.

"What is it?" she asked. "You want to tell me something?"

He nodded vigorously. Jade stepped toward him but Luke reached out a hand to stop her. "No way you're getting close to him. Let's just get the hell out of here. Nothing he says matters anyway."

"I want to hear." She pulled away from him and stepped over, removing the guy's gag.

"Did your boyfriend tell you what he did?" His voice was weak with pain but he smiled, giving Luke a look filled with hate and smug satisfaction.

"What?" Jade looked at Luke.

He shrugged. "I don't know what he's talking about. Let's just get..."

"I think she has a right to know." Kenner interrupted. "This asshole..."

"Shut the hell up!" Luke started toward him.

"No," Jade insisted. "Let him talk."

Kenner spoke to Jade but his eyes were on Luke. "He told your husband where to find you. Sounds like he sold you down the river."

Jade turned to him. "Luke?"

"He's lying. Let's go."

"If I'm lying," Kenner argued, "then how would I know..."

Luke smashed the butt of the Beretta on the back of the guy's head before he could finish. Jade gasped and whirled on him.

"What the hell is wrong with you? He was telling the truth, wasn't he? Otherwise, why did you shut him up?"

"I caught him calling DiMarco and I stopped him before he could say much. I just don't know exactly what he told him. I don't know what he was going to tell you but listening to his lies, listening to a sorry motherfucker who works for DiMarco isn't going to do you any good."

She looked at the unconscious man and shook her head. "He's hurt. We need to get him help."

"For God's sake, Jade. He works for Bryce. He's more than likely killed for him. He doesn't deserve to live but I didn't kill him. The sooner we get the hell out of here, the sooner I can call the authorities and have them come get his sorry ass. But we need to be long gone first. So, if you're really concerned about him, you'll leave with me now."

Jade nodded slowly, reluctantly following Luke from the room. She kept throwing suspicious glances his way.

She didn't fully believe him. She'd know soon enough that he lied to her but for now he had to. If she knew the truth, even though he had a good reason to do it, she'd be furious. He needed to keep her calm, keep her near him so he could protect her.

Protect her? You haven't been able to protect anyone else you loved, why would this be any different?

Luke didn't know. Maybe it wouldn't. But he knew he'd die trying.

One thing was clear. He did love her. And what a hell of a mess that was.

Chapter Eighteen

A white blanket of snow covered the ground below the jet. Bryce turned away from the window and smiled.

Colorado, huh, Jade? I always figured you for somewhere warm and sunny. Bet this wasn't your first choice, was it?

"What am I going to do while you're taking care of business?" Susannah whined.

"You're going to be flying."

"I'm what?"

"You're not staying. Once I'm off the plane, you're leaving."

She lunged to her feet and stormed to where Bryce sat. "Bryce DiMarco! You can't continue to treat me like I was some nothing. Like I was something to use and throw away. You know I won't stand for that."

"Yes, you will," he replied wearily. "You always have and you'll continue to do so."

"What makes you think that?"

Bryce looked up at her and gripped her wrist, pulling her down beside him. "Because. You love me."

"That's not going to last forever."

"Ok then," he said, twisting her wrist until she cried out. "Because you love living."

She stared at him for a moment, then nodded.

"Now, after you get to St. Louis, send your pilot back with the plane refueled." He looked to where his men sat at the rear of the plane. He'd brought four with him, one would be going back with Susannah. "My friend here will go with you. When the plane returns, it'll be just he and

194

the pilot and he'll call me when it lands and I'll meet him here and fly back."

"Why?" she was still petulant but not as upset as before. Apparently, the idea of him returning to her was enough to appease her.

"I have something to take care of. It's none of your concern." He would fly back all right, but not back to her. That was information he wasn't prepared to share with her. Not just yet.

****

Bryce rented a car, drove an hour to Solitaire and rented a cabin out by the lake. Then, he drove into town.

The first place he showed Jade's picture was a restaurant. He showed it to everyone inside, customers and employees alike. "Never seen her." He was told over and over again.

He stopped at a gas station. No one there recognized the photo. His frustration mounting, he went into a coffee shop. He showed the photo to a waitress and she slowly nodded. Excitement pumped through him.

He looked at the woman's nametag. "You know her, Brenda? You know where she is?"

"I seen her in here a few times but I don't know her. She comes in with a girl sometimes. I think the kid's mom works at Stony Point grocery down the street."

It wasn't a direct hit but it was a lead. Bryce thanked the woman and left.

He found the grocery store and went inside. It was small, one of those dinosaur mom and pop establishments that were quickly becoming extinct. He didn't see anyone right away but he heard voices raised in an argument. From what he could hear, it sounded like some kind of family squabble. He browsed the shelves, hoping they'd finish soon.

The voice of a young girl rose above the others. "Mom, this sonofabitch tried to rape Jenna!"

"Ashley! Don't you ever let me hear you say anything that horrible again."

Rape? Now this was actually an interesting family squabble. Bryce listened more closely, still staying out of sight.

"You heard her. You know she was telling the truth!"

A man's voice spoke up. "The lying cunt. Why would you believe her? You barely know her."

"Jenna's been better to me than you ever have, mom. All you care about is him."

"Now, young lady…" The woman's words were cut off by a screech of outrage from the girl.

"I hate you both!"

Damn. Better interrupt before they kill each other.

He walked around a shelf and saw the people that belonged to the voices. A pretty young girl and a woman who looked as though she'd seen her share of hard living stood in the center of the aisle. Even without overhearing they were mother and daughter, he'd have known. The resemblance was obvious.

A skinny, pockmarked, crack-head looking motherfucker stood next to the women. One of those white trash assholes whose only claim to fame was spitting tobacco further than his redneck buddies.

Before they noticed him, the girl went on another of her tirades. "You don't give a damn about me or Jon. I swear to you, we'll never live with this piece of shit. If you marry him, I'll…"

The woman saw Bryce. "Shhhh. We have a customer. We'll talk about this later." She plastered a professional smile on her face. "Can I help you?"

"Actually, I'm looking for my sister. She moved here a few months ago and I wondered if you might know her." Bryce pulled out the photo and passed it to the woman. "I have her phone number but she's not answering and I don't know exactly where she lives."

The woman glanced at her daughter, then back at Bryce. "Jenna is your sister?"

"Jenna?"

"Yeah." She tapped the photo. "This is our neighbor. Jenna Donovan."

The girl snatched the picture from her mother's hand. She turned to him with a wide smile. "You're Jenna's brother? She didn't mention she had a brother. Nice to meet you. I'm Ashley."

Jenna. That must be the name Jade was using. White spots danced before his eyes. His body tensed with rage. Jenna was the woman they'd been talking about.

The woman this motherfucker had tried to rape.

He'd tried to rape Jade.

Bryce couldn't breathe. His hands itched to reach for the knife. Itched to feel it jam into the asshole's gut. Rip him from navel to sternum. He didn't look at him. Didn't trust himself to look at him.

"Yeah. Jenna's my sister." Bryce's voice sounded almost normal. He didn't know how, when visions of this greaseball with his hands on his wife were all he could see. "We haven't seen one another in a while but she called and said she's having problems. I came to see if I could help but she didn't give me her address."

"She lives right down the hall from us. I'm sure she'll be happy you're here." The girl cast a resentful look at greaseball. "I'll show you where she lives."

"Ashley. You're not going off without me." The mother turned to Bryce. "Jenna lives in Sunrise apartments. I can tell you how to get there."

Bryce gave the girl a grateful smile, charm oozing from his pores. "Thanks for the offer, young lady. But your mother's right. She's obviously concerned about you. You're lucky to have a mother like her. I wouldn't dream of causing her any concern. See, the thing is," He turned back to the mom, "I don't know my way around here at all. I'm terrible with directions." That should earn some points with the woman. Men never admitted to being bad with directions. "Maybe your friend here could come along." He pointed at greaseball. "Keep your daughter safe. Would that make you feel better? I'd be extremely grateful."

She looked at greaseball, then her daughter. "Sure. That would be fine."

"Mom! I can go on my own."

"Now, sugar." Greaseball smiled at the girl. "Don't argue with your mother."

The girl crossed her arms and gave her mother a rebellious glare, then whirled and stalked out of the store. Bryce and the guy followed her.

The mom had actually bought his line of bullshit about being a good mother. *Yeah right, lady. You won't let your daughter go off with a stranger but everything's fine as long as a rapist goes along too.* Fucked up broad.

He followed the man's beat up truck to an apartment complex. One look at where Jade lived and he cringed. The apartments were old. Time and weather had worn the paint job almost completely off the building. The sidewalks had large cracks in them.

Inside wasn't any better. Chunks of tile were missing from the floors. An unidentifiable odor permeated the air. It smelled old...and cheap...and low class.

Jade had left their home to live in a hovel like this? She must have lost her mind. She'd almost been raped. She was living in poverty. It was time he came to her rescue. Eventually, she'd thank him.

Greaseball stopped midway down the hall. He pointed toward a door at the end. "Jenna lives in 1026B." He gave a quick look around. He seemed nervous. But not as nervous as he was going to be. "Ashley, we need to go back to the store and get your mom."

"I don't think so," Bryce said.

"What?"

He pulled a gun from his pocket and shoved it into the guy's ribs. "I don't think so," he repeated.

"What the fuck is this?" Greaseball's face faded to a starker shade of white.

Ashley backed away. She stared at Bryce as if she couldn't quite believe what she was seeing.

"Hey," He waved the gun toward her, then put it back into greaseball's side. "Come back here. I hate to do this to you because from what I saw, your life is fucked up enough with this asshole and your stupidass mom. But, unfortunately, your life is going to get even more fucked up."

She stopped, still not saying anything. Her face crumpled and tears spilled down her cheeks.

"What the fuck do you think you're doing, man?" Greaseball whined. "What's your beef?"

"Shut up and walk. Both of you. Walk slowly, no sudden moves. Take me to Ja...Jenna's apartment."

Finally, the girl spoke. "You're not really her brother, are you?"

Bryce laughed. "Just move!"

They reached Jade's apartment door. Bryce knocked. No one answered. "Jimmy the lock, asshole. Don't even pretend like you don't know how to pick a lock."

The guy shook his head. Bryce jammed the gun further into his side. He grunted and bent to work on the lock.

Bryce hadn't underestimated his skills after all. They were inside in no time. He made greaseball sit in a chair.

He pulled a rope from his coat pocket and tossed it to Ashley. "Tie him up." She stared at him, not moving, tears still streaming down her face. "Tie him up or I'll blow your fucking head off."

She tied him up.

"Sit down over there and be a good girl, got it?" She nodded and sat on the couch. Bryce bent toward Dennis. "What's your name, asshole?"

He gave a resentful glare. "Dennis," he spat.

"Okey dokey, Dennis." Bryce looked at Ashley. "No. I'm not her brother. I'm her husband."

He took a knife from his pocket and shoved it beneath Dennis' chin. The man's eyes rounded in terror. "That's right, asshole. You tried to rape my wife."

"No...No! I swear. She came on to me. She's a fucking tease. I swear I didn't do anything."

"You're a lying motherfucker." Bryce looked at Ashley. "Turn your head, little girl."

Chapter Nineteen

Luke stopped at an IHOP a few hours out of Solitaire. She'd barely spoken to him the entire trip. She kept seeing what he'd done to that man. He'd been like another person. Cold, heartless, determined. Yes, he'd done what he had to do but how could he bring himself to do it? And, was the guy telling the truth? Had Luke told Bryce where to find her? She glanced over at him. Silent and moody, he stared at the menu.

What was he thinking right now? If he had told Bryce where to find her, then why? She was so tired, still grieving over Katherine. She couldn't think about it anymore.

They gave the waitress their order and Luke pushed up his sleeves, revealing the leather wristband.

"You wear that a lot." She pointed to the wristband. She noticed writing but couldn't make it out. "What's that insignia?"

"It says 'Guardian Angel'."

Intrigued in spite of her exhaustion, she asked. "Where did you get it?"

His face closed and for a moment he didn't speak. "My sister gave it to me."

"You have a sister?"

"Had a sister. She died."

"I'm sorry. Want to talk about it?"

He looked at her as if challenging her to continue with the conversation. "You want to hear about it?"

She wasn't sure. She didn't like his tone. Or the look on his face. But she nodded.

"Her name was Angel. She was my baby sister. Only twenty-two when she died. Her husband beat the shit out of her on a regular basis. Each time, she would call me and I'd come to her rescue." He laughed but there was no humor in it. "Except the last time. I told her if she kept going back to him, not to bother to call. Well, she didn't."

Jade didn't want to ask but she had to know. "He killed her?"

"Yeah." It was only one word but in it she heard a wealth of guilt.

She wanted to reach out to him, erase the sorrow from his face. She wanted to tell him it wasn't his fault but she was afraid it would sound like an accusation. Instead, she said again, "I'm sorry."

He nodded and took a drink of coffee. An awkward pause followed. She tried to think of something to say to change the subject but anything she came up with seemed trivial after what he'd told her. She said nothing.

The chatter of the other diners and the clanging of dishes now seemed far away as she and Luke sat in a cocoon of silence. The food arrived and Jade stared at her plate, pushing the food around but not eating.

Luke didn't eat much either. They finished their coffee and he paid their check. They left, still not speaking.

The silence continued for the remainder of the trip. Jade finally spoke when they arrived in Solitaire and Luke passed the turnoff to her apartment complex. "What are you doing?"

"We're going to my hotel."

"What? Why? I need to go home."

Luke set his jaw and shook his head. "No. Not yet. I'm not sure what the situation is with the Marshal's office. They probably know what you did. They may be there waiting for you. We need to figure this thing out first. Besides, I need a hot shower and for now, you have to stay with me. We both could be in a lot of trouble."

She didn't like it but she went along. He could have his way for the moment but she was almost to the limit as far as taking orders from him. It wasn't like she fully trusted him anyway.

Luke's hotel room was tidy other than an open

suitcase on the bed. It reminded her he was leaving. Or had been until he'd jumped on his white horse and ridden to her rescue. Had he really been coming to her rescue or did he have a motive of his own?

"Sit tight, I'll just be a minute," he said as he headed to the bathroom.

She nodded. *A minute is about all you have, Butler.*

Jade lay back on the bed. Her body was weary but her mind worked overtime. How was this all going to end? How would they stop Bryce before he killed someone else?

Her eyes drifted shut. She was on the verge of dozing when the bathroom door opened. Steam from Luke's shower drifted into the room. And along with it, the scent of his cologne. God, he smelled good. She sat up and swallowed back the desire starting to grow. Sex was the last thing she should be thinking about right now. Especially sex with Luke. One screw up had been enough.

Sex with him could never be enough, a traitorous voice in her head reminded her.

She glanced at the bathroom door. Luke stood in front of the mirror, his back to her. Wearing nothing but a towel around his hips.

As if they had a mind of their own, her legs carried her to the bathroom door. She stood behind him, watching him spread shaving cream over his jaws. His crisp dark hair brushed the towel he'd slung around his neck.

God, she wanted him. Wanted him like she'd never wanted anyone or anything in her life. What was wrong with her?

Her gaze traveled downward. His taught bottom was clearly defined beneath the damp towel. Her fingers ached to touch him.

Stop it! Damn. This was insanity. Yet, it was out of her control. She moved a step closer.

For the first time, he became aware of her presence and half turned. He stopped in mid motion, the razor poised above his cheek.

They stared at one another, eyes locked. In his, she saw what she wanted to see. Like a fine whiskey, the amber flames burned in them. Burned for her.

She took another step toward him and brushed the back of her hand over the damp hairs on his chest. She trailed her knuckles lower to just above the towel. He gasped and the razor clattered to the floor. He whipped an arm around her waist and pulled her to him. Their mouths met in an explosion of desire.

Finally, gloriously, she ran her hands over his bottom where the damp towel clung. Yearning need swept through her. His hungry mouth plundered hers. She could taste the toothpaste on his tongue, feel the shaving cream as it smeared over both of them. The scent of his cologne wrapped around her in a cloud of warmth. She pressed against him and wrapped her arms around his neck, feeling his erection push against her belly. She realized she had too damned many clothes on.

Dragging her mouth away from his, she whimpered, "Luke..."

"I know, baby."

"I want you. This is crazy."

"This, sweetheart," he murmured as he rained kisses along her cheeks, her jaw line, her eyes, nibbling on her lips in between, "is amazing. Too real, too powerful to ignore."

She nodded and slid the towel from his neck as his lips once more found hers. "Mmmhmm," she moaned deep in her throat.

His hands began working the buttons of her blouse. In seconds, he had it undone and slipped it off her shoulders, letting it fall to the floor. He slid his fingers beneath her bra, teasing her nipples. Sharp waves of pleasure surged through her, pooling into damp heat between her thighs.

With all the craziness that had happened the past few months, with all the fear and anger she'd lived with since Bryce had gone mad, all she could think about now was this man and how good this felt. How right. Her heart squeezed with joy. Some small part of her mind asked a question. Did she love him? Is this what it felt like? No. She wouldn't think about that now. Wouldn't try to analyze it because in spite of how wonderful he made her feel, the thought of loving him was terrifying.

He lifted his head and stared into her eyes. She smiled. Her hands continued to roam over his shoulders...his chest.

His shoulder.

Her eyes dropped to where her hand had been. For a moment, her brain didn't register what it was seeing. And then it did and she was suddenly as cold as she had been hot before.

On his shoulder was the image of her nightmares. A wolf's head. A tattoo. Dear God.

"Jade?" His passion laced voice filtered through her mind.

She stepped away, backing further from him, shaking her head. Her skin tightened, her heart aching as she suddenly understood...so much.

"What's wrong, baby? What is it?" He moved toward her.

"No!" she screamed. She felt the dresser behind her and stopped. The gun. Luke had left his gun on the dresser. Her fingers reached back until they felt the cold metal. Then it was in her hands.

In one motion, she released the safety and brought the gun up, pointed at his chest.

"Jade? What the hell is going on?"

"You sonofabitch." Her words choked out on a sob. "You were working with him the entire time."

"What are you talking about?" Luke stepped toward her.

"Stop. Stop right there or I swear, I'll shoot you."

He stopped, shaking his head. "I don't know what's gotten into you. Talk to me."

"Talk to you? Okay, let's talk. Why the fuck were you working with Bryce?"

"I don't know what you mean."

Her body trembled. Her heart shattered. Nothing had ever hurt like this. Not what Bryce had done, not even Katherine's death.

Memories of what Agent Jackson had told her about El Lobo rushed over her. The vicious killings, how they hadn't been able to figure out who he was. She had figured it out. He was a dirty cop.

"The tattoo." She nodded toward his shoulder. "I saw that tattoo the night Bryce cut my throat. As I was losing consciousness, I saw the image of a wolf. I thought I was just hallucinating until right now. Now I know what it was. It was your tattoo. You're El Lobo."

His face paled. He lifted a hand and rubbed it over his eyes. "That's what this is about? I was undercover for the FBI. Good God, I would never work with that slimeball. What the hell is wrong with you?"

"Undercover?" The gun wavered as uncertainty surfaced. "Why didn't you just tell me that? Why keep your identity a secret all this time?"

"It was part of the operation. We weren't supposed to reveal our identities."

She shook her head. "Why did you lie to me even after the case was over? Once the operation was over with, you could have told me."

"No. I couldn't. Besides, what was the point?"

She needed time to think. Her mind wouldn't process the whole picture. She glanced behind her. A pair of handcuffs lay on top of the dresser.

She picked them up and tossed them to him. "Handcuff yourself to the leg of the bed."

He caught the cuffs but shook his head. "Are you out of your mind? I just told you everything. We don't have time for this. You need me."

"Yeah, right. I need another person in my life who pretends to be someone they're not. Who keeps secrets from me. Who uses me for their own agenda."

"I didn't do that, Jade. I was just doing my job. I swear. Why would I have tortured Kenner for information if I was working with Bryce?"

"I don't know. Maybe you didn't. You made me leave the room. Maybe you set it all up and you were trying to squeeze more money out of Bryce before you told him where I was."

"Jesus, Jade."

"Put the goddamned handcuffs on. Now!"

"You don't understand. This is crazy."

"I need to think. Need to decide what I believe. I don't want to shoot you, so handcuff yourself and I'll put the gun down."

He shook his head and dropped the handcuffs. "No way in hell. You'll have to shoot me."

She aimed toward his right shoulder, to the left of the wolf's head. She squeezed the trigger.

"Motherfucker." He whirled and grabbed his shoulder. Blood oozed from beneath his fingers. "You fucking shot me!"

Some part of her was horrified at what she'd done...but she shoved the sympathy aside. She hadn't hurt him. Not like he'd hurt her...and so many others. "I just nicked you, tough guy. I'm not playing, Luke. Handcuff yourself or the next one's lower. After all that's happened to me. After what Bryce has done. What I've seen you're capable of with that guy at the motel, I won't hesitate. I swear to God. I'm finished playing games."

He bent and picked up the handcuffs, snapping them to one wrist.

"Sit on the floor by the bed and put your hands behind your back."

He did as she said, eyes blazing with anger. "There's something I need to tell you," he said as she squatted behind him. She grabbed the cuffs and pulled his wrist back, securing the other hand behind the leg of the bed. "You really don't want to do this."

"Oh, I think I do. Nothing you say is going to make a difference."

He winced as she pulled his hands together and snapped the other cuff. "DiMarco is on his way here."

She dropped his hands. Her body trembled...realizing the exact extent of his betrayal before her mind did. "He's what?" she whispered through the pain.

"He's on his way to Solitaire."

She moved in front of him, holding the gun at her side. "The guy told the truth, didn't he? You told Bryce where to find me."

He nodded as his eyes searched hers. "I'm so sorry, Jade."

Tears blurred her vision but she swiped them away. "I knew it. I knew I couldn't trust you. You sorry motherfucker. You were working with him the whole time."

"No. That's not how it was. I told him how to find you so I could take care of him once and for all. He's never going to stop killing. You know that as well as I do. I figured if I brought him here, if I knew he was coming, I could take him out on my own terms. And protect you in

206

the process."

"I can take care of myself. I don't need your kind of protection, Luke. I don't need you."

"I'm sorry. I was wrong to keep it from you but now that you know, surely you see you have to let me go." He jerked against his restraints. "Bryce will be here. He will kill you. You have to set me free. You have to trust me."

She laughed but it sounded hollow with the anguish twisting through her gut. "Trust you? Yeah. That's a hoot. You know, I've found that I do a lot better when I don't trust a man than when I do. Fuck you, Luke."

"Jade, please. Maybe I handled it wrong but I did it to help you. To end this once and for all. You have to believe me."

She shook her head and backed away. "I don't know why you did it but I know you lied to me." She scrubbed a hand over her cheeks, angry that the tears wouldn't stop. "You know, the funny thing is, if you'd let me in on it. If you'd been honest with me, I'd willingly have been your bait. I'd have let you use me to stop Bryce. It looks like that may be what I'll have to do anyway."

"Wait. Please. I did all of this to protect you. Because I love you."

She brought the gun up and pointed it at his head. "Don't say that! Don't you *dare* say that."

"It's true. I swear. I've known it for a while but couldn't admit it, even to myself. But I can't fight it any longer. You're everything to me. I can't take it if I lose you, if something happens to you because of me."

"You're a lying sonofabitch. If you say that one more time, I'll shoot you again. I swear to God I will. Just shut the hell up!"

She snatched her blouse from the floor and shrugged it on. Taking a towel, she wiped the shaving cream from her face, trying not to think about how it had gotten there. About how his skin, warm from the shower, had burned against hers...his lips driving her mad with need...so much so that she'd overlooked the simple truth. He'd lied to her...betrayed her, just as the others had done. Stiffening her spine, she erased the images. She'd been a fool, but no more.

Grabbing Luke's cell phone, she shoved it in her

pants pocket. Jerking the motel phone cord out of the wall, she headed for the door.

"Jade! For God's sake, he'll kill you."

She stopped at the door but didn't turn around. "Maybe so," she replied, barely able to force the words past the stone in her chest. "But at least with him, I know what to expect."

Chapter Twenty

Like the blinding flash of a camera, the sun glinted off the snow-covered ground. Jade peered through the windshield of Luke's car, alternately turning on the wipers and brushing tears from her cheeks.

Heat blasted from the vents but she shivered. The cold she felt came from inside. She wondered if she'd ever be warm again.

At an overpass, a group of children slid down the hill on cardboard boxes. She couldn't hear their laughter but could see their smiling faces. How could everything still look so normal? How could the world go on around her when hers had just been torn apart?

She pulled into the parking lot of the complex but hesitated before getting out of the car. Was Bryce already in Solitaire?

He was coming. She knew that for a fact. Luke had told him where to find her. Nothing would keep him away.

She stared up at her window. Cold dread shivered through her veins. No. He hadn't had time to get here yet. It was a thirteen-hour drive. No way he could have gotten a flight here by now even if he were brave enough to show his face at an airport. She had time.

She would be ready when he arrived.

A warning bell clanged in her mind as she walked down the hallway. Something wasn't right. She could feel it. Was it just her imagination? Just the fear coursing through her bones or was Bryce here?

She held Luke's gun in front of her and turned the

209

key in the lock. She pushed the door open and stepped inside.

The curtains were closed and, in spite of the afternoon sun, the room was in shadows. In the dimly lit apartment, she could make out a figure sitting in a chair in the middle of the living room.

"Don't move," she shouted, aiming at the figure.

She flipped on the light and screamed. The figure was Dennis. But he couldn't hurt her. Not anymore. His head hung at a grotesque angle. Eyes fixed and distant, he stared at nothing. She would have known he was dead even without seeing the note impaled to his chest with a large knife. Blood coated the white paper, almost covering the red-streaked letters, but she could read them.

You're Welcome'.

She stumbled against the wall, still holding the gun in front of her. Her knees went weak. Her gun hand shook as she waved it around the room. Skirting the corpse in the chair, she crept toward the bedroom. She swallowed the lump in her throat and pushed the door open.

"Come out, you sonofabitch." Nothing moved. She searched the closet, then the bathroom but she knew he was gone. She could feel the emptiness of the apartment. She was the only living creature here.

She fumbled for her cell phone and almost dropped it when a shrill rang pierced the silence. A number she didn't recognize appeared on the screen. Along with a photo.

A scream left her throat. She went down on one knee, dropping the gun. "No. God, no." The photo showed Ashley, bound and gagged. Her horror filled eyes stared into Jade's.

The ringing wouldn't stop, so she jabbed the button and brought the phone to her ear.

"Hello, darling. Miss me?" The sound of Bryce's voice filled her ear. Bile surfaced and she gagged, trying not to puke.

"You hurt her, you sonofabitch, and I'll..."

"Now, now. Don't say anything you'll regret. You've seen what happens when you fuck with me. Right, Jade?"

"You're a sick bastard."

"Ah. I guess you found my little gift. You should

thank me. That cocksucker tried to rape you. I did you a favor, dear. Don't you find it romantic?"

Tears streamed down her face. Her breath hitched, causing the words to stutter out of her. "What do you want?"

"What I've always wanted. You."

"Please don't hurt Ashley."

"Well, that depends on you. Can you be a good girl and do exactly as I tell you?"

She closed her eyes, her voice a desperate plea. "Yes. Please. I'll do whatever you say."

"That's better. Those are the words I've longed to hear." He laughed and she cringed, clinging so tightly to the phone she thought her fingers would break. "I want you to head toward Clearwater Lake. Come alone. No cops, no Butler. Just you."

"Yes. Ok."

"If I get even a hint that you've brought someone with you, that you've told a soul, the girl dies. And it won't be a pretty death like it was with the rapist. Trust me on that one. I'll be in touch."

He hung up and she stood there, shaking with sobs. She heard a noise at the front door and whirled, pointing the gun.

Deb stood in the entrance, staring at Dennis. Her hand was clamped over her mouth and a low wail came from her throat. The wail became a scream of hysteria. "Dennis. Oh my God, Dennis." Her body shook and her head rolled from side to side. "No, no, no, no..."

Jade rushed over to her and grabbed her by the shoulders. "Snap out if it. Now!"

She didn't listen. Didn't see Jade. Her screams became louder.

Jade slapped her face. The screaming stopped.

"Listen to me." Jade shook her. "The maniac who did this has your daughter."

"What? Ashley?" She looked back at Dennis and pulled away. "No. How? Why?"

"I don't have time to explain. I have to go to her or he'll kill her. I need you to listen to me. Do exactly as I say."

"It's all my fault." Her voice was calm but tears

coursed down her cheeks. "I let her go with him. I'm a rotten mother and now my baby's dead. Oh God. No, please, no. I failed her. I failed them both."

Jade shook her again. "This isn't about you. We don't have time for hysterics. I need you to stay by a phone." Jade didn't know what her plan was but she needed to know there was someone she could call just in case. Besides, she needed Deb to feel like she was doing something worthwhile. Otherwise, she might go to the police and Ashley could die. "Can you do that? Do you understand?"

She nodded. "I don't have a phone."

Shit. She didn't. "Go to the store. If I find out anything, I'll call you there. What's the number?"

She gave Jade the number and she stored it in her phone.

"Momma?" Jade looked past Deb. Jon stood in the hallway, his chubby face scrunched in bewilderment. "Was you screaming?"

Jade pushed Deb out the door and closed it behind them. "Hey, Jon, how are you sweetie? Your mom just bumped her head. She's okay now, though."

He scowled. "Mom, bumped heads don't hurt that bad."

Deb gave a smile that was more of a grimace. "I know, son. I'm a big baby. We're going to the store to hang out for a while, just you and me, okay?"

"Can I bring my Gameboy?"

"Yeah. You can bring it."

Jade watched them walk down the hallway. Once they were out of sight, she closed her apartment door and hurried to the car.

****

Twenty minutes after Jade left, Bryce called again.

"There's a path off Sailboat Road just after the railroad tracks. Take that and follow it until it ends. You still being a good girl? Doing what I told you to do?"

"Yes," she snapped. She wanted to kill him, slowly and painfully. Wanted to make him scream. If she got the opportunity, that is exactly what she would do.

"So, where's your lover, Butler?"

"Don't you know? I bet you and El Lobo had a good

212

laugh over me this whole time. Dirty FBI agent and a psycho killer. You two make quite a pair."

"El Lobo?" The surprise in his voice confused her. Then his tone softened as if he'd just realized something he should have known all along. "I'll be a sonofabitch. That cocksucker was El Lobo. I should have taken his ass out along with that bitch FBI agent."

His words slammed into her with the force of a hurricane. *Bryce hadn't known.*

Luke really had been working undercover. Dear God, what had she done? It was too late to call Luke now. She hadn't left him with a phone. Besides, calling him would risk Ashley's life. She would have to face Bryce alone.

As she drove toward Bryce, a glimmer of foolish hope sprang inside her. If Luke had been telling the truth about that, maybe he'd meant it when he said he loved her.

Yeah? So what if he did? It wasn't likely she'd ever see him again.

It wasn't likely she'd live through the night.

****

Luke struggled against the handcuffs. Useless. Fucking useless. He stopped, panting heavily, sweat pouring from his face. Panic rose from his chest into his throat.

Jade. Bryce would find her. And it would be his fault. He'd brought him here. Led him right to her.

The look on her face when she realized he'd betrayed her...the hatred in her eyes when he told her he loved her...

She'd never forgive him. Even if she survived, she'd never speak to him again. She hated his guts.

Break your thumb. The thought popped into his mind and brought his head up. His hands were behind him but if he could manage to break his thumb, he could slip out of one cuff. It just might work.

He grabbed his left thumb with his right. Gritting his teeth, he began to pull, pushing at his left thumb knuckle as he did. Pain shot through his wrist and up to his shoulder.

Suck it up. Don't be a puss.

He squeezed with all his strength, then cursed in

213

frustration. It wasn't working. He lifted his hands and was about to slam them against the bed leg when the front door opened.

The hotel manager and Wayne burst through the door. Luke almost cried with joy.

"Wayne?" He shook his head. For a moment he thought he was hallucinating. But he was there. "I never thought I'd say this, but you, my friend, are a beautiful sight."

"You're not too bad yourself. Sitting there in nothing but a towel, wearing handcuffs. Kind of sexy."

"Fuck you. Just get me loose."

Wayne squatted to unlock the cuffs and noticed the blood. "What the hell happened to you?"

"A bullet. Just a flesh wound."

"Who shot you?"

Luke stood and grabbed a towel. He wiped the shaving cream from his face, then turned to the manager. "You have a bandage somewhere?" The guy nodded and disappeared. After he left, Luke looked at Wayne. "Jade."

"What? The woman you've been busting your ass to help *shot* you?" Wayne's mouth twitched. If Luke hadn't been so happy to see him, he'd have punched him.

"It's a long story." The hotel manager returned with a large band-aid. Luke wet a washcloth and wiped the blood from the wound, then covered it with the band-aid. He pulled on jeans and a gray Henley. "Not that I'm complaining, but what the hell are you doing here?"

"When you called me the last time, I'd had enough. I knew you were on the verge of some major shit and I was missing out on it. I wasn't sure if it would be DiMarco or the US Marshals but I knew someone was getting ready to fry your ass. I thought you could use the help."

"You have no idea how glad I am that you butted in."

"I tried to call your room. Ahmad here rang it but it showed out of service. I convinced him to open up and boy, was I surprised at what I found. Didn't think you'd take the time for kinky games with all the shit going down but I guess you never really know a person."

"Ha. Laugh it up, funny man." Luke winced as he shrugged into his leather jacket. "We need to go. Now."

"Go where?"

"I'm not sure yet, but we'd better find out quick. DiMarco is either here or on his way."

"How the hell does DiMarco know to come here?"

This was the part Luke dreaded telling him. It made him sound like the stupidest sonofabitch alive.

"He knows because I told him."

****

Jade eased off the accelerator as the icy road narrowed. Frozen tree branches reached out like the talons of a prehistoric bird and scraped against the car, sending shock waves of anxiety along her nerves.

She searched through the deepening dusk for Sailboat Road, barely able to feel the steering wheel beneath her frigid hands. She wasn't certain if they were frozen from the cold or fear for Ashley.

Her headlights reflected off a blue street sign. Sailboat Road.

Tendrils of apprehension buzzed through her system as the reality of her situation dawned on her. At any moment, she would come face to face with Bryce. Her heart stilled for a moment then beat with the intensity of a rock and roll drum solo. Her fear wasn't only for Ashley. She was also terrified for herself.

She turned onto the gravel road and only went a few miles before the road ended. She took the dirt turnoff as Bryce had instructed. Closer now. Closer to Ashley and to the evil hidden behind the mask of the man she'd married. The man she'd once thought she loved.

A figure stepped in front of the car.

She screamed, then clamped a hand over her mouth. *Bryce.* For a crazy moment, she was tempted to floor the gas pedal...send two thousand pounds of steel and rubber over his body, crushing his murderous soul. She couldn't do that though. He had Ashley.

She stepped out of the car. Bryce held out his arms as if inviting her into a hug.

Fat chance, motherfucker.

She pointed the gun at his chest. "Where is she?"

He dropped his arms and slipped his hands in the pockets of his parka. He smiled and it was as if Satan's demon's had painted the expression on his face. Pure evil radiated from him. How could she have ever thought him

215

handsome?

"Put that thing away, darling." He took a step toward her. "You would never hurt me."

"Wanna bet? Where the fuck is she?"

He moved closer and his eyes went to her scar. "Good God. I did that to you?" He looked away. When he turned back to face her, she thought she saw moisture in his eyes. He cleared his throat before speaking. "I'm sorry. You have to believe that I never meant to hurt you."

"Never meant to hurt me? You almost killed me. You've killed God knows how many people, including a woman who was like the mother I never had. And you dare to say you never meant to hurt me? If you've done anything to Ashley..." She raised the gun. "Tell me where she is. Now."

"The only way she goes free is if you stay with me. Waving that gun around will only get your little friend killed. Now give it to me." Bryce held out his hand.

She was carrying Luke's gun. Hers was tucked inside her boot. She handed the 9mm to Bryce.

"Turn around and put your hands on the car."

He'll find the gun. She stared at him, not moving.

"Do it now. I'm going to search you. We can either do it this way or you can strip right here in front of me. In the freezing snow. Which will it be?"

She turned and put her palms on the still warm hood of Luke's car. Bryce's hands roamed over her body beneath her jacket, lingering around her ribs, just below her breasts. She sucked in air, trying not to throw up as his touch went lower. *The gun. He's going to find the gun.* His hands pressed over the legs of her jeans, down to her boots.

"Sonofabitch. Sneaky little thing, aren't you?" He lifted her pant leg and unzipped her boot, pulling the gun from its hiding place. "You won't be needing this." He slipped it in his pocket. "Leave your cell phone in the car and come with me."

Resentment chased through her along with hopelessness. The gun had been her last chance to get out of this mess. What the hell would she do now?

She tossed the phone inside the car and followed Bryce through the snow-covered shrubs. She stumbled and Bryce took her arm to steady her. Revulsion, quick and sharp, shuddered through her system and she jerked away. His gaze turned as icy as the ground beneath them but he didn't respond. She followed him until he stopped near an abandoned mine.

"Good God. Is Ashley in there?" She turned to him in horror.

He smiled. "Yes, she is. In that cold, deep, dark mine." He gave a mock shudder. "Horrible, isn't it? Your worse nightmare."

"Wrong, asshole. *You're* my worse nightmare."

He shook his head. "When did you get such a smart mouth? You were always so loving, so docile. What's happened to you?"

You happened to me, she wanted to say. But that would probably please him. "I'm here now. Let her out."

"Oh, no. It's not that simple, darling. She stays right where she is. I just wanted you to know what she's going through. If you're a good girl and do exactly as I say, maybe sometime in the near future, I'll let her out. But she's my insurance policy. You see, I no longer trust you. You'll have to earn that trust once again." He reached up and brushed a hand across her cheek.

The revulsion returned but stronger this time. "Don't touch me!"

"That kind of attitude is not going to help your little friend. I have a place for us to stay. You'll like it, I promise. Not as lavish as the home we shared but at least we'll be together."

"You can't leave her here. She'll die. I'll go with you but you have to let her out." He didn't even know the extent of his cruelty. The girl's father had died in a mine just like this. Was that going through her mind? Adding to her terror?

Bryce grinned and reached into his coat. He pulled out a flashlight and held it out to her. "If you want her, go in and get her."

Jade took the flashlight from him. She hefted the weight in her hand. Did she have enough strength to knock him out with it? No. Not from this distance. And not with one blow.

A scream echoed from within the mine. *Ashley.*

Bryce's smile widened. He knew she was terrified of the dark. He didn't think she'd do it. She wasn't sure she would either. Wasn't sure she could.

She stared at him for a moment, then turned and ran to the entrance of the mine. She stopped. Darkness reached out to her. Much darker than the night around her. Black and deep. Evil. A shudder ran through her, her muscles clenching in dread.

I can't do it. I can't go in there. Hot tears scalded down her cheeks as a powerless groan left her throat. She wanted to help Ashley, but her legs wouldn't move.

She shook her head and backed away, her fingers going limp as the flashlight almost slipped from her fingers. Squeezing her eyes shut, she tightened her grip, searching for courage, but knowing that was something she didn't have...had never had.

As she stood there, with hopelessness and defeat weighing her down like the aftermath of a cave-in, Ashley's cries came to her from the pit. Jade's eyes flew open. She couldn't let Ashley down...couldn't let her die. Even though it was the most difficult thing she'd ever done, she had no choice.

Taking a shaky breath that ended on a sob, she stepped forward and plunged into the yawning mouth of hell.

Chapter Twenty-One

On the way to Jade's apartment, Luke dialed her cell phone over and over while Wayne called 'On Star' to track the location of Luke's car. No answer from Jade. Wayne was still on hold when they arrived at her door.

Once inside, Luke's guts seized. Bryce had been there. The thing in the chair was obviously his handiwork. He had no idea who the man had been...but he certainly wouldn't be able to tell them.

What now? Where was Jade? Did Bryce have her already? God, no. Please, no.

Luke searched the apartment, but she was gone. Wayne finally got through to 'On Star'. "Your car's about fifteen miles from here, near a lake," he told Luke as they headed to the parking lot.

They stepped to the bottom of the stairs and almost collided with a man and a woman. Special Agent Theodore Cummings and Special Agent Darla Blevins.

Luke looked at Wayne and his partner shook his head. "I didn't tell them."

"Luke Butler," Special Agent Cummings said, "We're here to take you into custody."

"What the hell is this about? I haven't done anything." Luke turned to the woman. "Darla?"

She looked at the ground, refusing to meet Luke's eyes. Darla Blevins was a stout woman with dark hair cut close to her face. She had been a friend of Delia's. Rumor around the agency was that she would have liked to be more than friends but after years of speculation, no one was certain of her sexual preferences.

219

"The Marshals' office called," Cummings said. "Apparently, you've done quite a bit. We have orders to take you in for questioning."

"You don't understand. A woman's life is in danger. Give me until the morning and I'll turn myself in. You have my word."

"I'm sorry, Agent Butler." Cummings held out handcuffs. "You're coming with us."

"Get Madsen on the phone." Panic built in Luke's chest. He couldn't tell them DiMarco might be here. That would start a manhunt that would endanger Jade's life.

"We'll call him from the car. Come on." Cummings pulled out his gun. His chin lifted and a glint came in his eyes. He'd like nothing better than for Luke to give him a reason. They'd never liked one another. Cummings was a straight arrow and resented Luke's unorthodox methods. He'd been waiting for years to see Luke brought to his knees.

Luke held out his hands and Cummings snapped the cuffs around his wrists.

"Where are you taking him?" Wayne asked.

"Denver. We'll catch a flight there back to St. Louis."

"I'll follow you," Wayne told Luke. "I'll talk to Madsen. We'll get this straightened out.

Luke nodded and followed the agents. His brain ticked off the seconds since Jade had left. Where was she now? More importantly, where the hell was DiMarco?

****

Jade held the flashlight with one hand and clung to the jagged surface of the walls with the other as she went deeper into the black hole. The smell of decay permeated the air. Coal dust coated her nostrils, her skin, even her tongue.

She clamped her lips together and tried to breathe through her nose but she couldn't breathe at all. A rush of dizziness came over her and she stopped for a moment. She closed her eyes, but that only made it worse. Now she knew what it would feel like to be buried alive.

"Ashley," she shouted. "Talk to me. I'll follow your voice."

"I'm scared, Jade. Please help me."

"I'm trying, baby. Just stay calm. Keep talking to me.

Are you hurt?"

"No. I'm okay." Ashley's voice trembled through the blackness, sounding like the wail of a lost infant. She rattled on about nothing while Jade moved toward the sound.

After a few disorienting turns and what seemed like miles, but was probably only about twenty feet, Jade was standing in front of Ashley.

The flashlight cast a grotesque glow around the frightened girl. Her arms were tied behind her around a wooden beam. Tears and black dust streaked her cheeks. She continued to babble.

"Shhh. I'm here, honey. I'll help you," Jade whispered. She knelt behind Ashley and tugged on the ropes that bound her.

"There's a knife in my back pocket," Ashley said.

Jade reached into the pocket of Ashley's jeans and pulled out a switchblade. "Where did you get this?" Jade asked as she cut through the ropes.

"My friend, Tanner, gave it to me. I told him what Dennis did to you and he wanted me to have it for protection. I've carried it ever since."

Bryce had searched Jade but not Ashley. It wasn't likely he'd search her again. Once Ashley was free, Jade slipped the knife into her back pocket. The large sweatshirt she wore might conceal it. She'd rather hide it somewhere less conspicuous but she might need to get to it quickly. She'd have to take the chance.

She took the shivering girl into her arms and held her for a moment, smoothing her hair. "It's okay now, honey. It's okay," Jade said over and over while Ashley sobbed into her shoulder.

When the trembling subsided, Jade pulled away and took Ashley's hand. "Come on. Hold onto me. We're getting out."

She hoped they were getting out. She wasn't sure she could find her way, even with the help of the flashlight.

By instinct or the grace of God, Jade retraced her steps and saw a glimmer. The opening of the mine. Although the stars provided minimal light, compared to the darkness of the coal mine, it was enough to assure her freedom was near.

They stumbled from the mine. Bryce stood outside the entrance, clapping his hands as he watched them emerge. "My, my. You're a much braver woman than I thought. I never dreamed you'd go into a dark, scary mine, even to save the girl. She must mean a lot to you."

"Let her go, Bryce. I'll stay with you. Just let Ashley go."

"I'm sorry, dear. I can't do that. You see, Ashley is never going home."

For a moment, rage and terror froze Jade's vocal cords. Then, she found her voice but her jaw ached with the effort of speaking without screaming out her fury. "What are you going to do?"

"Just to show you I'm not such a bad guy, I'm going to give the girl a choice. She can choose to die right now. Or, she can go to a whorehouse in Mexico. As you know, I have connections there." His white-toothed grin gleamed in the semi-darkness.

"You sorry bastard."

"Name calling won't help anyone." He looked over Jade's shoulder at Ashley. "You don't have much time to decide, little girl. What's it going to be? Die an easy death now or live your life as a whore?"

Jade's panicked mind raced. She wouldn't let him kill Ashley. That was out of the question but could she stop him from selling the girl to a whorehouse? What kind of sick freak was he? She knew what kind of sick freak he was, knew what he was capable of. Dear God.

Jade turned to Ashley. She took the girls cold hands and looked her in the eye. She raised her eyebrows and gave a slight nod. *Go along with me,* the look said. Jade hoped she understood.

"It's up to you, sweetheart. I'm sorry, but there's nothing I can do. You have to make the choice. Either way, you won't be there for your brother. Jon is on his own with your mom. You know how angry the wheelchair makes her."

As soon as she spoke the words, it occurred to her that Bryce might have seen Jon. He might know Ashley's brother was not in a wheelchair. She'd come too far now, though. She had to see it through. Taking a deep breath, she went on. "You're the only thing that stands between him and your mother's horrible temper. At least in Mexico you might someday escape. Maybe it won't be too late for him."

"Wheelchair?" Bryce's voice cut across her words. "What the fuck are you talking about?"

Jade turned to him as if annoyed by the interruption, praying he hadn't seen Jon. "Her little brother is crippled. Her mother's a drunk and takes her anger out on him. Ashley takes care of him. Or at least she did."

Uncertainty crossed his features. The gun lowered. "Shit." He brushed a hand over his eyes. He scowled, then pulled a cell phone from his pocket. He dialed a number and in a few seconds, began speaking. "I need you to come back to the mine. There's been a change of plans."

****

Luke shifted in the back of the car, panic crowding his brain. Darla called Madsen and put him on speakerphone.

"Butler, what the hell do you think you're doing?" Madsen's voice boomed in the confined space.

"You have to let me go, Madsen. Give me twenty-four hours. I'll answer whatever charges you have but Jade DiMarco's life could be in danger."

"You can't pull this shit, Butler. The authorities in Salina found a guy in a motel room who said you tortured him. *Tortured him.* What the fuck?"

"He's one of DiMarco's men. I tried to get DiMarco's location but I didn't hurt the asshole."

"Did you get the location?"

Luke blew out a breath and didn't answer.

Madsen's voice came over the speaker. "I didn't think so. Get your ass back here, now!"

There was a click and Madsen was gone. So much for that.

Darla finally looked at Luke. He could see the uncertainty in her eyes.

"Darla, I can find the bastard that killed Delia. I just need a little time. You have to talk some sense into him." He jerked his head toward Cummings.

"Forget it, Butler," Cummings spat. "I'm doing what I was told to do. Neither of us is risking our asses to help a loose cannon like you. Just shut the hell up."

Luke looked behind them. Wayne was there. Maybe he should have sent him after Jade. He couldn't have told him in front of the agents. Now it was too late. Shit.

A choking sound brought Luke's gaze back around. Darla's head was thrown back and she clutched her throat, making gurgling noises and thrashing in her seat.

Luke leaned forward. "Darla, are you okay? Cummings, for God's sake, help her."

Cummings looked helplessly at his partner, then at the road. "What the hell's happening?"

"How the fuck should I know? Looks like she's having a seizure. Godammit, help her or uncuff me so I can."

Cummings whipped the car to the side of the road and jumped out. As he headed to the passenger side, Darla's seizure stopped and she turned perfectly lucid eyes to Luke. "As soon as he's distracted, get the hell out. Find the motherfucker."

"What the..." Before Luke could form a complete sentence, Darla was back in seizure mode. Cummings threw the car door open and bent toward her.

"Air..." Darla choked through the gags. She pushed Cummings away and stumbled from the car, still clutching her throat. Cummings followed, frantically attempting to help the writhing woman.

Luke opened the door with his cuffed hands. Wayne had stopped behind them and was rushing to the agents when he saw Luke. Luke motioned with his head back toward Wayne's car. Wayne followed.

Still not quite believing what had just happened, Luke said, "Darla faked a seizure so I could escape. Let's get the hell out of here."

"Jesus." Wayne shook his head and opened the passenger door. Luke stumbled inside and slammed the door shut as Wayne got in the driver's seat and shifted the car into drive, nearly sliding on the ice as they took off.

"Did you get the trace?" Luke asked after Wayne unlocked the cuffs with one hand while holding the steering wheel with the other.

"Yeah. It's somewhere by a lake. We should be there in less than half an hour."

"Thanks, partner. I owe you." Luke's panic had eased

but not abated completely. There was hope for Jade now. But it all rested on his shoulders. He'd failed too many times before. He couldn't live with himself if he failed now.

"You owe me big time," Wayne warned. "After this shit, I can see my retirement turning into a stint in federal prison."

"I'll take the fall. I'll tell them I took you at gunpoint."

"Fuck that. If we go down, we're going down together." Wayne glanced at Luke. "You know, it's not your fault that she's in danger."

"I told him where to find her. How the hell could it not be?"

"He was working his way to her anyway. He had to be stopped. You were just trying to protect her and you could've done that if she hadn't shot you."

Luke shook his head. "Don't blame her. I'm the one who made the call. You know, it doesn't even matter whose fault it is. If anything happens to Jade..." The image of Delia's crumpled body flashed in his mind. The feel of her lifeless weight in his arms...ah, hell. That had been hard, gut wrenching, but to find Jade that way... No. He wouldn't think like that.

The main lake road wound through the mountains with smaller gravel roads every mile or so. The trace showed the car was just east of the road they were on.

Wayne turned on Sailboat Road, driving slowly as they searched through the ice-laden trees for some sign of something...

"Here it is," Wayne said.

They took a dirt road and had only gone about thirty feet when Luke saw it. His car, parked at the end of the road. His heart lurched. He didn't see anyone inside.

Wayne slammed the car in park. Luke jumped out and ran to the driver's side. He jerked the door open. No sign of Jade. No sign of blood either. Jade's cell phone lay inside. She hadn't gotten his calls. Maybe wouldn't have answered them anyway. She still didn't think she could trust him.

What to do now? Luke had no idea where DiMarco had taken her but he knew he had her. His shoulder ached but nothing compared to the ache in his heart. "Fuck." He kicked the tire and leaned on the hood. "What the hell are we going to do?"

"I'm sorry, man. We'll find her. Don't worry."

"How the hell will we find her? They could be anywhere by now." Luke's voice cracked. He felt tears at the back of his throat. "She could already be dead."

Wayne put his hand on Luke's uninjured shoulder. Neither of them spoke. There was nothing to say. He had DiMarco's number but there was no way Wayne could call for a trace. He couldn't take the chance. The bureau would be all over this by now.

****

Several minutes after Bryce's call, Jade heard the hum of a motor, then it switched off and in seconds, a bald, muscular, Asian man walked out of the trees.

"Take the girl." Bryce instructed. "I'll call you when we're safely away and you can release her. Don't let her out of your sight until I give you the okay."

"Sure, boss." The guy smiled, revealing the glint of a gold tooth.

Jade shuddered. How could she let Ashley go with a man like this? The question was, how could she stop it? And, would Ashley be safer with him than with Bryce?

Ashley clung to Jade and sobbed. "Please don't make me go, Jenna."

With all the will she could muster, Jade pushed her away. "Go on. You'll be fine."

"Hey, better than being dead, right?" He turned to the Asian. "I'll call you every hour. If an hour goes by and you don't hear from me, kill her."

"No," Ashley gasped.

Jade gave Ashley what she hoped was a reassuring smile but with the tears stinging her eyes, she had her doubts. "You'll be okay, honey. Just do what he says."

Ashley swiped at her tears, leaving a caked smudge of black dust on her cheek. She smiled and nodded but her lower lip trembled.

The Asian grabbed Ashley by the arm and jerked her toward the direction he'd come.

"Hey!" Jade cried. "You said you wouldn't hurt her."

"Take it easy, Chang," Bryce told the man.

"Sure." His hold eased as he led Ashley away.

Jade suddenly felt bereft. As if her last link to hope had vanished.

Bryce walked over and jerked Jade's hands behind her back, tying them so tightly, she felt her circulation slowly leaving.

He put the gun away and led her through the trees to a clearing where a silver Audi was parked.

"Where are you taking me?" she asked, her voice strong in spite of her terror.

"Somewhere warm and cozy to wait until our transportation arrives. You'll like it, I promise. It'll give us time alone to catch up, get reacquainted."

"Don't let him hurt Ashley."

"As I said before, darling, that all depends on you."

Chapter Twenty-Two

Luke's mind wouldn't function. Wouldn't give him a way to find Jade. He stood by his car, head bowed, alternately cursing and praying. Neither of them were helping.

"Let's go. Nothing more to do here," Wayne said.

"I have to find her."

Wayne turned and scanned the area. "We have no idea what happened here. No idea if he has her or what direction they've gone."

Luke lifted his head. "No, but it's pretty certain they wouldn't have gone back toward the main road." He pointed north. "You head that way and I'll head east."

"We probably shouldn't separate."

Wayne was right. If either of them found something, they'd have a hard time letting the other know. "Okay. We'll both head east but we need to keep a wide gap between us. Give a yell if you find anything."

"Right." Wayne nodded and the two of them set out through the wooded area. Wayne kept to the path while Luke searched through the drifts of snow among the shrubs.

Luke searched the ground for footprints, broken twigs, anything to indicate someone had been through here recently, although the chance of finding footprints was slim. Snow had been falling off and on throughout the evening.

After several futile minutes, he heard a branch crack nearby. He lifted his head and looked around. "Wayne?" he called.

No answer.

Luke headed toward the sound. He stepped into a clearing and came face to face with a man holding a gun. He pointed it at Luke's chest.

"Who the hell are you?" the man demanded.

Slowly, Luke raised his hands and purposely made his voice quiver. "Just a hiker, man. Please don't kill me."

The man's gaze moved up and down Luke's jeans and leather jacket. And lack of a backpack. "You're no fucking hiker." He raised the gun. "Put your hands on top of your head."

A shot sounded. The guy fell to the ground, clutching his leg. Blood leaked from beneath his fingers.

Wayne came out of the woods. "I didn't want to kill him. We need information."

"Right. Thanks, buddy."

The man rolled around in the snow, clasping his injured leg, howling with pain.

Luke pulled his Beretta from his pocket and knelt with one knee on the guy's chest. He pressed the gun to his forehead. "Tell me where he is or I'll blow your fucking head off."

"Who?"

"You want another hole, motherfucker? I know you work for DiMarco. You've got two point five seconds to tell me where he is."

"Shit." The guy groaned. "I'm fucked either way."

Luke pressed the barrel into his mouth. "You've never been fucked until you've been fucked by me. You're going to tell me where to find DiMarco. The only question is, how much I'll make you scream before you do."

****

Jade trembled in the passenger seat, even though Bryce had the heat on high. She was still cold...and the numbness in her hands had traveled up her arms.

Bryce looked at her and shook his head. "I still can't believe we're finally together. After all the searching. All I went through to find you. It's almost like a dream."

'More like a nightmare' would have been way too trite, so she didn't say it. She didn't want to talk at all. She wanted to figure a way out of this mess. A way to rescue Ashley. Maybe when they reached their destination...

At that moment, they did. Bryce slowed the Audi, the tires crunching over the snow as they came to a stop in front of a small cabin. It wasn't far from where she'd met up with Bryce, but it was a thousand miles from safety...a million miles from hope.

Inside were a wood framed couch and chair with southwestern print cushions and a coffee table marred with cigarette burns. A small pile of logs sat next to a fireplace, along with a wrought iron shovel and poker. A musty odor hung in the air, making Jade feel even more isolated as she realized the cabin probably hadn't been used in a very long time.

She turned to him. "Would you please untie me? My hands are numb."

He shook his head. "Can't do that. I don't trust you. But I'll loosen them a bit, how's that?"

She nodded and he stepped behind her. She felt him tug on the ropes and in seconds, her flesh started to tingle as the blood rushed back to her hands.

He turned her toward him and placed his hands on either side of her face. "God, I've missed you. You have no idea how much." His voice was husky with longing, sincere. As if she were a lover who'd returned from an extended absence rather than a hostage of his madness.

His hands on her face felt constricting, even though his touch was light. It was all she could do to keep from pulling away. She didn't want to antagonize him, not just yet.

"You do understand that all of this is your fault, right? If you'd just stayed out of it, none of this would have happened. You had it made. I treated you like a queen but it wasn't enough. Do you have any idea how many women would have loved to trade places with you?"

"You kidnapped girls and sold them into slavery. You almost killed me." She gritted her teeth with the effort of keeping her tone calm. "How can you possibly pretend that was a normal existence?"

He shrugged. "It was business. That's it. You should have never involved yourself in my business."

His eyes roamed over her face and he leaned toward her. Oh God, he was going to kiss her...she couldn't do it...couldn't cope with the feel of his lips on hers. She tensed, tightening her muscles in anticipation.

The kiss was light, but repulsive just the same. As if a serpent had pressed its revolting mouth to hers.

Bryce pulled away and released her face. "You'll come around, I promise you that." His voice was low, deadly. "When you realize what the alternative is, you'll be begging me to touch you."

Jade couldn't imagine any alternative that would be worse than having this despicable thing touch her. She would die first. She lifted her chin and said nothing.

Bryce pushed her down onto the couch and unable to break her fall, she landed with a thump, her elbow smacking the wooden arm. Shards of pain shot through her arm up to her shoulder and tears sprang to her eyes.

Bryce loomed above her. "Once we leave here, you're mine. You'll never escape. The only thing you can hope for is that I'm pleased enough with you that I let you live. And that I let the girl live."

Ignoring the threat to Ashley, but filing it away in her mind as a reminder that she had to tread carefully, she asked, "Where are we going?"

A smile split his face. The look was self-satisfied, as if he was the master of travel arrangements. "It's a surprise, but I'll give you a hint." His glacial blue eyes gleamed. "There are five very good reasons to go there."

Five very good reasons. Five million dollars. "The Cayman Islands?"

He made a sound like a game show bell. "Correct on the first guess, very good."

Despair weighted her down, sinking her heart into a pool of mire. If he got her that far...if they actually made it to the Cayman Islands, there was no way she'd ever escape. Other than in death.

****

After a little creative persuasion, Luke learned that the man's name was Blake Lawson and he did indeed work for Bryce DiMarco.

"Don't make me go with you," Lawson begged. "He'll kill me for sure."

Luke drove with Lawson in the passenger seat while Wayne sat in the back with a gun pressed to the man's

231

temple.

"Sorry," Luke said. "You're going with us. That way if I find out you lied, I can be the one to kill you."

"I swear to God, I can tell you where he is." He began to babble directions, looking from Luke to Wayne as if searching for his most likely ally.

"Shut up and listen," Luke interrupted. "How many men does DiMarco have with him?"

"I don't know."

"Don't fucking lie to me." Luke grabbed the guy's hair, keeping one eye on the road. "My friend here will put a bullet in the limb of your choice if you can't come up with a better answer than that."

The guy's eyes rolled back toward Wayne, then toward his injured leg. Wayne had used his scarf to wrap the wound, but the bullet was still there. Before long, he'd need medical attention.

"My leg is fucking killing me. Please, you have to get me to a doctor."

Luke twisted and the guy yelped. "Answer the fucking question and I'll think about it."

"I only know of a few. He could have more. I just mean I don't know exactly."

"Are they at the cabin with him?"

"He rented another cabin. We've been staying there, waiting for his orders."

Luke released his hold. "How many men are there?"

"It was me, Chang, and Reiker," Lawson said, rubbing his scalp.

"Call 'em."

"Which one?"

"Jesus. Start with Chang." Luke handed back the cell phone they'd taken from the guy when they searched him. "Find out where he is. Put it on speakerphone. If you say anything that makes me suspicious, you're dead. And be careful. I'm a very suspicious guy."

Lawson dialed the phone. A man's voice answered.

"Hey, Chang," Lawson said. "Are you with Mr. DiMarco? He asked me to check on the woman's car and I tried to call him back, but he's not answering."

"I don't know what to tell you. I just left him a few minutes ago."

"What about Reiker?"

"He's still at the cabin as far as I know. What the fuck's the problem?"

Lawson hesitated. He looked at Wayne, then down at the gun. "No problem. I just need to talk to the boss."

"I got my own shit to deal with. He sent the girl with me but he wants me to fuckin' babysit instead of havin' a little fun. Figure it out for your own goddammed self."

The call disconnected.

"What girl is he talking about?" Luke asked.

"I don't know."

Shit. DiMarco had another hostage? "How close is the cabin you were in?"

"It's right up here, why?" Before Luke could reply, Lawson shouted and pointed out the window. "There's Chang right there."

A blue van approached on the narrow road. Luke jerked the wheel toward the van, almost slamming into the oncoming vehicle. It careened to a stop and a large, oriental man jumped out of the driver's side.

"You stupid cocksucking motherfucker." he shouted, as if his biggest crisis was road rage. "What the hell..." The man pulled a gun and pointed it at the car.

Chapter Twenty-Three

Jade wasn't sure how much more she could take. Bryce sat on the couch next to her--so close, she could smell him with every breath--alternating between threats and contrition, one moment the vicious captor, the next the cajoling husband. Each time he touched her, it made her flesh creep and nausea rise to her throat. So far, it had been only the briefest of contacts. He'd promised more later...when she realized that giving in to him was not only her key to survival, it was what she wanted. Oh my God, did he really believe that? Could he possibly be that deluded?

The switchblade bit into her hip but she was grateful Bryce hadn't discovered it yet. How long had they been here? An hour? Longer?

Yes, longer than an hour. He'd called Chang once so it had to be.

He'd finally untied her hands, but had once more trained the gun on her, chatting as though he wasn't holding an instrument of death to her head.

Think, Jade, think. You're running out of time. He'd said the plane was due back soon. A call on his cell phone would indicate it had arrived. Then, they'd be gone. Forever. She shuddered, cringing at the thought of leaving with Bryce to fly out of the country, all hope for escape dashed indefinitely. She couldn't let that happen.

The phone rang...jarring her as much as the blast of a grenade would. *Oh God, was this the call?*

Bryce smiled as he listened. His eyes blazed with triumph. Jade stared at him, struggling to calm her racing terror. He stood to his feet and reached one hand down for her, the other still holding the weapon. She looked at his hand, then back to his demented eyes, one thought beating through her brain.

How long would it take to retrieve the knife...and could she do it before Bryce pulled the trigger?

She took Bryce's hand, cringing as his smooth fingers clasped hers. Without warning, the feel of Luke's calloused fingers sliding along her skin came back to her. *Luke.* Would she ever see him again? If she did, would he hate her for what she'd done?

"The airplane's here." His smile widened. "Almost to freedom. Your little friend is almost to safety, if you'll just be a good girl a little longer."

This was perhaps her last chance. She had to take it. Now or never. "Bryce?" she said softly.

His gaze was momentarily wary, but if he wondered about her change of tone, he didn't comment. He pulled her close and looked into her eyes. "Yes, darling?"

Reaching behind her, Jade pulled the switchblade from her pocket. She flicked it open and whipped it around, plunging it into Bryce's side, then jerked it out quickly.

A grunt left his throat. The gun clattered to the floor as he clutched his ribs and stumbled back, a look of disbelief on his face. He went to his knees, then fell onto his side.

For a moment, she was afraid she'd killed him. She needed him alive so he could tell her where Ashley was. Perverse relief shot through her when he rolled over on his back, moaning and clutching his side.

Head down, favoring his ribs, he attempted to get to his feet but Jade lunged on top of him. Fisting her knuckles, she jabbed them into his neck. He made a gurgling noise, his hands going from his side to his throat.

Blood seeped from his wound onto Jade's jeans but she ignored it, once more jamming her knuckles into him. This time, his chest was the target. Breath whooshed from him and he was still, staring at her with pain-crazed eyes.

"I learned a little something while I was away," she whispered. "It's called the death touch." She smiled down at him. "Just to show you I'm not all bad, I'm going to give you a choice. I can either kill you, or I can make you a fucking vegetable."

Bryce made a wheezing, howling noise and jerked beneath her.

She gripped his throat and squeezed. "Tell me where Ashley is or I'll make the choice for you." She knew his condition wouldn't last long. He would recover in a few moments.

"You won't do either." He managed to choke. "If you ever want to find her, you'll let me go. Even if you force me to tell you where she is, you won't know if I told you the truth."

Looking down at him, she was suddenly overcome with fury. The weeks of hiding...day after day of fear...and the innocent victims he'd claimed in his self-absorbed quest culminated in a rage that had no end.

Gripping his throat even tighter, she screamed down at him, "Who do you think you are? What gives you the right to destroy lives? The right to play God...to infect the world you're your evil?" With tears streaming down her face, she quivered in frustration. "If you don't tell me, right now, where she is, I swear I'll gut you like the pig you are." She pressed the knife to his throat. "Tell me where the fuck she is!"

"Godammit! You're out of your fucking mind!"

Jade had the crazy urge to laugh. A maniac like Bryce accusing *her* of being insane? "Tell me."

"I'll take you to her. You'll never find her if you kill me. And if I don't call Chang soon...she dies anyway."

He was right. The sonofabitch. Tamping down her wrath, she climbed off him and grabbed his gun from the floor.

"One false move, and I'll blow a hole through your sorry ass."

He lifted his hands in supplication. "Okay. I get the message. You're a bad ass now. Go figure."

"Move." She pointed toward the door with the gun.

She followed Bryce to the Audi, the gun trained on his back. She motioned for him to get inside and slid into the passenger seat.

"Drive, you sonofabitch, and you'd better drive

straight to Ashley."

A drizzle of snow and ice had started to fall while they'd been inside the cabin. Visibility was almost zero. Jade wasn't sure Bryce could see where he was going. She wasn't sure he was really taking her to Ashley but she had to believe he was. Right now, it was all she had.

****

Lawson opened the passenger door and bailed out of the car. He ran around the front, screaming, "Chang...help me!"

What happened next was either accidental or intentional, Luke didn't know or care. The oriental man's startled gaze flew to the guy staggering toward him in the dark and he pulled the trigger, shooting Lawson in the chest.

Wayne jumped from the back seat and knocked the gun from Chang's hand, then shoved the Beretta into his forehead. "Where's the girl?"

"Back the fuck off, dude. What're you talking about?"

Wayne smashed the gun against the guy's head and he went down like a toppled oak tree. He slapped handcuffs on the unconscious man while Luke threw the van door open.

Inside, was the girl he'd met at Jade's. Her hands were above her head, tied to the assist handle. Eyes the size of basketballs stared at him from her pale face.

"It's okay, sugar. Remember me?" Carefully, he crept toward the girl, keeping his voice low. "I'm a friend of Jenna's. You're fine now. We'll get you home."

She nodded. Then, as if a black cloud had opened up, tears poured from her eyes. Her hands shook so badly, Luke had to be careful to avoid cutting her flesh as he sliced through the ropes.

Once she was free, she dove into his arms and he held her. Her thin body felt fragile, like a twig that could snap with too much pressure. The sobbing turned to sniffling hiccups and he held her from him, helping her out of the van.

He led her to the car. "This is Wayne. He's a friend of mine. He'll take care of you."

"You two take the van," he told Wayne. "Put Chang here in the back and take him to the authorities after you

237

get her to the hospital." Luke looked at Lawson's inert form, then at Wayne. Wayne shook his head. The man was dead. Luke shrugged. He'd already told them all he knew. Let the buzzards have him.

"What about Jenna?" Ashley tugged on Luke's arm. "That maniac has her. He's taking her away."

"I'll find her, don't worry."

Ashley nodded but her brows creased in worry. She didn't believe he'd find her in time.

Let her be wrong, Luke silently prayed as he jumped in the car and sped toward the cabin.

****

Jade's gaze went back and forth between Bryce and the ice pelting the windshield like bullets. He gripped the wheel with one hand and his bleeding side with the other. Would he bleed to death before they got to Ashley?

Bryce shook his head. "Why?" The word came out as a strangled moan.

"Shut up and drive," Jade barked, not caring what he was referring to. She was tired of his shit. Tired of the whole sorry mess.

His eyes left the road and locked on her face. In the insane blue orbs, she saw no fear. The look he gave her was one of relief...and a smug contentment. He turned back to the windshield. She felt the car lurch forward as he increased his speed.

"Slow down," she commanded, afraid they'd kill themselves on the treacherous roads before they even reached Ashley.

When Bryce turned his demented smile on her, a flood of goose bumps shivered over her skin, and she knew that was exactly what he intended.

"Bryce! Godammit, stop! I'll let you go, I promise. I just want to find Ashley. Please stop the car!"

He didn't acknowledge her. He floored the gas, eyes glued to the windshield. She was going to die. She'd never find Ashley. Never see Luke again.

She aimed the gun at Bryce's right leg and fired. He yelled and jerked the wheel. His foot came off the accelerator but they were now in a skid.

The car tilted crazily to its side then miraculously, righted itself. Then it went into a full spin, the tires

238

refusing to gain traction on the slippery road.

The gun flew from her hand. Jade gripped the door pad, belatedly wishing she'd buckled her seatbelt, and prayed. With the force of a rocket launcher, the car slammed into a tree and came to an ear-piercing stop as metal scraped against wood and both air bags deployed.

Bryce's head slammed against the driver's window, then he was still. Even from the opposite side, Jade could see blood run from a gash on his temple.

She groped for the gun, trying to free herself from the deflated canvas prison. She couldn't find it, didn't know where it had ended up, but she couldn't worry about that now. She put a hand to Bryce's neck. Still alive. She shook him.

"Bryce! Wake up. We have to get out of here." Even as she said the words, she could smell gasoline.

A startled scream left her throat as her door was wrenched open. For a moment, her mind didn't understand what she was seeing. Her heart stuttered and her breath caught in her throat. She thought she'd died and was having one last wonderful dream. But it was real. Luke stood next to the car, his face twisted with concern.

"Come on, baby. Let's get out of here." He reached out a hand. She heard a hiss and saw flames at the rear of the car.

She ignored Luke and grabbed Bryce's arm. "Wake up," she screamed. "Tell me where she is...tell me where Ashley is!"

"Jade, let's go. The car's gonna blow. Leave him."

"He's got Ashley." She coughed as gas fumes filled her throat and watered her eyes. "I need him to take me to her."

"She's safe. We found her." Luke grasped her arm. "Please, baby, come on."

Jade looked at Luke, then back at Bryce. Bryce moaned and his eyes opened.

"Where is she?" Jade shook him, dizzy with the need for fresh air.

Bryce turned to her. With glassy eyes, he looked past her to Luke.

"Jade. Trust me," Luke begged. "You have to come

with me."

Jade looked at Luke's hand on her arm...at the amber eyes filled with anxiety. Could she trust him? If she left Bryce, would she ever see Ashley again? A popping sound came and simultaneously, a burgeoning glow as the flames reached closer.

Bryce was gaining his senses now, he was trapped beneath the wheel, but his hand shuffled around on the seat...stretched down toward the floorboard. He was looking for the gun.

He wasn't going to tell her where Ashley was. He'd been ready to kill them both on the icy roads. She had to believe that Luke had the girl. Had to believe he wouldn't lie to her again, not about something like this.

Without another glance at Bryce, she placed her hand in Luke's and he pulled her from the car. He kept his grip on her while she ran beside him, barely keeping up with his faster pace. They'd only gone a few feet when she looked back and saw the gun in Bryce's hand. How had he found it when she hadn't?

Suddenly, Luke jerked her down with bone-jarring force, covering her body with his. As her chest slammed against the ice covered ground, a shot rang out and an explosion ripped through the night air.

In spite of the deafening sound, Jade heard Bryce scream her name in an ear splitting mingle of rage and suffering. "J—a—a—a—d—e..."

The tortured wail abruptly ended and in its place came an agonizing scream, primal in its intensity.

Then there was nothing except the crackle of the flames as they devoured the Audi and the evil within.

Chapter Twenty-Four

Luke drove and Jade sat in the passenger seat, her brain trying to assimilate that it was over. It was really over and she was free of Bryce. She understood something now that she never had before. It wasn't the dark that held danger; it was the evil of the world. And evil could come in many disguises...and could come in the light of day.

She'd also discovered a courage she didn't know she possessed. It came from learning that you can't run from your fears, because when you turn around, they'd still be there. You can only face them...fight them...and hope to eventually conquer them.

"I know. I promise I'll be there in a few days and I'll explain everything." Luke was speaking on his cell to someone named Madsen. He rested the phone on his shoulder and winked at Jade as he reached out and squeezed her hand. "Yes. I understand. I'm sorry, sir."

He ended the call. "Sorry about that. My supervisor's kind of ticked. The only thing that might save my ass is that we got DiMarco and both you and Ashley are okay."

Jade nodded. "I hope you're not in trouble."

"They're sorting out the charges now. I've got some people on my side and it turned out okay so, they probably won't spank me too hard."

She smiled, grateful for Luke's attempt to keep things light. He'd helped her to her feet after the explosion, pulling her close against his warmth, stroking her hair as he murmured softly in her ear. She'd clung to him for a moment, then pulled away, mumbling something about checking on Ashley. She'd seen bewilderment in his eyes and maybe pain before he nodded and helped her to the car.

Jade called Deb at the hospital and the woman had gushed her thanks for saving her little girl. She swore she'd learned her lesson and would be a good mother from now on.

Her gratitude was hard to accept. Jade was the one who had endangered Ashley in the first place. Would Ashley hate Jade for lying to her? For pretending to be someone she wasn't? The very thing Jade despised in others was exactly what she'd done to Ashley.

She and Luke had been questioned by the police and released after promising to return the next day for a full statement. The US Marshals' service had told the authorities to let Jade know they'd need to see her tomorrow also.

Yeah. Tomorrow would be a big day.

"Have you thought about what you're going to do with all that money?"

"Money?" she asked.

"The five million in the Cayman Islands. Its yours, you know."

She shook her head. She hadn't thought about the money being hers, and as far as she was concerned, it wasn't. The thought of keeping cash that was earned by Bryce's evil deeds was abhorrent. "I can't take that money. Don't want it."

Luke nodded as if he'd expected her answer. "I understand, but nonetheless, it's yours. You could donate it to charity."

With his words an idea formed in her mind. An idea that might bring something good, some type of poetic justice out of this tragedy. "I could open a shelter for runaways," she said softly, thinking out loud.

Luke nodded again. "Yes, you could. That could work."

She fell into silence...her mind busy contemplating what it would take to put her plan into motion.

"Madsen said they intercepted a private plane at the airport with a pilot and one of Bryce's men inside." Luke's voice interrupted her thoughts. "Apparently, that was to be your getaway vehicle. It belonged to a Susannah Brennan. Do you know her?"

"Yeah." Jade gave a humorless laugh. "Bryce's ex-girlfriend. She and her parents ran in the same social circles we did. I bumped into her from time to time. She never seemed very fond of me." She laid her head on the headrest and closed her eyes.

"Are you sure you're okay?" Luke asked.

"I'm fine but I feel like I could sleep for two weeks straight."

"I'll take you back to my hotel. Your apartment is a crime scene now. You won't be able to go back for a few days."

Jade opened her eyes and cut a look at him. "Stay with you?"

He shrugged. "You can stay in my room or get your own but you need some rest."

"Yes. I'm so tired."

"Jade, there's something you have to believe. I *was* undercover when I worked with Bryce. We were sent in to bust his operation. I'd been assigned to the case for months."

"I believe you."

A rush of breath left his body. "How long do you think it will take you to wrap things up here and go back home?"

"Home?"

"To St. Louis. No need to stay now that Bryce is dead."

She shook her head. "My home is here now."

"You're staying?"

"Yes. I won't stay in the apartment." She looked out the window at the snow-covered pines. Glimpses of the lake flashed between the trees. In spite of the terror and near tragedy she'd experienced out here, she'd never seen anything more beautiful. "I'd like to find a place on the lake somewhere. But, yeah, I'm staying."

"What about us?"

She turned back to him. "What do you mean?"

"I meant what I said in the hotel room. I love you, Jade. I want to be with you."

Oh God. Not this. Not right now. "Please don't. I can't...I just can't. I don't feel that way about you." The lie settled on her tongue, tasting bitter and cold. She did love him. She'd known it for a while now, but with that knowledge came the dread and fear of the pain that would surely follow.

He pulled over to the side of the road and cut off the engine. Turning toward her in the seat, he searched her eyes. "You don't mean that."

She tensed. "I'm sorry but I do mean it. I care about you, but it will never work between us."

"Why not?"

"I'm just no good at love. I can't do it. I'm sorry. I just can't trust you. Can't trust anyone."

"Liar."

Her eyes flew to his face. "What?"

"You do trust me. You knew I rescued Ashley. You came with me because you believed me. That means you trust me."

She shook her head. "It's not the same kind of trust. I know you didn't lie to me and that you helped us. But I can't trust you with my love."

His eyes were burning coals and she realized his intent too late. But when he touched her, it was too late anyway. He gripped her arms and pulled her close. His lips met hers, firmly at first, then softening in a passionate caress. Instant heat pounded through her, raging through her body in a tingling explosion of desire. She opened her lips and slid her tongue against his, pressing closer, her flesh craving more of his touch.

Suddenly, he released her. Her breath came in rapid gasps, forming pockets of fog in the chill air of the car. She stared at him and put a trembling hand to her lips.

"Tell me you didn't feel anything." His voice was harsh. Slivers of lavender moonlight filtered through the windshield, illuminating the amber of his eyes as they bore into hers.

She wrapped her arms around her midsection and shivered, looking away from the intensity of his stare. "Of course I felt something. I won't deny the attraction..."

"Bullshit." He grabbed her shoulders and forced her gaze back to his. "That's bullshit and you know it. It's a lot more than attraction. What happened between us was more than just a fuck."

"Please, Luke." The windows had frosted over and chilly air pervaded the inside of the car. "Let's just go. I'm cold." She tried to pull away but he didn't release his hold.

"You're more afraid of loving me than you were of Bryce. What are you afraid of?"

She shook her head and didn't answer. Deep pain twisted through her, clogging her throat with unshed tears.

"You can't lie to me," Luke insisted. "I know how you feel about me. I've seen the way that little pulse in your throat jumps when I touch you." He brushed a finger across the base of her neck and she shivered again, only this time it wasn't from the cold. "It's not fear that causes it."

"Please don't do this. You're leaving, I'm staying. Whatever there was between us is over. We won't see each other again. That's the way it has to be."

"That's not the way it has to be. Dammit, Jade. After I go back to St. Louis and get this mess straightened out, fight whatever charges they have against me, I'll come back. If I haven't lost my job, I'll transfer to Denver. I can't lose you."

She shook her head. "I can't do this right now. I'm so tired. I'm freezing to death. I understand now why you did what you did. I believe you were working undercover and just doing your job. But my father spent my entire childhood 'just doing his job' while I was at home getting the shit beat out of me. We believe in different things. You're a good man and I care about you, but you're not the man for me."

He stared at her for a moment, a muscle working in his jaw. The only sounds in the car were the ticking of the engine and the wind as it howled around them.

"Forget it." He shifted around and started the motor, slamming the gearshift into drive. "Where to?"

"Uhm..." She couldn't think straight. Heart shrinking in misery, she realized she was getting what she wanted. He'd given up. If it was what she wanted, why did she feel this agonizing pain ripping through her heart?

"I'll take you to the Colorado Inn," he said without

looking at her. "That way, you won't have to be in the same hotel with me, let alone the same room."

She nodded but he didn't see. His eyes were fixed on the road ahead.

He didn't speak until they pulled in front of the hotel. "I'm sure you won't have a problem getting a room but if you do, call me. I'll have someone pick you up and take you to another hotel."

"Okay." She reached for the door handle. "Thank you for everything, Luke. I'm sorry."

He shook his head. "No need to be sorry. Shit happens. But, if you ever decide to stop punishing me for your father's mistakes, give me a call. Maybe it won't be too late for us."

On legs weighted down by gloom, Jade stepped out of the car and trudged through the snow to the hotel door. She heard Luke leave but didn't turn around. When her hand touched the door, a sense of emptiness, urgent and severe, rocked her, shuddering through her with the speed of a freight train.

"Luke." Her voice was panicky, desperate. She whirled and saw his taillights as he prepared to pull onto the road. A sense of doom washed over her. She was certain that if she didn't stop him now, it would be too late. May already be too late.

If it is, I'll live with this pain forever.

"Luke!" Jade screamed his name as she ran, sliding on the ice. She stumbled and went to her knees in the snow. She looked up just as his car pulled onto the street.

She knelt on the ground, tears sliding down her frozen cheeks.

You're a fool. A stubborn, frightened fool...

Over the thumping of her heart, she heard the slam of a car door and raised her head to find Luke coming toward her.

A grin tugged at his mouth as he gripped her shoulders and pulled her into his arms. "You know, you could have just called."

Joy seared her...warming her veins as giddy relief swept through her soul. "I was afraid if I let you go, it would be too late." Her breath caught on a sob. "That I'd lose you forever."

"No, baby. I was only bluffing." He pulled her closer and brushed a strand of hair from her face. "It could never be too late."

She clung to him, barely aware of the freezing wind whipping around her. She tilted her head back and looked into his eyes. "You know how you said I was more afraid of loving you than I was of Bryce?"

"Yeah."

"That's not true. I'm more afraid of losing you than anything."

His arms tightened around her. He leaned his forehead against hers, his eyes closed. "You'll never lose me," he whispered, his words almost lost in the screech of the wind. "I'll fight this thing at home, come back to you as soon as I can."

She put her hands on his face and lifted his head, staring up at him. "I want to go with you. I'll stay until we see this thing through, together."

His eyes shone, radiating happiness in their whiskey depths. He smiled. "You have to promise me one thing."

"What's that?"

He winced and glanced down at his shoulder. "You won't shoot me again."

She laughed. "Only if you can promise you won't make me angry again."

"Ah, I can see that life with you will be a bit of an adventure."

"Not really," she said softly. "I think I've had enough adventure to last me a lifetime."

He bent his head and touched his lips to hers. "You know," he murmured against her mouth. "We can continue this conversation somewhere a little less arctic."

She gave a short laugh that was quickly squelched by the heat of his mouth. Sighing, she relaxed against him, linking her hands behind his neck as she returned the kiss.

She no longer felt the cold. In its place was a thrilling warmth that pounded through her heart, filling it with love until there was no more room for the darkness...no more room for the fear.

A word about the author...

Alicia Dean was born and raised in Oklahoma, but now resides in Kansas City after taking a transfer with her job. She's a single mother of three, although she is now dealing with empty nest syndrome as her children, two grown daughters and a fourteen year old son, remained in Oklahoma.

Alicia's passion for reading started at a very young age and is only surpassed by her passion for writing. Mystery, suspense and the paranormal have always intrigued her and she's been inspired by authors such as Michael Connelly, Lisa Gardner and Stephen King.

Alicia is a member of Oklahoma Romance Writers of America where her friends and fellow writers have encouraged and supported her in the pursuit of her dreams.

Visit Alicia at www.aliciadean.com